The criti... ...aire
and...

"Roxanne St. C... ...ing—
more Bullet Catchers."
—Romance Novel TV

"Sexy, smart, and suspenseful."
—Mariah Stewart, *New York Times* bestselling author

"When it comes to dishing up great romantic suspense,
St. Claire is the author you want."
—*Romantic Times*

NOW YOU DIE

"The incredibly talented Ms. St. Claire . . . keeps the audience
on tenterhooks with her clever ruses, while the love scenes
pulsate with sensuality and an exquisite tenderness that zeroes
in on the heart."

—*The Winter Haven News Chief* (FL)

"A nonstop thrill ride of mayhem that leaves you breathless."
—Simply Romance Reviews

THEN YOU HIDE

"St. Claire aces another one!"

—*Romantic Times*

"Nothing short of spectacular, with the fast pace and the
tension constantly mounting."

—Kwips and Kritiques

THRILL ME TO DEATH

"Sizzles like a hot Miami night."
—*New York Times* bestselling author Erica Spindler

"Sultry romance with enticing suspense."
—*Publishers Weekly*

"Fast-paced, sexy romantic suspense. . . . A book that will keep the reader engrossed in the story from cover to cover."
—*Booklist*

"Roxanne St. Claire's got the sexy bodyguard thing down to an art form. . . ."
—Michelle Buonfiglio, Lifetime TV.com

"St. Claire doesn't just push the envelope, she folds it into an intricate piece of origami for the reader's pleasure!"
—*The Winter Haven News Chief* (FL)

KILL ME TWICE

"Sexy and scintillating . . . an exciting new series."
—*Romantic Times*

"*Kill Me Twice* literally vibrates off the pages with action, danger, and palpable sexual tension. St. Claire is exceptionally talented."
—*The Winter Haven News Chief* (FL)

"Jam-packed with characters, situations, suspense, and danger. The reader will be dazzled. . . ."
—*Rendezvous*

Also by Roxanne St. Claire

ROXANNE
ST. CLAIRE

MAKE HER PAY

POCKET STAR BOOKS

New York   London   Toronto   Sydney

Pocket Star Books
A Division of Simon & Schuster, Inc.
1230 Avenue of the Americas
New York, NY 10020

First Pocket Star Books paperback edition October 2009

POCKET STAR BOOKS and colophon are registered trademarks of Simon & Schuster, Inc.

For information about special discounts for bulk purchases, please contact Simon & Schuster Special Sales at 1-866-506-1949 or business@simonandschuster.com.

The Simon & Schuster Speakers Bureau can bring authors to your live event. For more information or to book an event contact the Simon & Schuster Speakers Bureau at 1-866-248-3049 or visit our website at www.simonspeakers.com.

Cover art by Chris Cocozza
Design by Min Choi

Manufactured in the United States of America

10 9 8 7 6 5 4 3 2 1

ISBN 978-1-4391-0222-0
ISBN 978-1-4391-2737-7 (ebook)

I give this one to Mia

Your life is truly a gift from the gods, a miracle from
the angels, the star I wished upon a thousand
times before you were finally in my arms.
My tiny dancer, my precious dreamer,
my lifelong best friend, my perfect daughter . . .
the world would be colorless, quiet,
and lonely without you.

ACKNOWLEDGMENTS

THE RESEARCH FOR this book was great fun, and allowed me to meet and talk to some of the most outstanding individuals in the world of salvage diving and treasure hunting. I thank them all. If any errors are made regarding treasure hunting, diving, or life in the Azores, blame me, not any of these people.

In particular, I'd like to send a huge hug and kiss to Pete and Gloria Mann, treasure hunters, divers, and all around fantastic friends (and bowlers!) who acted as escorts, making sure I had access, information, and a wealth of resources to help make my story more realistic. Especially Pete, who never ignored my calls and patiently explained the secrets of the sea. You two are the real buried treasure in this book!

Also, huge props to the friendly folks at the McClarty Treasure Museum and the Mel Fisher Center in Sebastian, Florida, who opened their doors, answered my questions, and gave me a chance to touch the treasure. Anyone interested in Florida treasure hunting must start in these two places.

A special tip of the dive mask to treasure hunting legend Robert "Frogfoot" Weller, whose writings guided me around the ballast piles, and maritime archaeologist and conservator Wyatt Yeager, who was a great source of information regarding the care and feeding of recovered treasure.

Also, awesome writer, dear friend, and former resident of the Azores, Lara Santiago, and Petty Officer Jennifer Johnson of the United States Coast Guard, who both took time from busy schedules to answer questions and fact check.

Obrigada to Barbie Furtado, who perfected my faulty Portuguese.

There's a crew of people who are on this ride with me book after book and I love them all. My dear writing friends, especially Kresley Cole, Kristen Painter, Cami Dalton, Allison Brennan, Toni McGee Causey, Marilyn Puett, and so many others who help me through the highs and lows and inspire me to dig deeper every time.

The entire publishing team at Pocket Books—most especially my beloved editor, Micki Nuding, along with literary agent extraordinaire, Kim Whalen. I may write the book, but without them, it would die in my computer.

And, finally, as always, my deepest gratitude to the ones who know me the best, and love me anyway, Rich, Dante & Mia. Without my family, none of this would be possible or even worth doing.

MAKE HER PAY

CHAPTER
ONE

"I DON'T NORMALLY make a habit of hiring thieves as security specialists." Lucy Sharpe met the cold blue gaze of a man she'd never imagined would return to the Bullet Catchers after she'd discharged him under a cloud of suspicion.

"Habits can be broken." Constantine Xenakis strode across the library and dropped into an antique chair that most men avoided, but his long, rugged body dominated the dainty seat, completely at ease. "Kind of like rules. And locks."

"Dan Gallagher mentioned you were as confident as ever."

"As I recall, that's a big plus for this job." A flicker of a smile softened his hardened expression.

"It helps," Lucy agreed. "First of all, thank you again for your assist on the kidnapping in Miami. Helping to find that piece of evidence was key and helped to save several people's lives, including Dan's son. I'm very grateful for that."

His smile deepened to show the contrast of white teeth against tanned olive skin. "I had to get creative to find a way back into this mansion, Luce."

"You could have called." She nodded to the Black-Berry on her desk. "The number hasn't changed in six years."

"As if you'd take my call."

In fact, she might have. "I tried to find you after the truth came out on that diamond drop, Con. You were exonerated and I wanted to tell you that I was wrong."

"You didn't try very hard, then—because you can find anyone, anywhere, no matter how deep under-ground they go."

"True," she conceded. "But by then you'd already taken a new career path, and I didn't like it. I still don't."

"Neither do I," he said quietly. "That's why I'm here."

She lifted a brow. "You've grown a conscience after half a dozen years of helping yourself to corporate se-crets, priceless jewels, and countless works of art?"

He bristled and she knew she'd hit his weak spot. "Let's get this straight. I didn't help myself to anything. I have never kept anything I've stolen. I have worked as a middleman between collectors with a lot of money, and the people and places who have things they want."

Lucy chuckled. "I've heard euphemisms for stealing before, but that one is in a league of its own."

"Think what you want, Lucy, but I don't want the stuff I've stolen. I've simply used the talents I was born with—skills I unfortunately honed too well as a teenager."

"You haven't been a teenager for twenty years."

"And as you recall," he continued, his voice low and deliberate, "I found that people *assumed* that because I had certain abilities, I automatically used them."

Definitely his weak spot. That would make the assignment, if she chose to offer it, even more challenging. "I *assumed* you helped yourself to diamonds because they were missing under your watch and you made no effort to dissuade me of that belief."

For the first time, he shifted his muscular frame in the undersized chair. "You hired me, Luce. Don't you trust your own judgment? Did I have to come in here and plead my case, or is the client always right?"

"If you wanted to stay a Bullet Catcher badly enough, it would have been a smart move." Instead he'd tested her, and they'd both lost. "And, no, the client is not always right. And neither am I. I have an open mind and am a reasonable woman, Con. There was no need for you to disappear and become a professional thief. You could have been protecting those things instead of stealing them."

"I made my choice, Lucy," he said simply. "And now I am here to unmake it."

"Dan told me you're serious about becoming a Bullet Catcher and I trust *his* judgment," she said. "And, I admit, the idea intrigues me. But only if I understand why, so that I can believe this sudden change of heart is real."

"It's real, and it's not sudden. The impetus was the case in Miami last month, when I saw one of your men in action."

"Dan Gallagher is one of the best."

"For good reason. So, I decided if I was going to steal anything worthwhile . . ." Humor glinted. "It should be his *job*."

She almost laughed at the idea that anyone could replace the man who'd been her right hand for the last five years. The man who she was already wooing to temporarily fill her chair when her baby arrived in six months. "That would be some steal."

"Let's put it this way. I don't do things halfway. If I work for you, I'd want to be the man you call one of your best." The conviction in his voice erased any concerns that the Con Man was doing a job on her.

A few seconds crawled by, punctuated by the pendulum swing of an antique grandfather clock across the room. Finally, without taking her eyes from his, she circled the writing table, settled in her chair, and reached for the dossier she'd been reading before he arrived. She couldn't go one more day without fulfilling this client's request, and the perfect man for the job was right in front of her.

"The assignment is tough, even for a seasoned Bullet Catcher." She handed him the file. "I need a diver."

"My time as a SEAL was brief, but I'm certified to dive."

"And I need a thief."

He lifted his gaze from the paperwork. "Excuse me?"

"Or someone who would know how to spot one." When he nodded, she continued. "The Bullet Catcher client is Judd Paxton. Are you familiar with him?"

"Of course. Paxton Treasures is the most successful

underwater salvage company in the world. But no one's diving in November."

"Yes, actually, someone is. Paxton is running a highly confidential dive about ten miles off the east coast of Florida that isn't an official salvage effort."

He frowned. "You mean it's not leased or claimed with the state?"

"Not yet."

"So there's no state rep on board cataloging everything they recover so Florida can suck its twenty percent of the potential bounty? That makes it a lot easier to sell anything recovered for full profit on the black market."

His knowledge of the inner workings of the salvage industry was another point in his favor, even if it was gleaned from the wrong kind of experience.

"Judd's not out to cheat the state or anyone out of money," she assured him. "He has a sponsor who wants to be the exclusive buyer for any treasure recovered on the dive, and that sponsor has insisted that the dive be kept secret, until they can confirm exactly what they've found. Evidently it will rock the salvage world, and when word gets out the area will be pounced on by poachers or, worse, pirates."

He looked intrigued. "What is it?"

"Are you familiar with the legend of the ship called *El Falcone*?"

"Yes," he said with a soft laugh. "I'm also familiar with Santa Claus and the Easter Bunny. It's folklore, Lucy."

"Well, Mr. Paxton doesn't happen to agree with

you," she replied. "The *folklore* of an unregistered ship that carried treasures from Havana to Lisbon would become *fact* if he is able to prove that's what he's found."

Con sifted through a few pages in the file, obviously unconvinced. "There's no manifest on record of a ship that wasn't registered, so this is pure speculation."

"The entire business of treasure hunting is speculative, but evidently some paperwork does exist, in various bits and pieces, and some of those are in the hands of Mr. Paxton's sponsor. The dive job is so confidential, I might add, that the crew and divers don't know what wreck they're salvaging."

He flipped the page, read some names. "Then why are they out freezing their backsides off, diving in November?"

"Because Paxton's paying a fortune. So, they're abiding by a no cell phone, no Internet access rule while on board. Since several of the Paxton ships were ambushed last season by well-organized thieves, the divers have been told the secrecy is for their safety."

He nodded. "That makes sense. So what's the assignment, protection from the potential pirates?"

"Not exactly. The threat, Judd thinks, is closer. They've recovered quite a few items already, and some are missing."

"Oh." His fingers rested on the diver and crew list. "So there's a thief on board—one of the crew or divers."

"It would appear so, but it's more complex than that," she said. "In Paxton's opinion, just as worrisome as someone helping himself to a few gold coins is a leak to the outside world when something more substantive is recovered. There are a few items in particular that are believed to have been on board *El Falcone*."

"What are they?"

"A pair of gold scepters topped with matching diamonds, made for the king and queen of Portugal on the occasion of their marriage in 1862. And not just any diamonds—the Bombay Blues, two of the most valuable blue diamonds ever mined in India."

He smiled, shaking his head. "That tale's been going around the art world for years. The Bombay Blues don't exist."

"Whether or not they exist doesn't matter. Our job isn't to find them," she reminded him. "It's our job to get on the boat and identify the thief, and if there is a leak, stop it."

He acknowledged that with a tilt of his head. "Flynn Paxton is the manager of the dive," he noted. "A relative?"

"Stepson. Evidently they have a contentious relationship and Judd is trying to smooth things out by letting him manage a dive. You'll go undercover as a new diver, infiltrate the crew, stop whoever has the sticky fingers, and figure out if someone's getting word to the outside world. No one, not even Flynn, will know your real reason for being there."

"Does Flynn know about *El Falcone*?"

"No one does."

"So Judd doesn't even trust his own stepson. Interesting." Con shifted through the file that contained in-depth backgrounds of the six divers, conservator, and crew on board the *Gold Digger*, then looked up at her. "Anything else?"

"Just check in daily. If you uncover anything or any-one suspicious at all, I want to know immediately. That day, that hour. We'll strategize together how to handle it."

"No problem."

"And remember that you're not on your own." She leaned forward, pulling his attention. "Bullet Catchers, even on individual assignments, work as a team. They might not be there with you, but we're just a phone call away, giving you access to all my resources, my infor-mation, my people."

"Sounds good. When do I start?"

"Immediately. My assistant, Avery, will arrange for you to have a bodyguard's license to carry concealed, and get you a satellite phone and a laptop, both pro-grammed to access this office with the press of one button or a keystroke. One of the Bullet Catcher jets is ready to take you home so you can pick up whatever you need, then fly you to the port where you'll be taken out to the Paxton boat."

She picked up her BlackBerry to check messages, clicking through what came in during the meeting. "Oh, and Con?"

He closed the file. "Don't tell me. One mistake and I'm out again?"

"And you'll go straight to the authorities, who I be-lieve are looking for you in three states."

"Four." He shot her a smile. "But who's counting?"

"I am." She held up one finger, then lowered it to point directly at him. "You get one chance, Con. That's it. Avoid trouble, stay in constant contact, and do the job exactly as a Bullet Catcher would."

"And then?"

She tilted her head to the side. "Those four states will never have heard of you, and you can arm wrestle Dan for his job."

"Tell him to lift weights." He gave her a cocky wink. "Thanks, Luce."

She was still looking at the empty doorway after he left, when Jack turned the corner and stepped into her line of vision.

"What are you staring at, Lucinda?" he asked, leaning against the jamb with his arms crossed and his smile aimed at her.

"The man I'm going to marry." She got up to meet him for an embrace, which was as tender as the kiss he added. "The father of this baby I'm carrying."

He tilted her chin to look into her eyes. "You're not going to change your mind, are you?"

She laughed. "Why would you even ask about that?"

"Because this . . ." He cupped her chin and scrutinized her face. "Is that very rare expression you wear when you're second-guessing yourself."

God, he knew her like no other man ever had. "Did you see the man who was just in here?"

"I saw someone leave, but I didn't talk to him. New client?"

"New hire."

"Really? You didn't mention you were hiring someone."

"I wasn't sure I would, until the moment I handed him the Paxton file."

"So you found the diver you wanted."

"I found the thief I wanted."

He inched back. "A *thief*?"

"Reformed. Or so he says. He's also a former Bullet Catcher, who I let go after some diamonds were missing from a delivery out of South Africa. He was eventually vindicated and cleared, but by the time that happened, he'd pretty much adopted the 'if you can't convince them you're innocent, then be guilty' mind-set, and went back to doing what he has an amazing gift for doing: taking stuff that doesn't belong to him."

Jack dropped on the sofa, studying her with a quizzical look. "So you brought him on board for just this job?"

"We'll see. He wants more. He wants Dan's job."

That got a soft hoot. "Not that I wouldn't be happy to see my old rival for your affections gone, but I seriously doubt Gallagher's going anywhere but in that chair . . ." He pointed to her desk. "At least for the first few weeks of Baby Culver's life."

"I'm still figuring that out," she said.

He reached for her and eased her next to him, a familiar and comfortable hand on her still-flat belly. "How is my boy, by the way?"

"She's fine. I'm not going to stop working, Jack," she said, a vague warning in her voice.

He just laughed. "No more than the earth will stop revolving. But you are going to have to restructure to some degree."

To some degree. "To the degree where I hire thieves to protect gold and diamonds?"

"Oh, come on, Luce. That's exactly why you did it: to test his loyalty and character."

"You know me *too* well." She nuzzled closer to him, her worries evaporating.

"So what happens if he fails?"

"I could lose one of my most important clients."

And, worse, she'd lose the chance to see Con Xenakis become the man he wanted to be.

The treasure chest. The recovery room. The booty box. The gold hold.

No matter what the crew nicknamed the dive ship's lab, where recovered treasure was bathed in acid and ash, tagged and numbered, then electrolyzed to its original glory, the place was fairly easy to break into.

But even if it hadn't been, Lizzie Dare would have made a go of it tonight.

Her watch alarm vibrated at three a.m., when the hundred-and-twenty-foot vessel was silent but for the hum of the generators. The other divers and the captain and crew were asleep in their cabins.

Secure in the fact that Flynn Paxton was on his boat anchored a hundred and fifty feet away, and certain that by tomorrow she'd never get her hands on the beaded silver chain that had been recovered that afternoon, she tiptoed barefoot out of her bunk.

Her feet soundless on the planks of teak of the narrow hallway of the quarters deck, she barely breathed as she glanced up the stairs to the main deck, where all was dark and silent after a day of diving, searching, and celebrating the recovery. If she were caught now, her excuse would be needing air. But once she turned the corner and took the stairs below, she'd have a hard time explaining herself.

Pausing for a second, she pulled a dark hooded jersey around her, took a deep breath, and darted to the steps.

At the bottom, the generators were louder, the engines and electrical systems clunking softly. Grasping the key she'd taken from Charlotte's stateroom during the hoopla when one of the other divers had emerged from the sea holding the chain, she headed toward the lab. In the midst of the chaotic celebration, it had been easy to slip down to the conservator's stateroom and steal the key unnoticed. She'd return it tomorrow while Charlotte and Sam Gorman had breakfast, no one the wiser.

The metal hatch of the cleaning lab squeaked, making her cringe, then she entered to suck in a noseful of salty muriatic acid lingering in the air.

Inside it was dark, except for one wedge of pale moonlight through skinny horizontal slatted portholes. She didn't need much light. She'd been in the lab enough times to know exactly how the worktables were arranged and where the chain would be hanging on alligator clips in an electrolysis tank.

She took a few steps to the left, reached out to touch the table, then glided her hands to the row of tanks. From her jacket pocket she pulled out a latex glove, slipped it on, then dragged her fingertips over the thin metal bar over the stainless steel plate.

But there were no clips draped with a silver beaded chain.

Hadn't Charlotte started the electrolysis yet? She'd

naturally done the initial cleaning that afternoon, and then she should have prepped the chain for electrolysis that would take up to twenty-four hours.

But the tanks weren't even on; there was no soft vibration of a low-volt current. So where had she put the chain?

Nitric baths, no doubt. Damn. There were beads on the chain and it wasn't all silver so Charlotte probably added a wash of nitric acid as an in-between step. Getting the chain out of a nitric solution would be much tougher.

But not impossible.

She pulled the other glove from her other pocket and headed to the closet-sized room at the opposite end of the lab, where the nitric acid baths were given to the treasure. They'd also found silver coins that day, and no doubt Charlotte had them each in an individual wash, the cups lined up along the worktable. She probably decided to do the necklace at the same time.

Lizzie slipped a pinpoint flashlight out of her pocket because a room with containers of nitric acid, even a five percent solution, was no place to accidentally knock something over in the dark.

Stepping deeper into the closet, she aimed the flashlight in the direction of the tiny worktable along one narrow wall and—

Thwack!

The door slammed behind her the very instant one powerful arm encircled her whole body from behind. A warm hand smashed over her mouth, silencing her scream as the flashlight clunked to the floor.

She jerked one way, then the other, but she was no match for the mighty arms that immobilized her. She tried to see him, but all she could get was an eyeful of shoulder. *Big* shoulder.

No shoulder she'd seen on this boat before.

"Looking for something in particular?" His voice was a low, menacing rumble, sending shivers over her skin.

She jerked hard, grunting into his hand. "Met me mo!" The demand was smashed right back into her mouth.

"No can do, sweetheart." He punctuated that with a squeeze, forcing her body against his, her backside right up against his hips.

A whole different kind of white-hot terror seized her. In all her dive trips and salvage efforts, she'd never been on a ship that had been attacked by pirates. But on Paxton boats? Entirely possible. Probable, even.

She tried to swallow, tried to breathe, but he just pinned her tighter. She fought again, but he was rock solid and unyielding.

"Mwat do you want?"

"What do *you* want? is the question."

She tried to wrest away one more time, but it was fruitless. She forced herself to be very, very still despite the adrenaline coursing through her, fueling her fight.

Three or four interminable seconds rolled by, her heart whacking at her rib cage in triple time.

"Good girl," he said softly, the tone ominous enough to almost stop that beating completely. "This is a very bad room for a wrestling match."

Yes, it was. Unless you had gloves and long sleeves on. Did she dare? Only her face was vulnerable.

What was worse? A minor burn or . . . rape and murder?

No contest.

"Now here's what we're going to do," he said, his mouth still pressed to her ear, his mighty grip strangling her whole body. "We're going to back out of this closet, very calmly and quietly, before you help yourself to a single item that doesn't belong to you. Then you'll pay for your misdeeds, and the punishment will be severe."

If he let go of either arm, she could grab a cup of acid and back toss it in his face. And scream like hell for help.

"Let's go," he said roughly, lifting her off the floor.

She had one finger free, her arm trapped under his. If she could just . . . close around his pinkie and *yank*.

His knuckle snapped and he loosened his grip just enough to free her arm. She stabbed straight for the row of tiny cups, seizing one in a gloved hand.

He jerked her backward but not before she tossed the contents of the cup over her shoulder. Instantly, he whipped them both to the right, hard enough that the acid splashed over the rim of the cup.

With a shriek, she flipped the whole cup just as he threw her to the ground, covering her body from the rain of acid.

"What the hell!" he grunted, writhing over her.

"Get off me!" She shoved at him, not knowing if any

of the acid had touched her clothes, or his. "Get the hell off me, you bastard!"

She tried to scramble away, but he snagged her sweatshirt. "Take it off!" he insisted. "Now! Take it off!" He grabbed the zipper and started to rip.

"No!" She slammed her hands into his chest, just as she felt the air on her arm, where a hole in her hoodie suddenly appeared and grew, the acid on it centimeters from her skin.

"You'll burn! You have to take it off!" He jabbed at the shoulders, pushing the jacket over her, stripping the sleeves as he pulled her to her feet and ripped off the cotton tank top, leaving her entirely bare.

"Your pants! Hurry before you burn!" He seized the waistband of her sweats just as she saw two gaping holes widening over her thigh.

"Off!" he demanded, dragging them down over her hips and taking her underpants with them. In one more lightning move, he flung them away. "Water! Wet your skin!"

He pushed her to the sink and flipped the faucet on, the water shockingly cold on her arm. Then he tore his dark shirt over his head and ripped his jeans off, whipping his clothes into the same corner he'd thrown hers.

"More water," he said, pushing her closer to the sink and cupping his hands. "Give me your leg."

Who *was* this man?

She lifted her leg and he started splashing handfuls of water over her thighs with one hand, and onto his shoulder with the other.

"Why the hell did you do that?" he demanded. "You could have blinded me."

"That was the idea. You *attacked* me."

He snorted softly, looking at her face. "I caught you stealing. Big difference." He lifted his own leg to the sink and started splashing.

"I was not—" She grasped the side of the sink, adrenaline dumping through her like a straight shot of whiskey, her body rubbery and wobbly as she stared at the huge, dark, naked, furious stranger next to her.

"Who *are* you?"

"The new diver."

Oh, no. Oh, *no*.

"The new . . ." Her voice gave out under the force of his laser-beam glare. Instead, she looked down, at the dark nest between his legs, his manhood fully exposed, lying against the soaking wet thigh he held up to the sink.

The new diver.

Oh, please. This wasn't happening to her.

She finally managed to meet his sharp blue eyes again, her stomach flipping around like a hooked fish. "I thought you were going to rape me," she said quietly. "Or . . . worse."

He stopped splashing water long enough to drop his gaze over her body, as if he were . . . considering it.

"This isn't enough," he said gruffly, still studying her.

"What?" What the hell did that mean?

"We have to shower. Now. There could be droplets on your skin, and they'll burn. They might already be burning. Come on."

She hesitated only for a millisecond; he was right.

"In my cabin." He shoved her toward the door.

He really *was* the new diver. The one who was coming . . . *tomorrow*. The one who was going to sleep in the small cabin next to the lab because it was the only unoccupied bunk on the boat.

The new goddamn freaking diver. "I thought you were . . ."

"I know. Rapist. Killer. Pirate. I got the picture."

"It's only five percent nitric acid," she said as she led him through the shadowed lab.

"It'll still burn you. And scar." She turned to look over her shoulder. His gaze was trained directly on her bare bottom.

Flynn had told them they were getting a new diver. But he failed to tell them the new guy was tall, dark, and so far past handsome that he was in another time zone. And she'd tried to burn that face?

He nudged her into the hallway and the first cabin, then whipped open the door to the head, a typical combination toilet and shower in one fiberglass closet.

With one hand, he shoved her into the tiny area, lifting the showerhose off its hook as he flicked the water knob.

"You know what they say, don't you, Lizzie Dare?" He stepped inside, stealing every remaining inch of space with his big, bare body. He pulled the door firmly behind him and looked down at her with a dangerous gleam in his eye as he pointed the ice-cold spray right at her breasts. "Payback's a bitch."

CHAPTER
TWO

SHE GASPED AS the water hit her, honey gold eyes flying open as she held her hands up to stave off the shock.

"You know my name?" she sputtered, backing up.

Con didn't answer but moved the nozzle to target that shapely little bicep she'd splattered. "Does it burn anywhere at all?"

She shook her head, a mop of shoulder-length blond curls already dampening from splashed water. "You?"

As if she cared, the treacherous little thief. "No, but like I said, that stuff can sneak up on you."

"Kind of like you did," she shot back. "What were you doing in there, anyway?"

A *pretty* treacherous little thief, with beautiful pink nipples that were beading up like pebbles before his eyes. "I heard you go in."

"There's no way," she said under her breath.

"There's a way," he assured her. No matter how silent she thought she'd been, Con could hear. He'd heard her breathe when she passed the bunk. He'd heard the key in the lock. And she, of course, never heard him follow her.

Could it be this easy? Could he have found his target less than three hours after he climbed on board?

"Other arm, Lizzie."

Her cunning eyes narrowed, forming a delicate crease that pointed straight to a pixie nose and a heart-shaped face that looked far too innocent and appealing to be a criminal's. Looks could be so deceiving.

Hesitantly, she stretched out her arm for washing. "How do you know my name?"

"I was given a list of crew members when I signed on."

"There are four women on this boat."

"And only one is five-four and a hundred and ten pounds." A hundred and ten well-distributed, nicely proportioned, sweet little pounds of *trouble*.

"The list had our heights and weights?"

"I'm thorough." Water sluiced over her breasts and down a clenched stomach. "This leg got hit, didn't it?" he asked. "There were holes in your pants on your right leg."

"Yes." She offered him her thigh, and he studied it for signs of burn dots. He saw none and his gaze moved up to the narrow strip of darkened hair between her legs. Beautiful, feminine, and wet.

No surprise, his cock stirred.

"Turn around," he said sharply, using his free hand on her shoulder to get her in the other direction.

When she did, he lingered over her back, taut and toned, straight down to a high, round ass.

"At least you're smart enough to take the treatment and not go all modest on me." So he could be equally smart, and not let his body respond to the visuals.

"I live on boats with divers for months at a time. Most of them are men, and all of our days are spent in bathing suits. I lost my modesty years ago."

He called up his mental file of Elizabeth Dare. Daughter of famed salvager Malcolm Dare. Highly skilled SCUBA diver with a recognized expertise in treasure hunting. Thirty, single, and commonly known as Lizzie.

It didn't say anything about smart-mouthed, pretty-faced, or smooth-assed. And Lucy thought she was so damn thorough.

He aimed the spray right between her legs, drinking in the curves of her heart-shaped behind.

"It's a shame I have to turn you in tomorrow morning."

"Turn me in?" She spun around, eyes on fire. "I wasn't doing anything wrong."

He just lifted a brow and turned the spray to his shoulder where a few drops of the acid had splashed on his T-shirt. "You were breaking and entering the cleaning lab and about to help yourself to the treasure. Define *wrong* for Mr. Paxton."

"Paxton?" She rolled her eyes. "That explains it. And I thought you might be one of the good guys."

"You thought wrong."

She grabbed the spray nozzle. "Here, let me get your back."

He relinquished the showerhead, turning so she

could see if he had any acid burns on the back of his shoulder. "Any spots?"

"Guess I missed," she said dryly.

He glanced back and caught her checking out his backside exactly as he'd studied hers. "Looks like I saved both our asses."

She lifted her gaze from his, not the least bit coy about having looked. "What the hell else should I have done?" she asked. "I thought you were going to hurt me."

"Someone has to stop a thief."

"I know you've made up your mind about this, but I wasn't stealing anything."

He turned to face her. "Yeah, right."

She aimed the water right in his face. "Any burns *there*?"

He blinked, dodging the spray, spitting water as he seized the nozzle. "Not for lack of trying."

"You got that right," she said, disgust rolling off her like the water cascading over her rock-hard nipples. "How was I supposed to know you were the new diver?"

"If I *had* been there to attack you, you moved fast and smart. Good thing I'm faster and smarter." He glanced down to his dick, which was dangerously close to coming back to life. He sprayed it, watching her eyes follow the water.

"Did I get you there?" she asked, nothing like apology or worry in her voice.

"Damn close."

The intensity of her stare and the iciness of the water canceled each other out, keeping his arousal at bay. But it wouldn't last much longer if he spent much more time in a two-by-two head naked with Lizzie Dare.

"Listen," she said, pointing a finger at him. "What you saw was *not* what it looked like."

How many times had he been in her situation, faced with an accuser, forced to manufacture some wild-ass excuse? A few.

"So, let me take a guess. You left something in there, woke up in the middle of the night, remembered, and went back for it?"

"No."

"I know," he said, snapping wet fingers and pointing to her. "You had a sudden urge to polish the silver."

"No."

Their gazes locked, their bodies close, their breaths matching. One more step and they'd touch.

But his orders were to get close to the crew. He might have the thief, but did he have the potential leak?

"Then what were you doing in there?" he asked.

She couldn't back up, so she jutted her chin up, pink lips pursed in defiance. "Can I trust you?"

"Honey, we're naked in a shower, a water drop apart, and I haven't laid a hand on you to do anything but make sure you're not hurt." He tilted his head to the side and gave her a lazy, inviting smile. "Of course you can trust me."

Lizzie blinked through the water on her lashes to study him more intently. This man was a study in contrasts.

His eyes were the color of a winter sky set against

olive-toned skin, and his ebony hair was short enough to qualify for the military, but he certainly didn't seem . . . safe. He'd jumped her like a man bent on killing, but saved her in one smooth, slick move. Despite a threatening body jacked with muscles and high-octane testosterone, he'd been positively protective since the moment she'd met him.

And he was right. They were naked and close, and the nitric acid wasn't the only chemical combustion going on between them. Still, he hadn't done anything but check her out.

He looked bad . . . but seemed good.

Could she trust him? Not with *everything*, but just enough to test his loyalties. "I just wanted a picture of something we recovered today."

"A picture? Then why not take it in the middle of the day, on the deck, with witnesses?"

"Because we're not allowed to take pictures of the treasure, of anything," she told him. "Didn't Paxton tell you that when you took the job?"

He shrugged, noncommittal. "I know things are a little different on this dive."

That was one way of putting it. "Do you know why they are different?"

"Security reasons," he said, parroting what the crew had been told.

"Right." She snorted softly, still assessing him.

He was a perfect stranger who could be sworn to loyalty by Satan or his stepson, and even if he believed her and wanted to help, he'd think she was nuts. But if she didn't tell him the truth—or at least part of it—he was going to rack up Brownie points with the boss by turning her in.

Then she'd be off the dive before her work was done.

"I'm trying to preserve history before Judd Paxton sells it on the open market, and uses the money to build another monument with his name on it."

He didn't react, but stared her down, considering that.

"I was trying to get some shots of the treasure before it disappears to a private collector," she explained.

"So you're just breaking the terms of your contract, not robbing our boss blind." He speared her with a smoky look that sent heat coiling through her, doused when his words hit her.

"Our boss?" One ding for the hot diver. "So you *have* been bought and brainwashed by Judd Paxton already."

"I've never even met the guy. I just take the pay-check—which, as you know, is better than most."

She surveyed his face, trying to read his indecipherable expression. Impossible.

"Come on," she finally said. "We're de-acidified. I want to get dressed. I'm freezing."

"You can't put those clothes back on," he said. "They still have traces of nitric acid on them. I'll get you something to wear."

"Fine." She tried to get by him but he grasped her elbow.

"After you tell me why you want to take pictures, Lizzie."

"In case we get caught out here. This dive is illegal. I don't know if you know anything about Paxton, but he's made his millions selling most of what his dives recover to private collectors. He gets to pocket a lot more if it's not reported. Not to mention that, without a claim or lease, we're a ghost ship out here. No one knows we're here. That's dangerous. Pirates—real ones—could board us at any time."

"So you're going to fight them off with pictures?"

"If that chain happens to disappear somewhere between this boat and the processing lab in Sebastian, then so does a little piece of history. Do you care about that, or are you just in this for the money, like Paxton?"

His gas flame eyes sent a blood rush from her toes to her ears. "So if you hate the company owner, resent his rules, and already have credentials, why did you take the job?"

For reasons he'd never get her to admit. "I needed the money," she said easily. "There's not a lot of salvage action in the winter, this beats cleaning heads on a ship in dry dock, and . . . it seemed like an intriguing opportunity."

He took another long, slow look at her body. "We better go get your camera, then, before someone finds it."

Hope surged. "Does that mean you're not going to turn me in?"

"That means I'm going to keep my eye on you." He stepped to the side, opened the door, and nudged her out. "And I like the rear view very much."

She was lying. Lizzie Dare had an agenda as sure as she had a blistering hot body, and he intended to find out a lot more about both.

"I'm afraid I don't have much you can wear," he said, glad he'd stashed his bag under the bunk, so all that she could see was a backpack and the clothes he'd shed when he arrived.

He grabbed them, pulling on khaki shorts and a shirt. He had a plan, and she needed to be undressed for it to work.

Taking a towel from a rack next to the head, he held it out. "Small, but it'll cover the essentials until I get back."

"Where are you going?"

"Your cabin to get you clothes. Is it unlocked?"

"No. The key's in my sweatshirt in the lab."

"I'll be right back."

He didn't think she'd run down the hall in that tiny towel, giving him enough time to do a quick search of her room.

In the lab he carefully gathered the clothes—which did include a camera in the pocket, as well as two keys—and dropped them into a plastic bag he found next to the sink where they'd washed. Carrying it out, he locked the lab using one of the keys she'd obviously stolen, and headed up to the quarters deck to her cabin.

He knew where every one of the crew slept; Lucy's file had a full layout of the boat. Lizzie's cabin was between the brother divers, Kenny and Walt Brubaker, who shared a double bunk, and the conservator and diver couple, Charlotte and Sam Gorman.

Would he even have to interview the other divers, or did he already have the person he'd come to find? She certainly hated Judd Paxton, and every excuse she gave was riddled with guilt and lies.

If things kept going his way, he'd be signing a contract with Lucy by the end of the week.

He slipped the key in and entered her cabin, far more spacious than his. The bed was unmade, the room just disheveled enough that he wouldn't leave any evidence that he'd searched it.

Dropping the plastic bag, he headed straight to the small built-in dresser next to the bed. The drawers were a jumble of bathing suits and underwear and tank tops, but nothing incriminating. Maybe the small work desk.

On top, a few paperbacks with two dive magazines, all well read. He flipped open each drawer, one with odds and ends, the next, a little makeup, some simple jewelry. The third, a deep file drawer, was locked.

Promising.

With a penknife, he opened it easily. Inside was a photograph of an older man on the deck of a boat, a gold trinket hanging from his hand, and another photo of the same man on another boat with two little girls about ten and twelve, each displaying huge smiles and shiny gold coins.

Either girl could have been Lizzie, especially the one with lighter hair, more curls, and the sweetheart face. Beneath the pictures were a few pages of computer printouts about treasure hunting. Then an article about Judd Paxton, torn from *Time* magazine.

And the flimsiest piece of cheap pressboard at the bottom of the drawer, not even close to the wood stain of the desk. A pathetically bad false bottom. It snapped right out of place, and under it he found a brown leather notebook.

He fluttered the pages, full of sketches of jewelry, brass buckles, a porcelain jar, some hand-drawn charts, notes in the margins in scratchy, shaky handwriting, and then, on the last pages, the large block-letter heading: *El Falcone.*

Gotcha, Lizzie.

Although it wasn't irrefutable proof that she was leaking the information. He studied the last few pages of sketches: a cross with jewels, a religious pendant, and an elaborate cup encrusted with gems. On the next page, no pictures, just three words. *The Bombay Blues.*

Oh, man. He definitely had his target.

He toyed with the idea of taking the notebook, but that would alert her and she was smart enough to know he had to have taken it. He returned it, feeling around for anything else and touched something hard, plastic, and thin.

A cell phone.

This really was ridiculously easy. He'd caught her red-handed and found the phone she wasn't supposed to have. How long it took her to discover it was missing would tell him just how badly she wanted it. He pocketed the phone, then replaced the false bottom.

He didn't have absolute proof that she was the thief, though. No treasure was hidden in her room.

He grabbed the first pair of shorts he saw, a top like the strappy one he'd stripped from her, and hustled back to his cabin, opening the door just in time to find her rifling through his backpack.

"Still looking for treasure, Lizzie?"

Not that it mattered. He'd hidden the Bullet Catcher dossier on the assignment the minute he got in the room, and nothing in that bag could incriminate him.

"Just trying to figure out who you are." She held up a book. "Besides a guy who reads—and annotates—*The Odyssey.*"

"Greeks are brilliant."

"Exactly what I would expect a man named Constantine Xenakis to respond." She fluttered his passport. "You've been a lot of places, Mr. X."

"Here you go." He tossed the clothes at her, giving her long, bare legs an open appraisal. "Don't rush dressing on my behalf."

She stood up and dropped the towel, a plucky expression on her face. "Thanks."

"Good thing you didn't burn that body," he said, taking a nice long time to appreciate the curves and angles of a well-toned woman, the dive suit tan lines drawing his eyes to the most private parts, the impact on his lower half exactly what she must have wanted. "Be a damn shame to wreck . . . perfection."

As she stepped into the shorts she smiled, her hair falling over her shoulders. "Now you're going to compliment me? Why do I think you have to have an ulterior motive?"

"Because thieves never trust anyone."

She stood, zipping the shorts, facing him as she reached for the top. "I'm not a thief, but I see there's no way to convince you of that."

He lapped up the last flash of pink nipples before they disappeared. "There might be a way."

She yanked the top on. "Forget it. I'm not going to screw you so you don't rat on me."

"That's not what I was thinking."

She notched her chin toward the bulge in his shorts. "No? Looks like you were."

"So I'm human. And you're hot. But I wasn't suggesting sex."

She flipped her curls out from under the tank top straps and shook her head a little. "So, what then? What's it going to take to buy your silence?"

"Maybe a cut of what you're getting?"

Her jaw loosened. "Excuse me?"

"You heard me. Take in a partner on this dive."

"You don't get it, do you?" She laughed softly. "I don't need a partner, because I'm not stealing anything. I'm taking pictures so when Paxton's treasures 'accidentally' disappear before the state of Florida even finds out we were diving for them, there's proof that they existed. No cut, X. There's no buyer for my pictures."

Was it possible she was telling the truth? There was something . . . oddly innocent about her, despite the feisty act.

"You been salvaging long, Lizzie?"

At the sudden change of topic, she shot him a sharp look. "I was practically born on a boat. My father was a marine archaeologist, and he took my sister and me on plenty of dives."

"Was?" He knew from her file that her father had died fairly recently, and the pain on her face said the grief was still pretty raw.

"He passed away a few months ago," she said, tucking some stray curls back from her lightly freckled cheek. "Diving accident."

That he didn't know. "What happened?"

She took a breath, tried for a casual shrug. "I don't know, I wasn't there." The ache was clear in her voice. "Nitrogen narcosis."

He thought about that for a second, frowning. "On a salvage dive? How deep was he?"

"Not a salvage dive." She waved her hand, dismissing the subject. "What are you going to do with my clothes?"

"Destroy them. And after you go to your cabin, I'll go clean the lab."

"So, then . . ." She gave him a questioning look and let her words fade away.

"Your secret is safe with me." He stood slowly, getting right in front of her, as close as he was in the shower. With one finger, he lifted her chin and forced her to look right at him. "For the time being."

She didn't flinch, didn't look away. "So, what, you can lord it over me whenever you want something?"

"That could work." He lowered his face one centimeter and saw the flicker of response in her eyes. A hint of pink rose in her creamy cheeks, darkening those few freckles, warming the skin under his fingertips.

Her lips parted to take in a soft breath, drawing him closer.

She stepped back, keeping the sly smile on her face. "Two can play the blackmail game, Mr. X." Without breaking eye contact, she reached into the side pocket of his backpack to slide out the satellite phone. "This is banned on the boat, baby."

He barely shrugged in response. "I'm keeping it."

"You do that. And tomorrow, remember that we'll be meeting for the *first* time." She dropped the phone back in the bag and wiggled her fingers in farewell.

He had her phone out and had started logging her calls before she'd even reached her cabin door.

CHAPTER
THREE

THERE WAS A damn good reason that salvage season took place during the summer, Lizzie thought as she dug through the clean pile to find thick sweats and an ancient University of Miami sweatshirt to pull over her diving suit.

It was freaking *cold* at sea in November, even off the coast of Florida.

The toothpaste was chilly on her tongue and she brushed furiously, working up a lather before she looked into the mirror in her head. She plucked at her wavy bang, which had gone way past needing a trim weeks ago, and let it tumble over her face. Was this how she looked last night, bare naked in a head with one of the most attractive men she'd ever met?

The thought tightened her belly again, as it had last night when he whipped off his clothes.

But it wasn't just the way he responded to that nitric acid—so protective and calm under pressure. Sure, he was a smart-ass, cocky as hell, and determined to paint her as a thief when she wasn't one—not technically, anyway—but there was something about him. And it wasn't just his gorgeous face and godlike body, although they didn't hurt the package.

She spat in the sink, rinsed her mouth, then checked the time.

Was it too early to call Brianna? Not that her twenty-six-year-old sister needed to be checked on, but worrying about that impulsive little spitfire had been Lizzie's job since Mom died when they were little, and the feeling of being the "parent" had intensified when they lost Daddy.

She yanked open her secret drawer and pulled out all the junk that covered the piece of pressboard she'd laid in the bottom, just in case some crewmember got nosy. It wasn't a masterful job, but—

Shit.

She moved her hand around, flipping out the cheap board to search more thoroughly. Where had she left her phone? She was sure she'd hidden it here the last time she called Bree.

Then another wave of panic hit her. Daddy's journal! She stabbed to the back, blowing out a sigh of relief when she touched the leather. Thank God. No one had taken her phone, or he'd have helped himself to the notebook, too.

So where did she leave it? She scanned every surface, flipping some clothes, books, magazines. She couldn't even call it, as she did at home when she lost it, because no one else had a phone.

Well, Constantine Xenakis did. But if she asked him

to come to her room and call her phone, then he'd have one more thing to blackmail her with.

She'd find it later. She had the morning dive so she didn't have much time, and the only thing she wanted more than to hear her sister's voice was to drink some of Brady's morning brew.

Heading out, she made it three steps down the hall when the stateroom door next to hers opened.

"Mornin', Lizzie Lou." Sam Gorman patted her back so hard, she almost lost her balance. It always gave her a start when he used Dad's special nickname for her, but she didn't have the heart to ask him to stop.

"Hey, Sam."

"How'd ya sleep?" He gave her shoulder a friendly squeeze, as he had many times on many boats for many years, his gentle blue eyes crinkling from thousands of hours under the Florida sun, his face looking every one of his fifty-some years and more.

"Eh, you know."

"I know," he said, nudging her forward. "Every day gets easier, dear, I promise. You have to move on. That's why you're here, and that's what Malcolm would want."

At her father's name, her heart hurt. "That and the paycheck, Sam."

That wasn't at all why she was here, but he'd done her a favor by getting her on this dive, and she wasn't about to tell him her real reasons for taking it.

"And you know what I smell?" he said as they headed up to the deck.

She laughed. "Gold."

"You got it! I smell gold in that water, Lizzie. And you know what they say?"

"The blondes find the gold." They said it at exactly the same time, with the same dragged-out intonation.

She gave him an elbow. "You haven't been blond for years, Sam. But I hope you're right. Will Char be down in the lab later?"

There might still be a chance to sneak in and get a picture without the big Greek breathing down her neck. Not that having him breathe down her neck would suck—just not when she was in mission mode. And her mission of the moment was to get the lab key back in Charlotte's room.

"Maybe," he said. "But Flynn said he'd be leaving later this afternoon to deliver what we have in the lab to the mainland for processing. Guess who you're sched-uled to dive with this morning?"

"You. I checked last night."

"Shoulda checked this morning." They reached the deck. "Dave changed the schedule and you got the new guy. Constantine Xenakis. Have you met him yet?"

She was diving with *him*?

"Actually . . ." The sound of a now familiar voice made Lizzie freeze. "We haven't had the pleasure," he finished.

She turned slowly, and miraculously managed not to let out a "wow" at the sight of him. But, *wow*. The man was even better in daylight.

"Hello, Constantine." She offered a hand, and a se-cret smile of thanks.

"Just Con." He shook her hand, holding it just a

little too long with a glint in his eye. "Constantine is kind of a mouthful."

Yeah. A mouthful of *man*. Shirtless, with muscles on full display from broad shoulder to broad shoulder, the top half of his wet suit open and hanging over narrow hips. He added a smile that would melt a glacier and squeezed her hand like they were just going to be the best diving buddies ever.

"You must be Elizabeth Dare," he said, not letting go until every possible nerve ending in her hand had been thoroughly . . . *warmed*. "I've heard so much about you."

His voice was rich with tease, their secret hanging in the air between them. If there *was* any air. He seemed to soak up all the air and light and space just by being there. If this really had been the first time she'd seen this dude, she'd break her "no shipboard romances" rule in a hurry.

"You can call me Lizzie." She managed to take her hand back, but could still feel the tingle he'd left behind. "And I don't know what you've heard about me, but gossip is as plentiful as fish in these waters, so don't waste your time believing it."

"I only believe what I see with my own two eyes," he whispered, close enough to send a little shiver up her spine.

She turned to the deck, already alive with action, the scent of seawater mixed with that of bacon and coffee floating out from the galley in the main salon. Along the starboard side, Dave Hawn flipped open the divers' lockers, air hoses already looped over his arms.

"Have you met our divemaster?" Sam asked Con.

"He's already given me an orientation. And my dive schedule." He gave Lizzie another direct look. "Looks like we go down together this morning."

"Looks like it." At least she'd have some control over what he did down there. But after last night, he'd probably stick with her like they were tethered to each other. If she found what she was looking for, it could get tricky. "But I need coffee first."

"Make it fast," Dave hollered as she headed to the salon, his shoulder-length blond hair sliding over broad shoulders. "Kenny's already blown coquina and we want to go right back to where Alita found that chain yesterday."

As if on cue, Alita Holloway slinked up the steps, her black hair tucked neatly into a *Gold Digger* baseball cap, a diving suit barely covering her voluptuous body.

"Awful early for you, Princess," Lizzie said, narrowing her eyes to look under the bill at the beauty-pageant face. "And with mascara and everything."

Alita shot her a withering look. "Actually, Lizzie, if you haven't had breakfast yet, I'll switch shifts with you." Her gaze shifted to Con and her dimpled smile deepened. "I'm just dying to go back to that spot where I snagged that chain. I'd love to show you, Con."

Obviously they'd met already. Which would explain the mascara.

"Fine with me," Lizzie said. She could get the key back and her dive would definitely be easier without him distracting her. "I prefer afternoon dives in this weather, anyway."

"Don't screw with my schedule," Dave called out. "No substitutions. There's a science to this, you know."

They all looked at each other with knowing smiles.

"The science is that Dave is a control freak," Sam explained to Con.

In the salon, Charlotte Gorman, tucked into the corner of one of the two dining booths, looked up from the chart spread in front of her, a frown of concern forming. "You feeling okay, Lizzie? You look flushed."

"I'm fine, Char." As she breezed through the aisle between the tables and headed back to the breakfast buffet, Lizzie reached out and tapped Charlotte's knuckles. Sam's wife of less than a year was not only the conservator, making her the one person who would have her hands on every single treasure before it left the ship, she was also the closest thing Lizzie had to a girlfriend on this boat. So the temptation to trust her and even enlist her help was strong, but Lizzie had resisted so far.

For one thing, if Charlotte assisted Lizzie in getting detailed pictures of recovered salvage and in making comparisons to the drawings in Dad's journal, then Charlotte would be an accomplice, and Lizzie didn't want to put her in that position.

She also didn't know her as well as she knew Sam. But, without help from someone soon, her whole plan would fall apart. That could happen any day, on any dive.

So who could she trust?

A soft breath moved the hair against her back, making her splash coffee mid-pour.

"Divemaster Dave says he's ready for us."

"I haven't had my coffee," she said, turning, bracing

for the proximity of Con's body and the sheer power of his eyes.

"I returned the lab key to its rightful owner." His voice was little more than a baritone rumble, the very sound of it like a sexy come-on. She glanced at Charlotte, but the other woman was deep into her charts again.

"Thanks for covering for me," she said softly, lifting her coffee mug to her lips. "Keep up the good work and I might let you have first hands on a gold coin."

"First hands?" His brow shot up. "I like the sound of that."

"Let's go, crew!" Dave popped his head into the salon with a sharp look at Lizzie. "We got a schedule to maintain."

She threw a wistful glance at the coffee and another at the man who made her miss it. "I hope you know what you're doing down there, Con. I can't babysit." She zoomed out to the deck, where she checked the stern blower while she stepped into her suit. Con came right over to her, zipping up and studying the murky water churning below.

"You ever dive with a blower, Con?" Kenny Brubaker's sun-kissed curly hair blew around his head in the breeze, but his eyes were blocked by the reflective shades he wore even on cloudy days.

"Not for a while," Con replied.

Lizzie threw a look at Kenny. Great, a rookie.

"Lemme just give you a primer." Kenny pointed to the two metal elbow-shaped pipes mounted onto the stern and swung over the prop. "Those are dusting about three feet of sand, and they'll run the whole time you're down there. You dive right under them and go to work when you hit the pan—meaning the hard coquina shell under the sand. You'll have the metal detectors, but stay next to Lizzie while you get the lay of the land down there. We'll be operating the air hoses and you can signal with them."

"What's the system of pulls?" Con asked.

"One pull on your hose means stop the blower. Two means start it up, three means you found something. Four means major find." Kenny grinned. "We like those the best."

Lizzie pointed to the air hoses that Dave was readying. "Just remember, we're down fifty feet and there's about a hundred feet of line, so feel free to take the tether room. The more we spread out, the better our chances of finding something."

Con gave her a knowing look. "You really don't want to dive with me, do you?"

"Just spelling out the guidelines," she said.

"Stay within sight of each other," Dave interjected. "Which is close, because it's bright enough to see a few feet away, but at this time of year, distance visibility is low." He nudged them toward the dive platform. "Use those detectors, and put your masks to the pan—especially the outer edge, where you'll have the best luck. If it shines or sparkles or makes that thing ding, we want it."

Kenny brought the metal detectors over to them. "First one to touch a treasure gets credit in the books, a *Gold Digger* baseball cap, and the biggest piece of Brady's celebration cake."

"That's 'first hands,' I take it," Con said.

"First hands aren't important," Dave replied, humorless as always. "And, just for the record, the second hands are mine or Flynn's; from there the goods go to Charlotte. We're not on this dive for caps or cake."

"I know why we're here," Con replied, giving Lizzie a meaningful look.

She pulled her mask down and shimmied to the dive platform, resentment burning. "If you have beginner's luck, I swear I'll kill someone," she murmured.

Con got closer to her. "Who says I'm a beginner?"

"Hookahs in!" Dave hollered. "Let's get to work, troops!"

Lizzie snapped her hose, checked it, then slid into the icy cold water. A second later, a warm, strong body was next to her, as close to her face as he could be with the air hoses separating them.

She knew it. She'd be wearing him on this dive.

Behind his mask, he winked, took her free hand with his, and pulled her deep into the murky water.

Con hated to dive. He could do it, and had, many times since that bad, black mission in Quezon City. But every time he submerged, he remembered that night, that save, that *choice*, and what it cost him.

Everything. It cost him fucking everything. So he hated to dive, which was probably one of the many reasons Ms. Machiavelli picked this job as his Bullet Catcher test.

They dropped straight down through the sandstorm blowing under the set of pipes that directed the prop-wash to the bottom. Con kicked through it, heading toward a two-foot-high pyramid-shaped ballast pile. These black stones were proof that they had found a bona fide shipwreck, since the pile of weighted rocks used to center the vessel was probably all that remained of the actual ship. There could be cannon down there and, of course, the cargo.

Lizzie started to swim to the edge of the pan, and he stayed right next to her, still highly suspicious of her, even though there hadn't been anything incriminating on her phone. The only person she'd been in contact with since she'd gotten on board was Brianna Dare, whom he assumed was a sister, though he hadn't asked the Bullet Catchers investigative team to verify that yet. Still, he wasn't about to let his little thief out of his sight underwater.

For one thing, the notebook she was hiding in her room proved she knew exactly which shipwreck they were salvaging. She was his number one target for the moment, which was why he'd subtly convinced the divemaster to let him dive with her.

If *he* wanted to steal treasure on a dive, he'd forget the stuff being recovered and processed. He'd take it right from the bottom of the ocean and no one would be the wiser.

Lizzie slithered in front of him, took his arm, and yanked him away from the ballast pile, using her metal detector to point forcefully at the perimeter of the coquina-shell pan.

He followed her lead, working tirelessly for almost an hour, recovering nothing but a nail, which she slipped into a zippered pouch on her weight bag. Periodically she checked the ballast pile, probably gauging a direction or specific spot where something had been found.

In one place, she mimed the line of a necklace around her neck. That must be close to where Alita found the chain. She pointed for him to go several feet away and start detecting while she worked where she stood.

In other words, go out of visibility distance.

Not a chance. He shook his head and she dropped her shoulders and glared at him in disgust. Then she tapped her dive watch, hard, and made a gesture of frustration. They were running out of time, she was trying to tell him. Meaning the discovery, if there was to be one today, might be made by the next dive team.

Reluctantly, he nodded, pointing to a place he'd go, still within visibility of her. She agreed with a half shrug, then flicked her hand as if to say, *Move it!* He swam there, splitting his attention between the sand on the pan and the woman who was now turned so he couldn't see if she dropped something into her weight bag.

How long would it have taken him to hone in on Lizzie Dare if he hadn't caught her in the lab? Not long, because he'd have honed right in on her anyway as soon as he met her. She might not have the lingerie model's body that Alita Holloway had, but there was something much more attractive to him about Lizzie.

He glanced over to watch her glide through the water, her concentration unaffected by a school of bluefish that swam between her and her magnetometer, her attention focused so intensely it was like watching a machine work the hunt.

The soft beep of her detector sounded, and she reacted. Instantly, he swam over, reaching her in two long kicks, setting his device down to move the dirt by hand.

She worked the detector like it was an extension of her body, following the speed of the beeps, faster, louder . . . closer.

He brushed a chunk of coral out of his way, and as it rolled, the underside glowed bright gold, like it had just been polished and put under a light.

Their hands smashed together as they lunged for it, but he was faster, closing his fingers over the metal and gently nudging it free. He heard her loud and furious grunt of frustration.

Con held it out for her to see, carefully brushing some loose bits of sand to reveal the shape as he turned it in the water.

Frustration gone for a moment, Lizzie just floated closer, drawn to the two-inch round brooch or medallion, a purplish crust around at least a half-dozen gemstones and something that ran straight down the center.

She reached out to loosen more coral, her fingers reverent and her movement slow. Through the water, he heard her low moan of reaction. Surprise and disbelief widened her eyes. Recognition.

She *knew* this piece.

Con closed his other hand around his hose, but Lizzie reached out, stabbing her fingers through the water to stop him from signaling, her eyes flashing at him.

She held up her hand as if to say, *Wait.*

Why wait to tell the ship they'd made an amazing recovery?

She put her hands together as though to plead with him, her eyes soft and begging. Then she reached for it, tentatively, holding up one finger as if to ask for just one minute with it.

As her fingers moved toward the treasure, her eyes met his with nothing but desire, and he couldn't deny her the moment. Obviously she couldn't steal it right in front of him. And he couldn't care less about having the "first hands" touch the treasure and getting credit for the find.

He let her take it, rewarded by a smile in her golden brown eyes.

She brushed the coral-encrusted piece with a gentle finger, holding it toward the sunlight that streamed through the water, examining it carefully. She turned it over, ran her fingers along the sides, counted the jewels, including the dent where one had been lost.

Her fingers trembled with awe, and her shoulders rose and fell as her breaths were obviously tight and quick.

Still holding it, she pointed at the spot where he'd found it, as if to say they should look for more.

No way. Part of his job was to protect the treasure, and this piece was a major find. With an easy snatch, Con took the medallion from her, getting a fiery look through her mask.

He tugged four times on his hose.

She twirled away and kicked hard, straight up. He unzipped the pouch on his weight belt, slid the medallion in, then bent over to pick up his detector.

She was already being pulled onto the dive platform by Kenny and Dave, and a group was gathering on the main deck, the excitement and noise palpable the minute Con popped through the surface.

"What did you get?" Alita called out.

"Hand over the goods," Charlotte said as she climbed down to the platform, a cloth spread out like a baby's receiving blanket.

"Gold or jewels?" Dave demanded, his voice rising with excitement.

Con hoisted himself to the platform and looked at Lizzie, who was shaking out her wet hair after pulling off her mask.

"What?" she said, a little hostility in her voice. "Just show them."

As he unhooked his air hose and flipped up the mask, Flynn Paxton came across the deck, the first time he'd made an appearance since Con had arrived. He had the same sun-bleached hair the divemaster sported, but his looked more salon-styled than surfer dude.

"What do we have?" He lifted sunglasses as he strode to the dive platform.

Alita put her hands on her hips and gave Con a glamour-shot smile. "We have beginner's luck, that's what."

"No beginner's luck," he said quietly, unzipping the pouch and kneeling down next to where Lizzie sat. "I just brought it up. Lizzie found it."

He felt her bristle, but she didn't say a word. He reached in, slid the piece out, then looked at her.

"Lizzie had first hands," he said.

Her expression softened momentarily.

Paxton clunked clumsily onto the platform. "Nice work, Lizzie." He seized it out of Con's hands and waved the medallion. "You brought us good luck, Con! Welcome aboard."

"Hey!" Lizzie choked, grabbing Paxton's arm. "Be careful. It's a hundred and fifty years old!"

"We don't know that yet, Lizzie," he said.

But Lizzie did, Con thought. She knew exactly what the piece was.

Con stood and turned to where Charlotte held out the cloth. "Let's handle it with the appropriate care, Mr. Paxton."

Ignoring the chastisement, Paxton put the piece in the cloth, bending close to it. "What is it?"

"A religious artifact," Con said. "Hard to tell until that crust is gone, but it looks quite distinctive."

"I don't know what it is," Kenny said, joining them with a brand-new hat, still folded from being in a box. "But I recognize greatness when I see it. That right there could pay for this whole excursion. Here you go, Ms. Dare." He handed her the cap with a flourish. "You are officially a Gold Digger."

For a moment, she just stared at the cap, then looked at Con.

He nodded. "Take it. You earned it."

She did, reluctantly. "It was kind of a tie," she said softly, still looking at him.

Paxton nodded to Charlotte. "Start the cleaning and conservation process," he ordered. "I want to get it off the boat."

"There's a lot of chloride on this," Charlotte said quickly. "I need twenty-four hours, then you can take it."

"Fine." Paxton glanced around as though sizing them up, and landed on Con. "You sleep in the lab tonight—we'll get a cot. I'm not taking any chances until we get this thing off board."

Kenny shot Paxton a disgusted look. "No one's going to take it."

"I'm not worried about the crew," Paxton said. "But after what happened on my dad's boats last summer, we're not taking any chances. Putting a person on guard is just added security."

Everyone on deck looked like they thought it was added bullshit, except Lizzie, who was staring at the piece as though she could memorize it, as though she would never see it again.

"And Lizzie," Paxton added, "we need to make an excursion to the mainland with Brady to get some supplies. I want you to come with me." Then he pointed to Con. "You don't leave that piece, and you have my permission to kill anyone who tries to touch it."

CHAPTER
FOUR

POWER. SOLANGE BETTENCOURT could swear she could feel the power of the scepter every time she picked it up, every time she stroked the plum-sized blue diamond that formed the handle. Maybe it *was* magical. Maybe it was imagined. Maybe it was just the fact that this stunning work of art was originally designed to be held by a king or queen, and used to force others to bend to their will.

Or maybe it wasn't power that Solange could feel, as she sat inside a three-hundred-year-old pile of stone cradling the scepter. Maybe it was just *irony*.

And irony made her laugh, something she'd stopped doing until she found this. Irony was a wonderful thing.

Especially the irony that Jaeger Bettencourt IV had shamed her, accused her of unspeakable things, then exiled her to a rock in the middle of the ocean . . . and that she had been stumbling up a hundred stairs on her way to throw her miserable body over a cliff and prove him right when she fell—literally, *fell*—on a loose stone and uncovered the very thing Jaeger wanted most in the whole world.

That's when the balance of power had shifted from Jaeger to her.

She had the greatest treasure ever lost, then found. Well, half of it. And if all went according to plan, she'd beat him to the other half.

A shiver skimmed up her arms when she thought about it.

Fortune had finally, finally smiled on her. And spat on the demon who made her an outcast. And all the despicable liars who called themselves *friends* as they whispered about her at fund-raisers and balls.

Solange is crazy.

Solange is suicidal.

Solange is taking a mental health break at one of the Bettencourts' vacation homes in the Azores.

As if this three-hundred-year-old dump and dingy old windmill would be a Bettencourt *vacation* home. He'd stuffed her away, made her take drugs she didn't want, planted a simpering fool of a nurse next to her, and stolen her life.

And inadvertently given her the treasure he wanted more than anything. She laughed out loud. Irony was pure fun.

The sound of her laughter bounced off the round stone walls, almost as loud as the never-ending groaning of the wheel and the cogs and the never-ending sweeps that blew the never-ending wind.

It had all seemed so never-ending . . . until she found this.

She tried to hold the scepter aloft, the way a queen might, but it was too heavy for her slender arm to manage. With two hands, she returned it to the white velvet bed she'd made for it, her attention shifting to the parchment papers spread over the rough-hewn wooden table. The words, despite the flourish of hundred-and-fifty-year-old script and a language barrier, were burned into Solange's brain now.

She'd even gone to that pathetic little library in town, found a Portuguese-English dictionary, and translated almost all the pages. Then committed them to memory.

She rubbed her arms against the coolness from the stone walls that surrounded her. Standing, she walked to the single door, the only opening in the whole windmill structure, looking out at the dark waters, blackness as far as she could see.

Was this the way it looked when Aramis Dare stole away in the night like the pirate he was, taking half of what he'd been paid to leave? Taking what belonged to the Bettencourt family, what now belonged to *her*?

She returned to the table, where the satellite phone sat silent. *Ring, damn it. Tell me what I want to—*

The soft beep of the phone thrilled her.

Oh, yes . . . she had *power*. And, God in heaven, she was going to use it to bring her husband the deepest form of misery he could imagine. As deep and miserable as the pit in her heart.

She answered, making sure she sounded commanding, and not breathless. Not crazy. This man was one of the only people who knew the truth about Solange. That she wasn't crazy, merely devious.

"I think we've got something."

His words tightened her insides. "Did you find—"

"No," he interjected. "But we found some proof that we're in the right spot. We're very close. The map you have is correct."

Of course it was. She'd copied it long ago from Jaeger's files—the minute she suspected that he was cooking up his plan to get rid of her. "What did you find?"

"There's a large jeweled pendant in the drawings. Are you familiar with it?"

"I'm not paying you to find a necklace," she said through gritted teeth.

"I know, Mrs. Bettencourt, but this is an important find. It tells us we're in the right place. Or at least, we have the right wreck. I need you to confirm some details."

"I have the papers here. I was just studying them."

"You shouldn't be touching them," he warned her. "Do you know how delicate they are? They could disintegrate in your hands. Be extremely careful. No oils should touch them. Keep them stored in the stone hold where you found them."

She closed her eyes and swallowed the urge to snap at him. They'd survived a century and a half under a stone stair in a windmill. A few hours in her hands wouldn't wreck them. But she needed this man too much to lash out.

"Describe the pendant," she said, carefully sliding out the parchment pages with the drawings.

"Look for something oval shaped, trimmed with

jewels, with a crucifix on one side and the mother of God on the other."

Mother of God was right. Her heart kicked a little as her eyes landed right on the image. They'd found it.

"The Our Lady of Sorrows pendant," she read the centuries-old script. "Seven jewels. Lots of curlicues and filigree. Is that it?"

"It could be," he replied. "Describe the shapes of the jewels."

"The top three are oval, the two on the sides are square, well . . ." She squinted at the faded drawing. "You could call them rectangular. The two on the bottom are round."

"That's it. We've got it. We've got it in our hands, Mrs. Bettencourt."

She was one step closer to seeing Jaeger weep with regret. "What kind of jewels are they?" she asked, more out of curiosity than anything. This piece wasn't important to her. She might use it to pay him off if—no, *when*—they found what she really wanted.

"One is missing, but the rest are diamonds on the side, and rubies. Decent size, and it's not sand-worn at all. The fact that this ship went down ten miles offshore is really in our favor," he said. "Much less damage from the coral reefs, and the stuff is buried so deep it should all be here—not picked over and not spread around. Now that we've found one piece, we'll start to bring up bounty every day."

Another thrill shot through her. They were getting closer. "Then dive and dig and call me every single time something is found."

"I'll do my best."

"And when you get the scepter, you know what to do."

"I do. I won't let you down."

"What about the crew and the other divers?" she asked. "Is everyone following orders?"

"Everyone is doing exactly what they're supposed to do."

She was dubious. People never did exactly what they were supposed to do. Wasn't she proof of that? Wasn't her famous and mighty fall from the pinnacle of society to a damn cow farm in the Azores proof of that?

"Remember, you are my eyes and ears," she reminded him. "That's what I'm paying you a lot of money to be. Someone could get very anxious to leak this activity now. If anyone—I mean *anyone*—leaks one word or shows any indication that they know or could beat us to it, then—"

"I've handled that in the past."

"Yes, you have. And what about Malcolm Dare's daughter?"

"She's right here, Mrs. Bettencourt. Ignorant and under constant watch."

"She'd better be ignorant." Of course, if Malcolm Dare had shared what he knew, his daughter would never have stayed quiet. Getting Lizzie on that boat was more proof of Solange's power and luck.

"I'll call you as soon as we make another recovery. In the meantime, this one will be hand delivered to safety and security on dry land."

"See to it that it is." She signed off and dropped the phone on the table, her gaze on the drawing of the pendant. A lovely piece. Very valuable. But not even close to what she wanted, and planned to have.

She lifted the scepter again. One without the other was like . . . well, a queen without her king. And Solange Bettencourt was willing to do just about anything to be queen again. And crush her king.

She gathered up the papers, heeding his warning to handle them with care, then put them in the metal box she kept them in. She took them first, glancing at the velvet-covered scepter. Should she try to carry both? No, it wasn't safe. Ana was in the kitchen and wouldn't renege on their agreement.

Ana gave her an hour alone each evening in the windmill, where Solange claimed to be "meditating" while Ana cleaned up after dinner, probably happy for the little reprieve from her charge.

Box in hand, Solange entered the darkened stairwell that encircled the inside of the windmill. Carefully, she climbed up, counting the stairs as they wended around the structure. The walls were rough, and the smell of the sea and old grain permeated everything.

When she reached the ninety-seventh step, the gears just a few feet away at the top were almost deafening. She bent over and lifted the stone on top.

Was it power or luck that made her trip over this stone the night she'd come up here to kill herself—her third failed attempt? How close she'd come to ending what was going to be a glorious existence.

She'd secretly stopped taking the meds, and of course the blackness in her heart had taken over her body like a cancer. It was going to be so easy . . . just throw herself from the windmill over a cliff hundreds of feet above the rocks of the Atlantic Ocean.

Proving every lie Jaeger had spread to be the truth.

Then she'd tripped. And there, like a miracle, lay the scepter. And then she'd checked every other step for secret hiding places and found the paperwork.

She gently laid the box in the hole.

"*Senhora* Bettencourt? Are you here, ma'am?"

Ana.

Her first thought was the scepter, out in the open on the small worktable. Oh, Lord, what if she found it?

Solange stayed very still, listening for movement. How could she explain it? A gift from her husband? Ana would know if something had been delivered. She remained still, flattened to the wall. Listening for the sound of Ana leaving.

But if she left and took the scepter! No, that just couldn't happen.

"*Senhora* Bettencourt?" The voice was closer, the Portuguese-accented English echoing over the stone as the young woman rounded the stairwell. "Are you fine, ma'am?"

Solange scrambled up the rest of the steps, pushing open the planked door to the gear room. She hated this place. A narrow ledge, not two feet wide, circled the top of the round windmill. There was no railing, no protection. One misstep, and you could fall right into the massive, grinding teeth of the gear turned by the windmill blades.

An ugly thought coiled around her brain. If Ana had the scepter . . .

She had to hide. Wait it out. Ana would leave if she thought Solange wasn't here. That main floor was dark. She might never see that scepter on the table.

But if she did . . . Solange needed a solution fast.

She followed the ledge to the door that led outside, the only way to get to the three giant sweeps that turned constantly in the wind. She could hide here, watch through the door, see if Ana had—

Whoosh! The giant blade spun right in front of her, the force almost knocking her over. She pressed herself against the rounded stone, the chill seeping through her, too terrified to look back to see if Ana followed her up there.

"*Senhora* Bettencourt!"

She had. Solange remained silent, willing the young nurse to just go away.

"*Senhora* Bettencourt!" The door opened slowly, and the first thing Solange saw was white velvet.

"*Senhora!* Do not do this!" Her brown eyes were full of sympathy, no doubt certain she'd found her boss about to commit suicide again. It wouldn't have been the first time. She held up the scepter in the velvet. "Where did you get this? Do you know what value it is? There is a tale of this, a folklore!" She practically quivered with excitement.

"What are you talking about?"

"You found this? Here in the mill? It is . . ." She lifted it as though making an offering to the gods.

"*Mine.*" Solange took it from her.

"Oh, no, ma'am. This belongs to Portugal!" She let it go, but only because she needed to put a hand on

Solange to coax her back inside. "There are stories, oh, madame, wait until I tell you what you've found. Here! On your farm! You will be famous!" She beamed in the moonlight. "You will be the most famous person in all of Portugal. This will go into museums. It will travel the world!"

But that wasn't what Solange wanted.

"Come," Ana said, affection and excitement making her eyes dance. "Come back down, *Senhora*. You have been doing so well for months. You don't need to do this."

As Ana turned, urging her inside, Solange gripped the wrapped scepter, nudging the huge diamond handle behind Ana. "No—I don't."

The push was hard, furious, and full of strength Solange didn't know she had. Ana gasped, reached out for balance, and when she did, Solange slammed the giant diamond into the young woman's back with enough force to topple her.

For a split second Ana seemed to hang in the air, just long enough to look right in Solange's eyes and realize what was happening to her. Then she plunged forward and the giant windmill sweep whooshed by with enough force to blow her off the side, her blouse billowing as she fell into the air, her scream lost in the wind as she tumbled down, down, down to her death.

The sound was lost in the crashing waves and the constant, aching groan of the windmill gears.

Solange cradled the scepter. *All that power.*

CHAPTER
FIVE

THE TAP ON the lab door surprised Con, and so did the stab of disappointment that it wasn't Lizzie. Was she *still* out with Paxton?

Alita lifted the corner of a napkin covering a plate, offering it to him along with a slow, sweet smile. "It would be a crime for you to miss Brady's Bacardi Double Chocolate cake just because you're babysitting the treasure."

"That was thoughtful of you." He took the plate and she raised a brow, obviously waiting for an invitation. He'd had long chats with Kenny and Walt Brubaker today but only a few minutes with Dave the divemaster in his effort to infiltrate the crew. Guess it was time for Diver Barbie. "Have you had any? I'll share."

Dimples deepened. "I hoped you'd ask, since I'm sacrificing the last piece for you. I thought Walt would stab me with his fork when I reached for it."

Con stepped to the side to let her in, his gaze sliding over the skin-tight jeans and T-shirt. "I'm getting the impression Brady is the most beloved crewmember on the boat."

"He is a masterful chef," she said, breezing in and giving the lab a visual sweep. "And he only bakes dessert when we make a great recovery, as motivation." She turned and trained deep blue eyes on him, the dimples still at work, a lock of dark hair sliding over her cheeks. "Where is it?"

That didn't take long. "Locked up."

She pointed to the cake. "That should buy me a look, don't you think?"

"I don't know." He pulled out a stool from the center table and offered it to her, taking the one next to it. "Haven't tasted it yet."

She slowly ran one finger over the icing, gathering a clump on the tip, then lifted it to his mouth with a look of pure sex. "Then have some."

He took the lick she offered and managed not to make a face. He didn't like sweets, and he didn't like pushy women. But he'd play her game, because his job wasn't quite done here.

"Very good."

She smiled as if he'd paid her the compliment, and not the cake. "So, I hear you were a Navy SEAL."

He'd told Kenny, who'd been in the Navy. "Word travels fast."

"On a boat with a dozen people in each other's face 24/7? You bet it does. How long have you been diving?"

"A while. How about you?"

"A few years."

He took a small bite of cake, avoiding the frosting. "What's your background?" He knew, of course. Dropped out of the University of Miami from a marine biology program, married a boat captain and started diving, divorced him a year later, kept diving.

"I'm a marine biologist."

And a liar. "Who dives for treasure."

"Hey, someone around here has to understand the environment. I know, I don't look like a marine biologist. But you *do* look like a Navy SEAL."

"I wasn't one for very long," he said, never comfortable with the idea that people thought he had some long and illustrious career as a SEAL. "How'd you get into diving?"

"The way all women get into a lifestyle change."

"A guy?"

She shrugged. "Of course. But he's gone."

"And you're still diving."

"It's an addiction, as you know." She tapped the tabletop with her nail. "So let me see it. It's not against the rules for me to look at it."

He pushed off the stool to unlock the cabinet. "Lot of rules on this boat, aren't there?"

"When Judd Paxton's signing the paychecks, we follow the rules." She came up next to him, letting her body brush his, her smile flirtatious. "Most of them, anyway."

He opened the steel-encased door and took out the medallion that had spent the afternoon soaking in a vinegar solution and under the ministrations of Charlotte Gorman's well-trained hands. The coral was gone from the gold, which gleamed, and the jewels were almost perfect.

"Charlotte thinks it needs some more cleaning, but . . ." He angled it for her to see. "It is a beauty."

She nodded, her eyes widening appreciatively. "And worth a ton."

"Have you seen anything like it before?" he asked.

"Nope." She ran her finger over the crucifix. "Makes you wonder just what we're searching for here."

"Doesn't it, though? What do you think?"

She shrugged, still studying the artifact. "We're too far out for the 1715 or 1733 fleets, so something independent, probably. Something that didn't go down in a hurricane, or it would be closer to shore."

"Any ideas?" he asked, holding her gaze, knowing the eye contact might open her up to talk.

"Not a one. I'm just here for the money."

He inched away. "I thought it was an addiction."

"I'm addicted to money." She laughed, leaning into the space he'd left between them. "Is that something you find unattractive?"

"Not passing opinion on it." He returned the medallion to the cloth bedding Charlotte had made for it and reached to close the cabinet door, but Alita put her hand in his arm, stopping him.

"You need to see it again?" he asked.

"I just . . ." She leaned over and let her shoulder press into his arm. "I kind of want a picture of it."

Another one with pictures? "No can do, sweetheart. That would be against Mr. Paxton's rules."

"Screw Mr. Paxton."

"I suppose you could try that and see if he lets you take pictures."

She put a hand on his bicep and squeezed. "Is that *your* price?"

Con spun at the sound of a shuffled foot and a tap that pushed open the entry that he'd left ajar.

Lizzie stood there, a knowing smile on her face. "That didn't take long."

For a moment, he just looked at her, a sensation kicking him that was exactly the opposite of what he'd felt five minutes ago when Alita arrived.

"As you know so well," he said, closing and locking the cabinet door, "things aren't always what they seem."

"Well, I *seem* to be intruding, so see ya later." She nodded at Alita and turned to leave, but he reached her in two steps, getting hold of her elbow as she stepped into the hall.

"Wait."

Surprise darkened her amber eyes. "What?"

"How was your excursion?" Dumb question, but he didn't want her to leave.

She smiled, almost as though she got that, but behind him Alita cleared her throat and Lizzie's gaze slid past his shoulder.

"We're just about done," he said softly.

She flicked a playful finger at his unbuttoned shirt. "I see that."

"Don't leave." He still held her elbow and gave it a squeeze. "I want to talk to you."

She slipped out of his grip, her gaze skimming his face, stopping at his mouth, then going back to his eyes. "Stop by later."

"I will."

"On one condition," she added. "Bring your phone."
She mouthed the last three words so Alita didn't hear.

She headed away slow enough that he could watch
the sway of her faded jeans, a siren call of a backside
he'd already seen in the flesh, and wanted to see more.

He turned his attention to Alita, wondering how
quickly he could get rid of her.

She was on his makeshift cot, thumbing through *The
Odyssey*.

"Color me impressed, Constantine."

"Don't be."

She laughed, leaning back on two hands, letting her
sizable rack jut forward, a toss of thick black hair com-
pleting the come-on.

He reached for Alita's hand and her eyes sparked, but
then she realized he was helping her up from the cot.
"And I need to get back to reading."

"You're kicking me out." There was a note of surprise
in her voice. She probably didn't get turned down too
often.

"Thanks for the cake."

She gave his hand a little squeeze and sent a regretful
look at the closet where he'd locked the medallion, con-
firming that she wanted it, or a picture of it, as much or
more than she wanted him.

Could *she* be the traitor?

"Hope you're just as lucky tomorrow," she said as
she headed out. "Brady said he'll make strawberry
cheesecake."

"I'll do my best, but Lizzie found that medallion."

"Yeah, right."

"You don't believe me?"

"Lizzie never finds anything," she said, stepping out into the hall. "Since we've been on this dive, she comes up empty-handed every time. Then she goes down with you and, bam, she brings up the best recovery of the trip so far. You were a sweetheart to let her have credit for it."

"Maybe I'm good luck."

Or maybe she wasn't showing her finds to the crew. Maybe she was slipping them into her weight belt when no one was watching. And then maybe she was contacting someone who secretly met her at night and she handed them off. Maybe he'd better get up to her bunk, now.

"Well, I'd like to dive with you tomorrow," Alita said. "So I can rub up against some of your luck."

"That's up to Dave, I suppose."

Even after he closed the door, he could hear her footsteps on the stairs. He waited long enough for the sound to disappear, for Alita to go into her bunk, or maybe up to the main deck where some of the crew was watching a movie and eating cake.

He retrieved Lizzie's phone from the hiding place, then slid it into the pocket of his jeans next to his own.

Locking the entry with a new dead bolt he'd installed, not bothering with shoes, he moved soundlessly up the stairs to the quarters deck, paused to make sure the hall was empty, then took a few long strides to her door.

One tap, and it was open.

"That was fast," she said, then she peeked around him. "Or did you bring your new girlfriend?"

He grinned. "Stop, or I'll think you're jealous."

She rolled her eyes and stepped back, letting him in.

"You cleaned up," he said, looking around. It wasn't exactly pristine, but he could see more surfaces than before.

"That's why I need your phone," she said, holding her hand out. "I lost mine. I need to use yours to call it. And don't even think about giving me shit for having one. We all signed papers, and I bet half the crew has them."

"Who's so important that you'd trust me with your secret?" he asked, pulling out his phone.

"My sister. I have to check on her." The answer was guileless, and, if his gut was correct, honest.

"What's wrong with her? Is she sick?"

"She's alone, that's all."

"How old is she?"

"Twenty-six."

He laughed. "And no babysitter?"

She snagged the phone he offered and dropped on the bunk. "I just like to talk to her every day. We're all we've got now."

"You can call her from that, if you like."

"That's okay. I just want to find my own phone."

Normally he'd have dialed, not wanting her to see how advanced the phone was, but he needed her to look at the keypad. When she did, he surreptitiously slipped her cell phone from his pocket and flicked it under the blanket.

In a second, the bed vibrated with a soft hum.

"Oh, thank God," she said on a sigh of relief. "How in the heck did it get under there?"

"You should try making your bed."

"We all have our flaws." She lifted the sheets and blankets and dove halfway under them as she sought the source of the vibrating. She glanced up from the sheet cave, shaking her head a little as she looked at his exposed chest. "Well, some of us do, anyway."

He smiled at the compliment. "I have plenty of flaws, believe me."

"Faults, maybe." She whipped her hand up, victoriously producing the phone. "But flaws? You have none. You're great looking, have a charming personality, an excellent diver, and you share the wealth and credit with your crewmembers. You even worried about my burns before yours last night."

"Yet you were ready to think the worst of me when you saw Alita Holloway in the lab."

She nodded. "I was, but since you came to my phone rescue so quickly, I believe you can add 'avoiding her charms' to your list of attributes."

"If you're not careful, you're going to start to like me."

"Don't worry. Won't happen."

He laughed softly. "Why not?"

"Because I'm . . ." She trailed off as if she'd said too much.

"You're what?" He trailed a finger up her arm to coax her. "Why don't you finish that sentence?"

"I don't want to." She looked at her phone again. "I wish I could trust you, though," she said softly.

"Because you have secrets, don't you?"

"Everybody has secrets."

Bracing his arm behind her, he leaned closer. "Tell me yours."

For a second, he thought she would. Then she jerked away, pushing herself up from the bed, but he grabbed her arm.

"Never mind," he said reassuringly. "I'm not interested in your secrets."

She settled back on the bed, not quite as close, but near enough for Con to feel her warmth. "You're interested in something," she said, eyeing him. "I haven't figured out what it is yet, but you're after something."

"Two guesses, Lizzie." He let his gaze drop to her mouth, brushed a curl out over her cheek, and kept his eyes open so he could watch hers close as he kissed her. "First one doesn't count."

CHAPTER
SIX

THE CONTACT WAS so light, Lizzie was more aware of sweet, warm breath than the feel of his mouth. Her eyes began to close but his didn't, so she fought the urge to sink in to the kiss. Instead she held his eye contact, as electrifying as his mouth, as sexual and sensual as anything she'd ever felt.

Silver blue. Intense. Locked on her.

He angled his head slightly and added an infinitesimal amount of pressure, just enough to make it a real kiss and send a wave of warmth from her mouth to her . . . everywhere.

His fingertip grazed her jaw, a whisper of a touch, barely a caress. She breathed in a little, and that seemed to pull him deeper into the kiss, the tip of his tongue softly, slowly circling the opening of her mouth.

Her eyes heavy, her hands achy, she finally closed her lids and lifted her arms to rest on his shoulders, turn her torso toward him, and pull closer. He met her halfway, his chest against hers, their thighs pressed on the bed.

The instant they had body contact, he slid his tongue into her mouth, stealing more breath and sending more heat through her. A soft moan vibrated her mouth, and she wasn't sure if it was him or her or both, but the sensation just made her want more.

As natural as the next breath, he guided her on her back, the move so sweet and easy, she just let it happen, falling on the unmade bed like it was a cloud.

"You're seducing me."

He smiled into the kiss. "Man, I hate to be so obvious."

She broke the kiss, but he just added some body pressure, gently rolling against her hips, taking his lips from her mouth to her jaw and down her throat.

"Why are you doing this?"

This time, he laughed. "You really don't get out much, do you?"

Still, the sense that there was an ulterior motive lingered. "I mean why . . . me and not Alita?"

Lifting a little, he frowned. "Dumb question. Bad timing. But I'll answer it if I have to."

"You have to."

"You're cute and sexy and funny and . . ." He kissed her again, with a quick stroke of his tongue. "I like you."

As if that was all that needed to be said, he returned to kissing her so completely she couldn't stop the twisting ache low in her belly, the fiery sparks making her want to slide her leg over his hips and pull him into her.

Her heart hammered and he lowered his head, dragging that tongue over her, as if he were going straight to the source of all the noise in her chest and could simply . . . *lick* it.

Her fingers tightened on his head, tunneling into thick, soft hair, lifting his head before he reached his destination and she was gone for good.

"You like this, or you like me?"

A soft puff of air escaped with his frustrated chuckle. "Both. I like you. I like this." He rocked his hips against her. "But honey, if you just want to talk for a while . . ." His tone left no doubt he didn't want to, but the offer stood.

Did she? Too much time, and she'd tell him everything. And she still couldn't be sure he was trustworthy. So why was she horizontal on her bed, when she was supposed to be calling Brianna for an update . . .

"You're thinking too hard," he said, inching his hand up her waist, perilously close to the breast that had just escaped his mouth. "Don't think, Lizzie."

"I don't just . . . do this with anybody."

"Good to know." One more inch. His thumb grazed the underside of her breast, the thin fabric of her shirt somehow making the contact positively incendiary. " 'Cause I'm not anybody."

He fooled her, lowering his head before his fingers moved again, closing his lips right over the hardened tip of her nipple, the cotton no match for his tongue.

The room spun, and her body went boneless and helpless and lost.

He pressed his lower half against her, that beautiful manhood she'd admired in the shower fully erect now, pulsing with each move of his hips, finding her center as he shifted so their bodies met.

The concept of stopping faded with every suspended second of sweetness, her lower half completely melted, her brain just as mushy, and all she could do was clench his shoulders and let it happen.

Just as he glided his hand around her breast, circling it with certainty, the fog started to lift. How far was she going to let this little session go? Far.

His other hand slipped under her shirt, sliding toward the bottom of her bra. He timed the next roll of his hips perfectly, just as he dipped his fingers under her satin bra and closed over her breast.

The shock of his hand on her flesh exploded through all her senses.

Then he jerked upright, almost completely off her.

"Con." She slipped her hand behind his neck, pulling him back.

"Someone's out there," he said in a harsh whisper. "Outside your cabin. Listening."

"How do you— I didn't hear anything." Except the Niagara Falls of blood rushing in her ears.

He put a finger on her mouth and shook his head.

She forced herself to be perfectly still, to concentrate on the sounds outside her bunk and not on the shadow of whiskers right in front of her, or the pressure of his hard-on, or the bare chest she was surely going to feel against her about-to-be-bare chest.

The knock was hard and swift. He gave her an "I told you so" look and flipped off the bunk in one easy move.

"Lizzie!" Oh God—*Flynn Paxton*. "We need to find Con! Do you know where he is?"

Before she could formulate a cover for him, Con had the cabin door open.

"I'm right here. What's the matter?"

"The medallion is missing."

Lizzie's heart stopped slamming as she sucked in a breath.

"I hid it," Con said, blocking the entrance and giving her time to sit up, straighten her clothes, and check her top, soaking wet from his mouth. "It's in a locked cabinet in the lab."

She scanned the bed and desk, desperate for anything to pull over when her gaze fell on the cell phone he'd dropped on the table.

"No, it's not," Flynn Paxton insisted. "That cabinet is hanging by a hinge and the medallion is gone. Nice work."

As Con swore under his breath and bolted into the hall, she launched up and made a grab for the phone. The second she slipped it in her pocket, Paxton stepped into her cabin, his glare as dark as anything she'd ever seen.

"I knew he was in here."

"Good for you, Flynn," she said.

"So if the medallion's really missing, we have you to blame." His gaze dropped over her kiss-dampened T-shirt and he made a smirk, then followed Con down the hall.

With a sigh, she sank on the bed.

If Paxton hadn't shown up, there was no telling how

far that would have gone. Yes, there was—it would have gone all the way.

So if she trusted the man enough to give him her body, shouldn't she trust him enough to give him her secrets?

It was time to find out.

Con stared at the hole where his padlock had been. *Gone.* It couldn't have been shot off—he'd have heard it. Someone just picked it. Totally outsmarted him. He marched to the metal cabinet, which hung from a hinge, having been ingeniously unscrewed from the outside. A trick he'd used many times.

"Fuck!" He slammed his hand on the counter with a thud.

"Perhaps if you hadn't been trying to do just that, this wouldn't have happened."

He spun at the sound of Alita's voice, her flirtatious smile reduced to an unattractive smirk.

"You're the only person who knew it was in this cabinet," he ground out.

"Thank you for the compliment, Con, but I'm not capable of that." She nodded toward the destroyed cabinet. "Anyway, I told the entire crew where you had it when I went upstairs."

"Why?"

She shrugged, and he took a few steps forward, using his size and fury to threaten her.

"Why?" he demanded again, in her face.

She met his gaze, unintimidated. "I knew you went to her room."

"So, what? You were jealous?"

"Of Lizzie Dare? She wouldn't know what to do with a man if one bit her."

She obviously didn't know the power of her competition. Or maybe she did.

"That's why you advertised the hiding place of the most valuable item on board?" He couldn't keep the disgust out of his voice.

At least he knew now that Lizzie wasn't the thief . . . or not the only one, anyway. While he was busy trying to screw the truth out of her, someone else had screwed him. He blew out another curse, just as Paxton powered in.

"Get out of here, Alita," he said. "I need to talk to Con privately."

She speared him with a look, and left.

"There's a thief on board," Flynn said.

No shit. "Whoever it is, they're still on board, and so is that medallion," Con replied. "We need to search every room, every hold, every bag, every corner until we find it."

"Do *we*?" Paxton practically spit out the words.

"As you may recall, you gave me the assignment to secure the treasure this afternoon."

"And you failed."

Had he been set up? "Who on this ship has this kind of capability?"

"Plenty of people," he said. "And if we don't find that medallion soon, you're going down as the one who took it."

Con shot him a look. "You know damn well I didn't take it."

"I don't know anything." He turned to leave, then paused. "I don't even know how you got this job."

He disappeared into the hall, leaving Con to examine the broken cabinet and search for clues that a second-rate thief might leave behind. There were none. An hour later, he'd finished reattaching the cabinet and headed to his own cabin, not bothering to lock the lab.

Paxton had taken all the treasure that day to the mainland, and the medallion was gone. He stepped out into the hall and stopped when he saw Lizzie sitting on the floor outside of his bunk.

She put down something she was reading. "You have a minute?"

He nodded, noticing that she'd showered, changed into a loose, blousy top, and looked even fresher and prettier than when he'd left her.

Standing, she held out a brown notebook he knew he wasn't supposed to recognize but did. "I want to share something with you."

Part of him was disappointed. The part that wanted to *seduce* the answers he wanted out of her.

"Come on in," he said, unlocking his cabin. "Your reputation's probably pretty trashed by now anyway."

"Like I care."

He shot her an appreciative smile. "Tough girl."

"Seriously, I don't care about these people."

"One of whom is a fairly skilled thief."

"At least now you know it's not me."

"Unless you're working with someone," he shot back. "That was a pretty thorough distraction technique you employed up in your cabin."

"You think that I *planned* that?"

"No," he admitted. "You're not quite that devious."

She took the chair, her posture stiff and awkward. Was she nervous? "Don't be so sure."

He gave her a quizzical look and indicated the notebook. "What's that?"

"My father's journal."

Lowering himself to the bunk, he leaned his elbows on his knees. "I've already got a good book going, so I guess you must have a reason for bringing this in here."

She took a breath and nodded. "I was going to sleep with you."

"Did you change your mind?" And what did it have to do with that journal?

"I changed my mind about you. I think you're . . . one of the good guys."

He laughed softly. "That's what you call them now?"

"I mean, you can be trusted."

That must have been some make-out session for her. It left him hard as a rock, but trustworthy? He was better at this than he thought.

"Con, I need some help."

Her tone was dead serious, so he matched it. "For what?"

She held up the notebook. "Have you ever heard of a legendary ship called *El Falcone*?"

Whoa. He was *much* better than he thought. "I've heard the folklore."

"Do you know the captain's name?"

He searched his memory banks and the little information he'd read. Nowhere had a captain's name been mentioned.

"His name was Aramis Dare," she said, a look of absolute expectation on her face. When he didn't respond, she leaned forward.

"Aramis *Dare*."

"A relative of yours, I take it."

"Yes, I am a direct descendant of Aramis, who was my great-times-something grandfather. His name isn't known to many people in history, but those who do know it, and believe the legend of *El Falcone,* also believe him to be a pirate and a thief."

"Was he?"

"I don't know. I'd like to find out. More specifically, my father wanted to find out, and he was very close to doing just that when he died." She handed him the notebook. "Quite a bit of it is in here. The information about *El Falcone,* a ship that carried two of the most spectacular diamonds ever mined, set atop matching royal scepters that were commissioned as a gift for King Luis I of Portugal and his bride, Maria Pia."

He just listened, taking in the gleam in her topaz eyes.

"A few months before my father died, he went to Havana and scoured the libraries and manifests and old documents and found many answers, and plenty of questions. It was his lifelong mission to find out the truth, to salvage *El Falcone,* and, mostly, to clear Aramis Dare's name and prove that he was no pirate; he was a merchant."

"Okay. And . . . how are you fulfilling this mission?" He knew, of course, but wanted to hear her say it.

"My dad's theory was that *El Falcone* wasn't lost in a storm. It was shot by cannon fire, taken down by a man who was Aramis's sworn enemy, a man who tried to renege on paying for the very scepters and diamonds he'd commissioned artisans to make."

Con leaned back, considering what he should say.

She stared at him, that look of expectation brightening her eyes again. But she wasn't going to say it. He'd have to.

"You think we're salvaging *El Falcone*."

"I know we are. And you know what else? Judd Paxton knows it. That's why all the secrecy. I don't know if he knows all that my father knew, but he knows enough. And he's going to rip this wreck apart piece by piece, selling all of the treasures to his high-bidding private collectors. A tiny portion of it will be in a museum, if any, and no one is going to look for the truth about what happened to the ship, leaving the world to think Aramis Dare stole everything because every item on the ship was *sin registrada*."

"Not registered."

"Exactly. No official manifest exists. Aramis was selling the goods to private buyers. He bought the treasures himself, and didn't officially register the ship. That's why he was considered a pirate. But he was just a shrewd businessman."

Kind of like Judd himself.

"Paxton's already stripping up the treasure," she said, slapping her hand on her thigh with anger. "Don't you see that? He's *stealing* treasure he found on the bottom of the ocean and selling it. Aramis Dare paid for his treasures and was selling them to a third party for profit, which is perfectly legal. If he didn't get paid for them, then he kept them himself. And according to what my father found, he *didn't* get paid for them. Therefore . . ." She stood. "I own everything we find on this dive."

Con just stared at her. "You want to keep all the treasure?"

"Not all of it, and not for profit or glory," she shot back. "I want to do what's right with the treasure. Display it. Exhibit it. Share it. Tell Aramis's story and make it a testament to him."

Really?

She leaned forward, her golden brown eyes wide and sincere, searching his face. "I can trust you, right, Con?" She reached for his hand. "I don't know you well, so this is a huge risk, but I have this powerful gut instinct about you that I can trust you."

Trust him to turn all this over to his boss and her client, sure. "Yeah."

She took a deep breath. "It's all about the scepters and the diamonds, as you can imagine. Those matching blue diamonds sitting on top of matching golden scepters created for a king and his bride, that's the big draw, right?"

"If the diamonds are sizable and really match, of course."

"So if the scepters are found and taken off this boat, and turned over to the state authorities before Paxton goes through the claim filing, he can't keep them."

"Is that what you're trying to do?" Con almost

laughed. "Single-handedly find two matching scepters and two of the world's most valuable diamonds, figure out a way to somehow bring them up without your dive partner seeing them, get them off this boat, and report him to the state, using the scepters to prove that this is *El Falcone* and that some kind of Cuban paperwork says they belong to your family?"

Her smile was slow at the end of all that. "Yeah, that's pretty much it. Would you help me?"

"Why would I do that?"

She put one hand on his knee, squeezing softly. "Because you are one of the good ones, Con. I see it in your eyes. In your attitude. I see a good man. Will you help me?"

When she found out the truth about what he was doing, she'd hate him. Not that it mattered what this spunky little blonde thought of him. He had a job to do.

And helping her, in some way, might actually be *doing* that job. He'd know if she found anything, and then he could let Lucy know.

"What are the chances," he said slowly, buying some time as he thought this through, "that you are going to find two golden scepters and matching diamonds at the bottom of the Atlantic Ocean? They could be anywhere."

"Anywhere," she agreed with a twinkle in her eye. "Absolutely anywhere."

Slowly, her eyes dancing, she lifted the large, loose top she wore, revealing hips in low-slung jeans, then her bare waist, then the elastic bottom of a sports bra.

With one hand, she reached into her cleavage. "One might even be right here."

In one smooth move, she held out her hand, opened her fist, and presented a pale blue diamond the size of a baseball.

"Holy shit," he muttered, staring at it.

"You can say that again."

"How long have you had this?"

"Got it the second day. The second day! Can you believe that?"

He just stared, every hair on his neck standing in awe. "And the scepter?"

"That's where you come in."

He finally looked up at her. "How?"

"This came right out of the scepter, which I hid— pretty damn well, I might add—under the ballast pile. I've been waiting to pick the right person on board to be my accomplice." She held out the diamond, inviting him to touch it. "And now, I've found him."

CHAPTER
SEVEN

WHEN HE REACHED for the diamond, Con's icy eyes darkened and they were, for just that instant, precisely the color of the Bombay Blue. Lizzie let him take it, as pleased with his expression of awe and desire as she was with her plan. And her choice of partners.

"Con," she said, dropping to her knees in front of him to get in his line of vision, which was locked on the rock. "This belongs to my family." She seized the book and waved it over the diamond. "The proof is in these pages."

He might have heard her, but he was still turning the diamond over in his hands, his jaw loose, his fascination clear.

"This is incredible." His voice was barely a whisper.

"It certainly is," she agreed. "Which is why we can't let Judd Paxton sell these on the black market. Treasures like this belong in a museum, for the whole world to enjoy." She grabbed his forearm and demanded his attention. "You realize that I don't want to keep this or profit from it. It's for posterity, not prosperity."

He finally looked at her. "Excuse me?"

"It was my father's favorite saying about treasure hunting. It should be done for posterity, not prosperity. Which is why he hated Judd Paxton. One of the reasons, anyway."

"What were the others?"

She rocked back on her heels, unwilling to go back to the chair. She liked being close to him, liked looking up into his rugged face. Liked it a little too much.

"My father was always obsessed with the fact that we are descendants of a great maritime family. If you go back another hundred years, there's another famous Captain Dare in history. You may have heard of Captain Antoine Dare, the only captain to steer a boat in the 1715 fleet *out* of the storm that took down eleven Spanish galleons off the coast of Florida."

He nodded, dividing his attention between the diamond and her face.

"The 1715 galleon wrecks are all up and down this coast, and every few years another one is uncovered. Years ago my father found one, and because a Dare had been part of the armada, the wreck meant a great deal to him. Long story short, Judd Paxton swooped in and claimed it as his own. He's got the reputation and he's got the money, and he's ruthless like that. Other people find the wrecks, and he takes the credit and the cash. He steals as much as any pirate. He just does it by buying off half the officials in the state of Florida."

Con held the stone up to her, his expression still troubled. "You can't keep this diamond on this boat."

"I know that. Can you imagine if news got out? We'd be attacked."

"I will help you."

She almost sighed with relief. "Good. Because I can't bring that scepter up alone at night."

He shot her a disbelieving look. "I meant I'll help you hide this. I can get this to the mainland, and get it somewhere safe."

"What?" She tried to grab the diamond, but he held it tight. "I *know* where it'll be safe—in my family's safe-deposit box."

"How are you going to get it there?"

"I'll figure that out. You just have to help me get the scepter out of the water."

"Lizzie, it's worth *millions*—"

"Many of them," she agreed. "And even more with the scepter, and I will not, under any circumstances, for any reason, separate that diamond from its scepter. It killed me to leave it down there in the ballast pile."

"That's what you were afraid I was going to find when I looked in the ballast, weren't you?"

"Of course I was. And obviously someone will, if I risk too many more days. I have to get that scepter up without anyone seeing, then get them both to the mainland. I need you to work the air hose while I dive at night, when everyone is asleep."

He just stared at her. "You're going to night dive and get the scepter?"

"Yes." To make her point, she got up and sat on the bunk very close to him, turning his sizable shoulders so he'd face her and listen. "And that's all I need from you,

Con, I promise. You don't have to get in any deeper than that. I'll handle getting them both to the mainland and hidden."

He didn't say anything, but finally set the diamond down on his pillow behind him, then picked up the journal. "What kind of proof is in here that all this is true?"

She didn't like his tone but understood the skepticism. "Notes, copies of documents and letters, proof that Captain Aramis Dare sailed to Portugal to sell the scepters and quite a bit of other treasure that he had legally purchased in Havana. Some paperwork that supports the theory that he had a buyer lined up in Portugal, that that buyer tried to swindle him, and Aramis took off with a lot of the treasure still on board. They chased him down to here." She pointed down, indicating the very water they floated on. "And shot *El Falcone* down."

"Surely, if that's true, they boarded the ship and took the bounty."

"He threw it overboard as they were being attacked. It's deep here, almost fifty feet, and they probably didn't have any diving equipment on board. Salvaging was done in shallow waters back then. The guy who chased him—and before you ask, I don't know who that is, because Aramis only refers to him as CB—might have gone back to land or even home to put together the equipment necessary to salvage the area. But whatever happened, no one ever recovered the Bombay Blue scepters. At least, they've never turned up in the past hundred and fifty years."

He fluttered a few pages. "How did you get on this dive if you hate Paxton so much? How did you know that this was *El Falcone*?"

"A little serendipity, a little hunch, and friends. Before he died, my father developed the cannon theory, and surmised that the ship wasn't in shallow water, and knew it had probably been about ten miles off the coast. He was killed before he could figure out a way to finance a site exploration, and I decided if I ever could figure out a way, I would do it. But, man, does that take money! So when Sam Gorman called and told me about this secret, high-paying dive, I was interested."

"But you couldn't have known that it was *El Falcone*."

"No, but then I found this." She opened to the last page and pulled out a sketched oceanic chart and pointed to a spot in the Atlantic Ocean. "The map my dad had. Out of curiosity, I called Sam and convinced him to tell me the exact location of this salvage effort. When he did, I said I'd go."

"Does Sam know?"

She shook her head. "And believe me, I've been tempted to tell him."

"Why didn't you?"

"I don't want to get him involved. I could get into a boatload of trouble, and he has a reputation to maintain."

"And I don't?" His half smile was so droll, her heart rolled over at it.

"You seem like you could handle a little controversy. Plus, I told you, I'll keep you out of it. All you have to do is work the air hose for me on a night dive." She dug her fingers into his arm. "I swear, that's all."

He didn't say a word.

She pulled him closer, drawing him around to face her again. "My father died with this one dream that mattered to him. I'm all he has to make that happen. I mean, I didn't promise him, because he died when I wasn't there . . ." She fought the lump in her throat, the strangling guilt and remorse. "But if I had been, I would have sworn on our name that I would do this for him."

"Lizzie, does anyone else know what you're doing?"

"My sister, Brianna. And believe me, she's batshit that I'm here without her. But I couldn't risk bringing her into this, plus she had to stay home and go through all of Dad's files. I convinced her that was as important as what I'm doing. And we're keeping each other posted when we find anything important."

For a long time he didn't respond, but paged through the notebook, glanced at the diamond, considering it all. Finally he shook his head, and disappointment lurched in her.

"No, you won't help me?"

"You can't dive with no blower down to the ballast pile in the middle of the night and bring up an eighteen-inch-long hunk of gold and hide it."

"*I* can't," she agreed, hope making its way up into her chest again. "But *we* could."

"Will you answer a question for me, entirely honestly?"

"I've been completely honest with you," she said defensively. "You can ask me anything."

"Have you taken anything at all from the treasure hold?"

"I've taken pictures, so I could match items to the sketches I had. And I've taken that diamond and hidden that scepter. That's all, I swear."

"Then there is a thief on board this boat."

"Flynn Paxton would be my guess."

"The boss's stepson?"

She rolled her eyes. "The boss's albatross is more like it. Have you ever seen a company dive manager do a more pathetic job? He's not even on the boat, sleeping in his own cabin cruiser like some kind of royalty."

"I got the impression he was being groomed to head the company when Judd retires."

She snorted softly. "There's no love lost between those two. Flynn was sixteen or seventeen when Judd married his mom, and though he took his stepfather's last name, there's a lot of animosity there. I don't like Judd Paxton, but I give him grudging respect for being a hard worker. Flynn? He's like a rich kid, breezing in and out of dives, never serious except to get the treasure off and out as fast as he can. If anyone is dipping into the gold till, I bet it's him."

Con turned a page of the journal and tapped a drawing. "Someone has that."

"The Our Lady of Sorrows medallion," Lizzie said, turning the page to look at it. "I bet Flynn took it."

"I considered that," he admitted.

"He knows that medallion is very, very valuable."

He nodded in agreement.

"And see what a big deal he made about appointing you

to watch the treasure, then blaming you for losing it? And now he's got that medallion, and he probably has a buyer for it. He left me dangling on the dock for two hours today while he went to some meeting. I was his cover." She tucked her knees under her, determined to get into his face to make her point. "Can't you see that I'm right?"

"I can see the possibility," he conceded.

"The possibility? I bet you a million dollars he's got that medallion. If we could get on his boat tonight, we'd probably find him fondling it right now."

"You don't have a million dollars, Lizzie."

"No," she agreed, turning toward the diamond on the pillow. "But I have that."

He looked hard at her. "Then let's make a bet."

"A bet? For the diamond?" She laughed softly. "Not a chance."

"If Paxton has the medallion, if he really stole it from me and set me up, then you're on. I'll help you."

"And if he doesn't?"

"You're on your own, kid." He stood up, scooping up the diamond in a flash so fast, she didn't have a chance to get it first.

"Hey!"

"I'm keeping this for you."

"You are not," she said, practically lunging at him.

He held it out of her reach. "Lizzie, you are not safe with this in your cabin. If someone knows you have it, you could be killed for something that valuable. I'll keep it." As she started to protest, he held up his hand. "First of all, no one knows I have it. Secondly, I'm armed and dangerous and will kill anyone who tries to get near it."

Her eyes widened and her jaw opened, but he stepped forward and closed it with a single finger. "Regardless of that, I *am* one of the good guys. Now go back to your cabin. Wait for me to come and get you in about ten minutes, and be sure you have your camera."

"What are you going to do? Take pictures of the diamond?"

"Nope." He finally lifted his finger, only to graze it under her chin, lifting her face a fraction like he wanted a kiss. "We're going to settle our bet."

"Flynn, I have to go now."

Alita's announcement, delivered with a poke of her fingers, pulled him out of a dream, forcing Flynn to roll over with a grunt. "So row back."

"You would let me do that? At four in the morning?" Alita's voice grew shrill. She was a great diver, a terrific source of inside crew information, and a fine fuck, but, Jesus, the woman could whine.

"You rowed over here at one in the morning. What difference does it make?"

"It's just *crude* to do me and send me back in the middle of the night."

He pushed himself against her. He could get hard again. Maybe.

"Can't I just stay?" she singsonged.

For about twenty minutes. "What would Dave say when he saw you in the morning?"

She propped up on an elbow. "He'd say, 'Lucky Flynn Paxton, gettin' it on with the hottest diver in the business.' "

That made him smile. He liked her ego, and the fact that he was the beneficiary of her very active libido on this dive. He'd heard enough rumors to know someone on board always got a piece of Alita.

"Honey, I need this to be a secret." Because Judd the Dud would have his ass for screwing the help. "Otherwise no one will talk to you, and there is some nasty shit going on over there and you are my . . ." He ran his hand over her rear, then worked his way up. "Conduit."

"Nasty?" She launched up. "*You're* the one who took the medallion. It really wasn't fair to set Con up like that. He's a nice guy."

"Yeah, but he wouldn't split the cash with you. I will." He gave her boob a quick massage. "And just in case you're getting all creamy down below over him, he's already giving it to Lizzie, so forget it."

She jerked back and threw the covers off. "You really can be a prick, you know that?"

"You like my prick."

She blew out a breath and stood up. "You totally don't get it, Flynn."

"Get what?"

"I have feelings, too." Grabbing her underpants, she stepped in, hopping a little on one leg, then the other, making her boobs bounce.

"I'm teasing. Come on back to bed."

"Fuck you."

"Precisely." He rolled closer and reached for the lace edge of her panties. "I'll row you home. I promise."

She snapped out of his touch, then jerked toward the porthole. "What was that?"

"What?"

"That flash."

"Lightning?"

She gave him a look like he was crazy. "That. Did you see that?"

He did, and it wasn't lightning. He bounded off the bed out to the salon, onto the deck just as it flashed again.

"Motherfucker," he mumbled. "Someone's out there. Taking pictures of our boat and location. Shit."

Alita was next to him in a second. "I don't see a boat. It's pitch-black."

"Someone's found us." His stomach rolled. If their location got out, Judd would be down here in a heartbeat. That'd screw up everything.

On the other hand, he already had a buyer for the medallion, and this gig was going to be up soon.

"What are you going to do?" she asked.

Do? Why the fuck did he have to do anything? Because he was the company manager on the dive and had to do something. Or act like he was.

He puffed his chest up with a deep inhale. "I'm going over to the boat."

"They could be pirates."

Jesus. "They could be poachers. Or someone from the state trying to figure out what we're doing here." Or, he hoped, some ambitious fisherman he could scare off. If not, he'd avoid them altogether. "You stay here. No one knows you're here. Just get back in bed and stay low. I'll check it out."

"Are you sure?" She looked up at him, a little of the admiration he wanted to see back in her eyes.

"Of course I'm sure." He headed back to the state-room, on the way glancing at the cabinet where he'd hidden the medallion before she showed up. That *had* to go tomorrow.

He dressed, counting three more flashes. Feeling protective and strong, he gave her a kiss and headed out, climbing into the motorized raft that he hoped would make enough noise to scare them off. He moved very slowly, taking his time to close the hundred and fifty feet between his boat and the *Gold Digger*.

The whole time, there were no more flashes. Approaching the boat head-on to the stern, he went around the starboard side, even though he thought the flash had come from the port side. Slowly, he cruised alongside of the vessel, which looked completely still and dark. When he got back to the stern, he braced himself, but saw nothing. A few of the rafts tied up. The deck quiet. The starboard side looking completely calm.

Could it have been lightning?

He continued around the boat, reaching back with one hand to steer the raft, the motor puttering softly. Suddenly he saw some movement on the deck.

"Flynn?" a woman's voice called.

"Is that you, Lizzie?"

"What are you doing out there?" she asked.

"I thought I saw some flashes. Thought someone was taking pictures of our location and I came to investigate."

"Really? I didn't see anything and I've been out here for a while. Maybe you imagined it."

No, he didn't imagine it, and he had Alita as a

witness. But he wasn't about to tell her that. He maneuvered around as she aimed a flashlight onto the water.

"There's no one here." The sea was indeed empty as far as the beam of light showed. She swiped over the water, all the way to the black horizon. Nothing.

"That's strange," he said. "Are you sure no one boarded?"

"Absolutely. I've been sitting out here for a while now. Can't sleep."

Would she be out there taking pictures? No, that didn't make sense. "Well, you ought to," he said, working the raft around. "You have to dive tomorrow morning."

"I know. I was just on my way to my cabin when I heard the motor."

"I'll check out the rest of the perimeter of the boat," he said, sounding brave, and actually feeling that way now.

"All right. G'night." She disappeared into the shadows of the deck, and he took a few more minutes to circle the whole boat again.

By the time he tied up the raft to his cabin cruiser, he was wide awake and ready for sex. Feeling heroic, strong, and ready for another round, he bounded back to the stateroom, hard for Alita.

She must have liked his heroics since she barely asked any questions, fucked him for a good half hour, then dressed and left, a happy little camper.

Life was good, and he'd soon be a couple hundred grand richer. Screwing Judd the Dud had become his favorite pastime.

CHAPTER
EIGHT

CON HOISTED HIMSELF up over the dive platform, not even shivering, although he had to be freezing without a wet suit, even that short distance. Lizzie stepped out of the shadows, searching to see if he had anything in his hands. If he managed to find that medallion, then she was certain she'd picked the right man for the job.

"Did you get it?" she asked, slipping down to the dive platform.

He lifted his hand.

Oh, yes. The absolute right man. She wanted to reach for the medallion, but she couldn't resist getting closer to him, feeling the waves of cold from his skin, and flattening her hands on his bare chest. She knew how much that kind of cold hurt, but he didn't seem fazed, except to let out a soft grunt when her hands made contact.

"Come on, let's go," he said, moving her back into the darkest part of the deck and toward the stairs. "My cabin. Now."

She kept up with his long strides back to his cabin, him dripping water from his bathing suit and body, but still not giving in to what she knew had to be the urge to just shudder with the bone-deep chill of swimming in the ocean on a November night. He unlocked the hatch and nudged her in without a word.

"Let me see—"

He yanked her right into his chest, pulling out a shocked breath from her, his flesh cold even through the thickness of her fleece sweatshirt.

"God, you're warm." He nearly moaned the words, squeezing her tighter.

She understood instantly and obliged by wrapping her arms around him, rubbing her hands over the hard muscles of his back. She'd dived without a wet suit before, and human contact was like heaven to the whole body.

"Why don't you take a hot shower?" she suggested.

He just shook his head and pressed himself against her from head to toe. "This is much better. You're like a human heating pad."

He punctuated that with a little more pressure on her legs and hips, riding her enough to dry his skin on her clothes. She curled one of her legs around his, using the warm cotton of her sweatpants to dry and warm his thigh and calf.

He sighed again, sliding one more time as if he could wipe his whole body with her warmth.

"You better let me have that damn medallion since you are totally taking advantage of this situation," she teased.

He backed up just enough to reveal his open palm. And the gold.

"Oh." She let out the word in a little breath of air. "I told you Flynn was the thief."

"You were right. He's a thief and more."

Her eyes bugged. "He had *more* treasure in there?"

"Depends on how you define treasure. This piece wasn't worth much, in my opinion." At her look, he lifted a brow. "Did you know he was sleeping with Alita?"

"Alita? Did she see you?"

"No, she stayed in the stateroom and this was in the salon. Not very creatively hidden, either."

"Alita." She shook her head. "I never picked up that vibe from either of them."

"It explains how he knew exactly where that medallion was hidden. She told him after I showed her, so they're a team."

"Why did you show her, anyway?"

"To test her." He bent over, rubbing his legs. "She failed."

"What do you think'll happen when Flynn discovers it's gone?"

He shrugged. "He won't have the nerve to nail me on it, and the crew will assume whoever stole it had second thoughts and returned it. Maybe he'll think Alita double-crossed him."

She took the gold with her to the edge of the bunk, sitting down to admire it. "They're scum, both of them. And him, stealing from his own stepfather. I told you their relationship is a mess." She turned to him, her smile widening. "And now I've won the bet."

He stood up and pulled a canvas duffel bag from under the bed, dragging out a pair of jeans and taking them into the head. He didn't close the door, giving her a perfect view of his backside as he shoved off his wet bathing suit and gave himself a cursory rub with a towel.

God, the man had a beautiful body. He stepped into the jeans, pulling them over his bare hips, giving the zipper a half tug that didn't make it to the top, not bothering to snap.

The medallion forgotten, she stared at his bare chest, the cuts of muscles disappearing into the jeans, the bit of dark hair peeking out from the half-zipped fly. Her throat went bone dry.

"So we dive tomorrow night," he said, approaching the bunk slowly.

What was he talking about? Diving. Gold. Scepters.

That's why she was in this room, eating up her new partner with her eyes. She lifted the medallion and laid it against her chest as though it could help slow her rapidly increasing heartbeat.

"I dive tomorrow night," she corrected. "You work the air hose and cover my ass."

He reached the bed, looking down at her. "*I* dive tomorrow night," he countered. "*You* work the air hose and cover *my* ass."

She started to stand up. "No way. I know where it is."

He put his hand on her chest, over the medallion, and eased her all the way down. "You can show me tomorrow. We dive together first thing in the morning."

"You can't change the rules, Con."

Smiling, he took the medallion, grazing it over her breasts with a wicked gleam in his eye. "I can do anything I want."

Wordlessly, he laid the medallion on the nightstand and in one smooth move, was back on the bed, kneeling over her, his knees sliding right between hers. "And since I can do anything I want" —a zing shot straight up her body—"I'm going to dive for the scepter tomorrow night."

He loomed over her, bare-chested, practically unzipped, exuding sex and control and power . . . and changing the rules.

Her fingers curled into the thin blanket under her, awareness flaring through her.

"It's a dangerous dive," he said, easing her legs open a fraction with his. "It'll be dark, with no blower."

That was true. "But if I do it," she said, managing not to let her voice crack, "I'll be down and back in seven or eight minutes. I know exactly what to do. I've visualized it."

"I've visualized it, too." He leaned over her, putting his hands on either side of her, letting his weight drop so that his biceps tightened. "And I'm making the dive."

His face was very close, his gaze fierce, his lips almost curled in a smile.

"You can't do this."

His smile said he could. "I know your secrets now, Lizzie. And you need me."

Need. That was one word to describe the heat in her body. "That doesn't give you the right to take over my plans. I'm in charge of this and you're following my instructions." She put a hand on his chest, his skin still icy from the water, but he just pressed himself closer.

"I'll dive. You work the hose. And we . . ." He closed

the space and brushed her mouth with his. "Will be partners. How's that?"

Partners. What kind of partners?

"The kind Alita and Flynn are?" Onboard lovers. Right now, it sounded really good.

"Way better." He kissed her again, a little more potent this time, enough to intensify the need between her legs and make her whole body want to rise up and meet his.

He opened his mouth, breathed into hers, and kneed her legs open one more inch. Every cell screamed more. Every inch of her wanted to bow her back, and feel all that hardness against her.

He rose just a little, as though tempting her higher, luring her.

Glancing down, she saw the tip of his hard penis threatening to burst out of the half-zipped jeans. Her mouth almost watered.

Very slowly, he stood, his abdomen clenching as he straightened, his gaze right on hers. He put his hands on the zipper and her eyes dropped, watching, waiting, anticipating the scrape of the teeth as he freed himself. She tried to breathe, but all she could do was watch his fingers, his flesh.

He was going to do this. He was going to . . .

Zip up.

He closed the jeans, snapped, and reached out a hand to her. "You better get some rest, Lizzie. We dive early. And late."

She let out a breath and relaxed her elbows enough to drop an inch. "Don't ever do that to me again."

"What? Change your game plan?"

In one move, she rolled off the bed, away from the trap of his legs and steel slice of his gaze. "Don't tease me. I don't like it."

She was halfway into the hall when she heard him whisper, "Neither do I."

Speaking of changing the game plan . . . Con hadn't called Lucy once since he got on this boat.

Puffing a breath full of frustration, he double-locked the door and waited until Lizzie's footsteps disappeared and the ache in his groin lessened a little. Very little.

Let's see, Lucy had, what? Four rules for this assignment?

Check in every day. Nope, hadn't called once.

Report anything suspicious. Everything was suspicious.

Turn in anyone he found stealing. Or, just steal it back.

Inform the client of any crewmember who might know the wreck they were diving was El Falcone. Not aid and abet her plans to ruin Judd Paxton's recovery effort by assisting in a secret ploy to steal the most coveted artifact on the dive, remove it from the premises, and hide it on the mainland.

After blowing every rule she'd set out for him, sex with a target who had a personal vendetta against the client and a plan to ruin the entire dive probably wasn't going to make a dent on his already battered employee evaluation.

But that wasn't what stopped him from doing what

he—and Lizzie—wanted to do. At least he could admit that truth.

Running his hand through his hair, he grabbed the satellite phone, dropped onto the bed, inhaled enough to get a whiff of Lizzie's perfume, and dialed.

She answered on the first ring. "You didn't call yesterday."

He laughed softly at the greeting. "So that rumor's true."

"There are a lot of them. Which rumor are you testing?"

"That Lucy Sharpe answers her private line 24/7."

"For now it is," she said. "But you've probably heard the rumor that my 24/7 days are numbered."

He'd heard she was pregnant but doubted that would slow her down much. "Until they are, I'm afraid I have to take advantage and wake you to tell you what's going on here."

"It's about time. I told you to check in daily."

"Trust me, Luce, that's the least of the regs I've been wrecking."

"Great."

In the background he heard movement and a soft comment from a man. Jack Culver, her partner in every way. He waited, imagining the lithe, long-haired woman leaving her bed to walk down the hall to her office.

"All right. Talk to me, Con."

"There is someone on this boat who knows we're salvaging *El Falcone*, and she's already located one of the diamonds, kept it for herself, is planning to do the same with the scepter it was separated from, then is going to take it to the mainland and hide it until the other is found."

"Whoa. Good work. Nice and fast, too. Who is it and what's your plan?"

"Elizabeth Dare."

She waited a beat. "And your plan?"

"My plan is to help her recover the scepter and help her hide it on the mainland."

She was stone silent.

"Because she's not the person he's looking for."

"She's not? Sounds like she is."

"She's not. She does have an agenda and it isn't friendly to Paxton, but she's not stealing any treasure."

"You just said she has one of the diamonds and scepters."

"Any *other* treasure. The leak of treasure and information is Flynn Paxton, aided by Alita Holloway. I just went to great pains—swimming in cold water and testing my exemplary 'recovery' skills—to prove that, taking something back that he'd stolen earlier this evening."

It was quiet, but for a paper shuffling in the background. "Elizabeth Dare is the daughter of the late Malcolm Dare," she said.

"She's not our target, Lucy. Her issues are personal and family driven. I can keep an eye on her."

"Sounds like you already have been."

Resentment bubbled. "Not to the point of blindness," he shot back. "If I don't work with her, she'll do what she wants anyway. This way, I know exactly where the treasures are and have her under my thumb."

"That's a plan, although not my first choice. What about Flynn?"

"Depends. How will our client take finding out the thief and traitor is his stepson?"

"Hard to say. They have a volatile history, and Judd's trying to mend fences with him. They've had a rocky relationship since Judd married Flynn's mother about ten years ago. Giving him responsibility for this dive is Judd's way of showing he thinks Flynn has potential to run the business, but in my opinion, Judd has no real intention of leaving his fortunes and reputation to his stepson."

"Flynn probably knows that and is taking what he can get, when he can get it," Con said, encouraged by Lucy's willingness to see the whole story and not jump to the obvious conclusions. "If anyone has an outside contact and is selling items taken from this dive before they get logged into the Paxton system, it's Flynn."

"But you're certain it's not this lovely blonde with big brown eyes and a sexy body?"

"You have a picture or you taking an educated guess?"

She laughed softly. "I guessed on the body."

"And correctly. What's probably not in that file is why she's doing it, of her family's connection to the ship. *El Falcone* was captained by Aramis Dare, her great-times-seven or so grandfather. She's on a personal mission to finish her father's life's work. Nothing nefarious."

"Except stealing a priceless treasure and taking it off the boat to hide it."

"Okay, a little nefarious. But I don't want you to get

all bent out of shape over Lizzie when the real target is Flynn. I just need a little more time to prove it, since Judd will undoubtedly want a lot of irrefutable evidence against a family member. While I'm at it, I think it's smart to be sure that diamond gets off this boat, along with the scepter, and that I know exactly where it is so I can return it to the client when we're done."

Lucy was quiet for a moment. "Compelling argument."

"Just a smart one."

"Still, I'm going to dig a little into Lizzie Dare's background, check out her story, and her family."

"Good idea." He doubted she'd find anything.

"And I agree with you," she continued. "By knowing exactly what she has and where she's hiding it, we're actually doing a service for our client. But Con, if that diamond and scepter are not returned to Judd Paxton, you will be held responsible."

So she still didn't quite trust him. How come Lizzie was so certain he was one of the good guys, and Lucy was still on the fence?

Because Lucy was a better judge of character.

"Oh, and Con? Pirates and thieves don't make good partners."

CHAPTER
NINE

LIZZIE STEPPED OUT of the head and blinked at the sight of Con sitting on her bunk, more stunned that he'd gotten in through her locked door without making a sound than the fact that she wore nothing but a bra and sleep pants.

"You should be dressed," he said, his gaze hot on her chest as she gaped at him. "Not that I mind."

"How did you get in here?"

"Trade secret." He tossed her a T-shirt from the bed. "I told you to be ready at three."

A little frisson of irritation skittered over her at his tone. This was her secret plan, and he'd hijacked ownership of it ever since she'd shown him the diamond.

"You'll need a jacket, too," he said. "It's colder tonight than last night."

"You were up there already?"

He pointed up. "Listen. You hear anything?"

She stood still, frowning as she absorbed the normal sounds of the boat. "No."

"Good. The air compressor's on."

"It is? I was worried about that. It seems so noisy during the dives." She pulled the sweatshirt over her head. "How did you do that?"

"I rigged it up so that it's not vibrating the deck. That's what the noise is, not the actual compressor. Let's go. Everyone's asleep. I want to do this fast."

He wanted to do it. "Then let me dive. I can find that thing in my sleep."

"In the time it would take you to put on a wet suit, I'll have the scepter in my hand."

Possibly. In their earlier dive that morning, when they were supposed to be treasure hunting, she timed him moving the ballast stones and the dirt to get to the scepter. It had taken about four minutes. A minute down and a minute up meant six total.

"You really are going to do this with no wet suit?"

"Of course. I can last six minutes in fifty-nine degrees. I checked the water temperature already."

"But—"

He put his finger over her lips. "Not another word. Even on the deck. We go up, hookah in, you keep watch, and I'll dive."

He led her down the hall. Barefoot, they didn't make a sound, and heard nothing until they reached the main deck. The compressor hummed softly from a new spot, resting on rubber strips. He'd already hooked in the air hose and the reserve tank.

She might not have thought of the rubber strips to dull the sound, and even if she had, she wouldn't have been able to lift and maneuver the compressor since it was four feet square and heavy.

So, she really did need him, she rationalized as he attached his harness and mask and grabbed the hookah. Plus, skipping a wet suit saved valuable minutes.

It's just that ever since she'd brought him into her plan, he'd taken over everything. Including her thoughts.

He slid down to the diving platform, and she handed him the air hose.

"Yank three times when you have it in your hand," she said.

"More important. Yank two times if someone comes on the deck. You know what to say."

Night diving was not unheard of, although it was generally done during the warmest months. The only person who would be truly furious was Dave since, as divemaster, he had to grant permission and log any dives.

"Just hurry." She handed him the hose.

In an instant, he disappeared into the black water, the slice of moonlight offering almost no chance to see him, or even the bright yellow air hose.

So, she just stared at her watch.

When she reached the five minute mark, she looked over her shoulder to check the air compressor, which still hummed along quietly. The hose stayed still in her hand. One more minute and a man with so little body fat in sixty-degree water would be in trouble.

At six and a half mintues, she set the hose down and walked to the compressor, just to make sure it was working properly. The belt was moving. The relief valve was open, which would be normal. The reserve tank was doing its job cooling the air. The . . .

"Oh my God." She stuck her hand around the remote air intakes. Gone. Both of them. He was breathing carbon monoxide.

Snapping the motor off, she didn't even take a minute to think. She had no time to harness or set up a clean air system. No time to get a wet suit on. Grabbing a light hanging by the closest locker, she popped over the side, slid to the platform, took a huge breath, and threw herself into the water.

The scepter. He couldn't drop the fucking gold scepter. But ever since Con had it in his hands, he'd been disoriented. It was heavy, even in the water. He dropped his flashlight but didn't care, knowing there was only one way to go now. Up.

He kicked. He breathed. He spun around. Was he even going up?

A sharp pain stabbed his head at the same time his heart rate ratcheted up.

Somewhere, in the back of his mind, he knew what was going on. But he couldn't lose the scepter. She'd be furious. Disappointed. Down here after it herself.

Lizzie. He blinked and saw her face.

Lizzie . . .

Then she was there. With no mask, no suit, her mouth clamped shut, her cheeks exploded with a held breath. In one move that seemed both sudden and slow, she twisted his regulator, cutting off the air.

What the hell?

She yanked him, kicking the water, kicking him.

Pulling him. He squeezed the scepter. Couldn't drop it. Couldn't. But he couldn't fight her, either.

They rose. He started to tread water, more out of instinct than anything. He let out a bubble of air. She did the same, her eyes, sparking from a flashlight she carried, burned on him, her insistence clear. Swim, those eyes said. Swim harder.

And he did. Harder, faster, then slamming through the surface and gulping in air as she did.

"Con!" Her voice was a harsh whisper. Or maybe she screamed. He couldn't tell.

Damn it!

He shook his head, sucked in more air. Held onto the gold and blinked at her, still treading, still swimming. And so freaking cold.

"Are you okay? Con? Are you?"

He held up the scepter. "I got it."

She nodded, water sluicing from her hair over her face, fury and fear over every feature.

"Carbon monoxide. You got that, too," she said, tugging him toward the boat, yanking his mouthpiece out for him. "Do you know that?"

His head spun a little, but he kicked along with her, the first cohesive thought finally taking hold of his disoriented brain.

Carbon monoxide. Of course that's what this was. *How?*

"Just swim. Stay with me," she said, her teeth cracking against each other.

God, she must be so cold. She was so small and thin. He kicked harder, staying with her, oxygen finally seeping through his body and blood along with a determination to take over, to swim *for* her, not *with* her.

And not drop her damn scepter.

She yanked him to the boat, hoisting herself up the dive platform first, then turning to him. He lifted the scepter to her, and she barely looked at it, taking his arms in her hands instead and pulling.

"Just get up here, damn it."

He threw his body onto the deck, and only then did she take the scepter with one hand, pulling his mask off with the other.

"Are you all right?" Her whole body shivered so hard she could hardly say the words. "Do you know your name? The date?"

"Your lips are blue," he said. "Inside. We have to go inside."

"Your name?" she insisted.

He ignored her, standing and helping her up, his brain almost clear but for the sharp, stinging headache and the cold that felt like it went right into his spine. "Turn the compressor off."

"I did."

"I'll pull in the hose. You get in a blanket." He turned, tugging at the air hose, which they had to coil up again. And he had to move the compressor back, leaving no evidence of what they'd done.

Holding the scepter in one hand, she thrust the hose back to the deck. "Let it go. You want to die? Who cares if we leave it? Dave'll go batshit tomorrow. Inside, Con. Now!"

"I never leave . . ." He almost said "evidence," but his head was clear enough to stop, and she was right.

With a cursory glance around the deck, and fairly certain no one was around, he followed her, but stopped at the air compressor.

"How'd you know?" he whispered.

"The air intakes were removed. When you didn't come up in seven minutes, I worried."

He stuck his hand under the valve and felt the empty slot. Son of a bitch. He'd checked them. He'd checked them both when he moved the compressor, checked the gas level, too.

Someone took them out while he was getting Lizzie from her cabin.

She pulled his hand, her body quivering with cold. "Come on. You have to get warm. We both do."

He followed her, instantly warmer inside the stairwell, but she was still shivering.

He was clearheaded enough to close and lock her cabin without making a sound. "Hot shower. Strip."

But she was already in the head, reaching into the shower stall, turning on the water in the head with one hand, and pulling at her sopping sweatshirt with the other. He shoved his trunks off as she got the top off, both wet pieces coming at once. She skipped the bra, but was shaking so hard she couldn't untie the drawstring of her sweatpants, so he just pushed her under the hot water, getting in with her and closing the shower door to keep the heat in, grateful her cabin was more deluxe than his.

"Are you okay?" she asked again, color finally returning to her lips. "You still didn't tell me your name."

He choked a laugh, pulling her into him so they were both completely under the stream, which wasn't nearly as hot or hard as he would have liked it to be. "We've done this before. Does that prove I know who I am and who you are?"

She nodded, pressing against him, the warmth finally getting through his skin. And then she put her head on his chest and he felt her whole body relax.

"I thought I was going to pull up a dead man," she murmured.

"You thought I was going to lose your precious scepter?"

"No." She looked up at him. "I really thought . . . never mind."

They didn't move, letting the water warm and soak them. Finally, she looked up at him. Her lips weren't blue at all anymore. They were pink and wet and parted, and he ached for their warmth. Tunneling into her soaking hair, he pulled her up to meet his mouth and kissed her.

She folded right into his arms, the only thing between them a stream of warm water and her very wet pants, which molded to his body. She stood on her toes, opened her mouth, and kissed him back, still shuddering.

One hand stroked his face, as if she were kissing him out of continued concern, but her hips nudged forward and her breasts pressed against him in a way that had nothing to do with concern.

He slipped his tongue between her lips, slanting his head, which only sent more water cascading down their cheeks and into their mouths, the sensation sexy enough to make his whole lower half tighten.

Flattening one hand on her back, he pulled her harder against him, the heat and wet and womanliness of her body like an elixir, sweet and irresistible.

She finally broke the kiss, but her eyes stayed closed and she swayed a tiny bit in his arms.

"Now who's disoriented?" he asked.

"I'm just . . . warm."

He kissed her forehead and tilted her face up so that she opened her eyes and he could drink in the whiskey color, her lashes thick with water, her pupils wide with arousal.

"That's the idea," he said. "Body warmth."

"This is your cure for hypothermia?"

He smiled. "Don't knock it." Once more, he kissed her, harder this time, not even trying to fight the rush of blood or the response. With one hand, he reached behind her and twisted the knob of the shower, stopping the spray.

"Don't move," he murmured, opening the door and grabbing a towel. He was back in the shower in an instant, as much to get close to her as to keep the warmth and steam captured around them.

He wrapped the towel around her shoulders like a cape. "Hold this on you."

She did, clutching it with both hands as he moved to untie the drawstring of her pants.

"These have to go. They're soaked and you'll freeze in them," he explained, giving the wet string a good tug and finally freeing the knot. He pushed them over her hips, the sopping material taking her panties with it.

"You've seen me naked twice now," she said.

He dipped lower as he dragged the pants down, his face eye level with the towel, and then her hips and the dark tuft between her legs.

"Gets better every time." And different. No fear of acid burns this time, no certainty that he had the target of his investigation. This time, he had a woman who'd just risked her life—and her objective—to save his life.

The thought shot through him, hardening an already stiff erection even more as he crouched on the balls of his feet in front of her.

He had the pants to her ankles, lifted one of her feet out, then the other. She backed into the fiberglass wall. He didn't look up. He wanted to, wanted to see if there was invitation or warning in her eyes, but the gentle pressure on his shoulders told him what he'd see.

He kissed the inside of her thigh, softly, and heard her exhale a slow breath.

"Con."

He kissed the other thigh, this time stroking the flesh with his tongue in a slow, small circle.

Her fingers tightened on his shoulders, so he licked higher, closer to her center, a long, slow trail of tongue on skin that tasted so sweet and warm he let out a soft groan of his own.

Her womanhood glistened in front of him. Beautifully pink, slightly swollen, scented with remnants of saltwater and sex. He inched back, looking up to meet her gaze.

But her eyes were closed, her head was back, and her hands gripped his shoulders as though they were the only thing that could keep her from falling into his mouth.

Getting closer, he put his fingers on the soft flesh of her inner thighs, easing them further apart, as he took the first delicious swipe over her.

Her legs buckled, but she hung on to him, rocking her hips forward. He licked her again, curling his tongue in the folds of her flesh, tasting warmth and salty, tangy woman.

Closing his hands over her hips, he crouched lower, to get under, get his tongue in deeper.

"Con." She dug her hands into his head. "What . . . are . . ."

He sucked gently, kissed the inside of her thighs, adjusted his position to kneel right in front of her.

"Hypothermia treatment," he said softly, glancing up and letting his eyes do the smiling. "To be sure you're warm."

He curled his tongue inside her again, magnetically drawn to the taste of her, his cock throbbing a full erection from the sight and smell of her woman's body. He wanted to be inside her.

"I'm . . . oh . . . warm."

Snap.

His head jerked back at the sound.

"Wha—"

"Shhh." He held up a hand to silence her question, rocking back and propelling himself up to a stand.

The click of a latch was barely audible over the blood

in his ears, but Con was up in an instant, using every cell in his body to pinpoint the source of the sound.

"I didn't hear—"

"Don't move." He spun and shoved open the head door and stepped into the cabin, his attention on the knob as it turned. He held up his hand to silence Lizzie behind him, walking to the door, wanting the full impact of surprise on his side.

The hatch slowly creaked open, separating from the rubber strip with a suction sound.

Charlotte Gorman's nose peeked in first, then her face, her eyes popping at the sight of Con. "Oh."

"Can I help you?"

Her gaze dropped over his torso, her color rising as she jerked back behind the door in embarrassment. "I was looking for Lizzie."

Lizzie bounded forward, the towel wrapped under her arms and knotted now, passing Con with a quick look. "It's only Charlotte."

He held her back with one hand, pointing to the scepter on the bed, the silent message clear. *Don't let her in.*

"Let me just talk to her," she whispered, nodding to assure him she wouldn't let her in.

"She was breaking in."

"She has a *key*." She stepped to the opening, keeping it cracked just enough to peek out. "I'm, uh, kind of busy, Char. What's the matter?"

Con stood right behind Lizzie, glaring at Charlotte, who ignored him. "It's Sam. He's really sick."

"What's wrong?"

"I don't know. He's been moaning. He has chest pains." The older woman's eyes looked pained, with deep circles and a feathering of lines all around. "Can you come and see him, Lizzie?"

Lizzie glanced over her shoulder at Con. "Would you know the signs of a heart attack?"

He nodded.

"Then . . ." She faltered. "Could you check on him?"

"Lizzie." Charlotte reached to take the woman's hand. "I need you there. Please. I'm scared."

Con pulled Lizzie deeper into the cabin, against his chest. "Give us a minute, Mrs. Gorman. One of us will be over in a minute."

She finally looked at him, her expression a mix of pain and relief and a little distrust. "Sorry to interrupt. But I'm scared."

"We'll be right there," Lizzie assured her. "You go stay with Sam. If we need to get him to the mainland to a doctor, we will. We'll do whatever we have to, I promise."

When she left, Lizzie turned, but Con didn't move.

"We have to help her," she said.

"She was breaking in."

"Con, she has a key to my cabin. She's my friend. And her husband's sick." She pushed by him and started lifting up random clothes looking for something to wear.

"Why didn't she knock?"

"Maybe she heard the shower or didn't want to wake the rest of the crew. Maybe we didn't hear her. The shower was on, and we were . . . breathing heavy."

Stepping out of his grasp, she gave him a little nudge. "Please get dressed and we'll hide that and go see him. The man could be dying."

She hadn't knocked. Con knew that for a fact. He watched the towel fall, leaving Lizzie naked, damp, pink. "You warm enough now?" he asked.

She nodded and glanced over at him as she pulled her panties on. "You still disoriented?"

He smiled. "I was just getting there when the 911 call came."

"Timing is everything," she said with a shrug.

"Yeah. And hers was impeccable."

CHAPTER TEN

BRIANNA DARE SHOULDERED her travel bag and powered through the streets of Lisbon. Lizzie was going to kill her, but then she'd throw her arms around her and get all emotional about how she had to watch out for Brianna because they didn't have a mother. And now they didn't have a father, Lizzie was worse than ever.

At the base of the funicular that would take her up a steep hill to another noisy, crazy, insanely gorgeous part of the city, Brianna climbed on board. A man muttered something to her in Portuguese and checked her out. A woman elbowed past her to get onto the Santa Justa elevator to Upper City. Smells and colors and sounds swirled around her, and Brianna couldn't wipe the smile from her face. Freedom felt *so* freaking good.

She was out of Vero Beach. Out of that stifling, suffocating house with nothing to do but organize Dad's pile of chaos and look for paper clues, while Lizzie had all the fun on a dive.

She'd left her cell phone at home—it wouldn't work

over here anyway—and hadn't told Lizzie what she had decided to do. Her sister would be furious, but if she was successful on this trip, Lizzie would forgive her in a heartbeat.

From his notes, it was clear Dad had wondered about the identity of "BC" and how he or she fit into the legend of *El Falcone*. Brianna was about to find out, and it was something Lizzie wanted to know almost as much as she wanted the treasure itself. Without that piece of the puzzle, it would be hard to prove their ancestor was anything but a slimy pirate.

As the car started to ride up the rails, Brianna reached into her bag to double-check the address and directions. Maria Rossos Della Buonofuentes spoke enough English that they could communicate over the Internet, and according to her directions, Brianna was one stop and a quick walk from her destination.

Off the funicular, she headed up another hill, so steep that the cobbled streets were like steps. Everywhere, her senses were assaulted with foreign beauty and sounds and smells. Creamy stone church spires curled into a blue sky right next to candy-colored storefronts, their balconies festooned with laundry. Vendors and fishmongers cried out as she passed, tempting her to stop and taste and experience it all.

But she had a mission, and she was focused on that.

At the entrance to a large park, she saw the café across the street. *Solar do Vinho*. Exactly as Maria's directions said. She waited for a brightly painted trolley to rumble by, then dashed across the street and into the wine bar.

It was almost five, so she was a few minutes early,

and the tiny café was nearly deserted. Except for a woman who sat in the far corner, a bright orange scarf around her head, just as she'd promised.

"Hello, Maria." Brianna plopped down across from her, letting her bag fall to the floor. "I'm Bree Dare."

Dark, sad eyes crinkled with a smile. She was younger than Brianna had imagined and really pretty. She held out a cool hand and clasped Brianna's, not in a classic handshake but more of a knuckle squeeze.

"You have made it." Her English was flawless and musical.

"I didn't even see my room," Bree admitted with a laugh. "I just left my bags with the concierge and came right here. Do you have it?"

Maria crossed her arms. "I do. It took quite a bit of research, but I have finally located the property for you." She drew a cylindrical roll from her bag and spread the paper out.

A map. An island. "Where is this?"

"This, my friend, is Corvo. The farthermost island in the Azores, with a population of less than four hundred, if you include the horses and cows, and one very, very tiny town. Many windmills that are not like any you'll find in the world. Stone windmills with remarkable machinery that never stops, no matter which way the wind blows. Corvo is famous for them."

Windmills? Whatever. "This is where the family I wrote to you about, the Bettencourts, live?"

"One of them. Bettencourt is a common name in the Azores, but I believe this is where the branch of the family you are looking for once lived."

"Are you sure?" Brianna frowned at the map. "It's really . . . out there."

"You are looking for Carlos Bettencourt, and this is the land that was in his family name. I've run genealogy on many of the lines of this family for other clients. This particular branch goes back to Corvo, although that tree is so large that even a seasoned genealogist like me has trouble keeping them straight. Most of the family lived on Terceira, one of the other islands in the Azores, and there is even a palace there named for them."

Brianna nodded, dividing her attention between the map and the woman. It was like a little rock a thousand miles away.

Lizzie would *really* kill her if she went there. But after what she found in Dad's office . . . how could she not?

"Did you find anything out about this Carlos guy?"

"A small amount. Evidently, he broke away from the family and was exiled to this home." Maria tapped the map. "I had a long conversation with a historian at the University of Lisbon, who said that Carlos Bettencourt was willing to do just about anything to get back in the good graces of his wealthy, renowned family. One of the things he did was commission a gift for the king and his bride to commemorate their wedding in 1862."

Brianna tingled all over. This was the right Carlos Bettencourt. They'd found CB! Maybe. "Do you know what he gave them as a gift?"

"Nothing. Apparently he registered to give them

scepters and promised they would include two of the most beautiful, rare, matching blue diamonds from India. But no such gift was ever received."

Somehow, Brianna managed not to react. This woman was simply a paid consultant; she didn't need to know the emotional value of her information. She might charge even more then, and Brianna was already paying a small fortune for this whole trip.

If Carlos Bettencourt paid for the scepters and Aramis Dare ran off with them, then history's recounting that he was a blackhearted thief was correct. But if Carlos had refused to pay Aramis, as one letter Dad had uncovered said, then the scepters, when found, belonged to the Dare family.

Her heart hammered with hope. "So what happened to the scepters? Are you certain they were never given to the king and queen?"

"There is a list of wedding gifts in the archives of the Palace of Queluz, one of Portuguese royalty's main residences. They are mentioned as promised by Carlos Bettencourt, but never delivered."

"Did the historian you talked to know what happened to Carlos?"

"According to the family records, he traveled by ship to the Americas and never returned. His property on Corvo, however, has stayed in Bettencourt hands for over a hundred years, which isn't unusual in the Azores. One family can stay in a house for many generations."

Bingo. And would that family have any records she could study?

She had to find out. "Thank you, Maria. This, on top of the information you provided about my own ancestors, is so valuable."

"Valuable indeed." The other woman raised her eyebrows and waited.

"Oh, of course." Bree reached into her bag and handed Maria the envelope, swallowing guilt. Lizzie would have paid that much, too. And Dad would have paid ten times the amount for the identity of the mysterious BC.

Brianna stood, taking the map. "This property, you said it's a farm?"

"Probably. There's a main house and a windmill. Habitable, but very rural."

"How do you get there?"

"A flight from Lisbon to Terceira, then I'm afraid just a very small plane can land on Corvo, which has a treacherous little airport." She smiled. "It's very windy on the archipelago of the Azores. Not for a faint flyer."

"Good thing I'm not." Brianna grinned back, loving the possibility of the adventure. "And you're sure that Bettencourts live there now?"

Maria tucked her envelope in her bag and stood. "The deed is in the name of an American named Jaeger Bettencourt, so it is hard to say who might actually be living there. It wouldn't be unusual for a local family to rent it and run the farm for an American, or an Azorean family could live there. It could be abandoned, for all I know."

With luck, there would be someone there. Maybe

even a Bettencourt. And hopefully, they didn't care about some ancient folklore and lost artifacts.

Brianna was about to find out.

A few minutes before dawn, Lizzie slipped out of her bunk and tiptoed up to the main deck to coil up the air hose and hide the evidence of what they'd done. But someone had already put the deck back together.

Had Con done this? After they'd spent about an hour with Charlotte and Sam, certain his pains were heartburn brought on by his weakness for Brady's hot salsa, and not a heart attack, Lizzie had gone to bed. But not to sleep. And not with Con, which was a shame.

She walked over to the air compressor, which had been replaced in its normal position. Bending over, she put her finger on the valve to check—

"They're back on."

She spun around to see Con at the top of the stairs, a black T-shirt making him look even bigger and badder. "Did you do this?"

He shook his head. "I came up here about five minutes ago, and the place was neat as a pin. I was just checking the lab, which is still locked. The engineer and his assistant are awake, and Brady and Flo are cooking. The rest of the crew is still down."

"Flo might have cleaned this up, although that—" she indicated the neatly coiled air hose—"has Divemaster Dave's signature all over it."

"Would the cook's wife have noticed the air intakes were out and replaced them?" His look was as skeptical as his tone.

"Well, she's responsible for housekeeping, but that doesn't usually include the deck." She blew out a troubled breath. "I need coffee, stat."

In the main salon, Lizzie mentally flipped through every person on the boat who could have come up here and covered their tracks. The same way she'd flipped through everyone who might have tried to kill one of them last night.

And *why*?

Could someone know she had the diamond? The need to get it off the boat burned hotter than ever.

"I still think Dave came up here earlier and cleaned up," she said softly to Con as they walked toward the galley buffet table. "He's a hound about recoiling the air hoses."

"And checking the air intake?"

"Of course. That's his job. Maybe—"

She stopped as Brady came around the buffet with a steaming pot of coffee.

"Mornin', Lizzie. Con."

"Hi, Brady," she said. "Are we your first customers this morning?" Maybe the cook could give them some insight.

"So far." He set the pot on the warming pad and flipped two mugs down from the shelf for them. "You're not diving this morning, Lizzie, so how 'bout I make you some Sunday morning pancakes?"

"You're too good to me, Brady."

"I'll take some, too." Flynn ambled in. "Fast. I'm going to get that medallion into the Paxton lab, now that it mysteriously showed back up in our lab." He flicked his gaze at Con, but Lizzie stepped forward to seize the opportunity.

"I'll go with you to the mainland, Flynn." He scowled, and she continued, "I really need to get down to see my sister."

"To see your sister?" Flynn half-laughed. "In the middle of a dive? I don't think so, Lizzie. You're not paid for vacation days."

"Flynn, please, she's . . . she's had a hard time recently and I just want to pop in and see her for a few minutes."

It wasn't ideal; she'd planned to figure out a way to get there during the week when the bank was open and she could get the scepter in the family safe-deposit box. But this opportunity might not arise again soon, and she had to get that thing off the boat. Her sister could be responsible for it overnight, and secure it in the box tomorrow morning.

"You're going through the Sebastian Inlet, right?"

He nodded. "There's no time to get up to the port and back."

"Vero's just twenty minutes away from the inlet. I'll be back at the boat before you're back from the lab. I promise."

He shook his head. "I don't know, Lizzie. That's a rough ride through the inlet—even I wouldn't attempt it after sundown. If you get stuck in Vero, I can't wait for you, and God knows how long it could be till you get back to this boat. I don't think so."

She hated having to beg this son of a bitch for anything. "Flynn, really, she lives so close—"

"I'll go with you," Con said.

Flynn looked up from his coffee, surprised. "That won't assure she'll be any faster."

"I'll keep her on schedule, but more important, I can help you navigate the inlet. I know it well, even in the dark. You should have a second pair of hands on board going through that place, anyway."

Lizzie swallowed her arguments. What was she, *no* hands? She didn't really want him to come, but if it got Flynn to agree to take her, then she'd accept it.

Flynn eyed them both, obviously enjoying the little power trip of granting permission to his minions. "You better have a way to get to Vero Beach, Lizzie, because I'm not driving you down there. I have things to do."

"I've got that covered," Con said.

"Great," she replied. *Maybe.* She got what she wanted, but would Con call every shot? "Then I'll get my stuff together and pass on breakfast, Brady. I'll meet you up here in twenty minutes or so."

Con would bring the diamond, so she had to get the scepter wrapped and hidden in a bag. In her room, she dragged her canvas zippered tote, then pulled out the mattress from the bunk where she'd hidden the scepter.

And stared at the empty spot, her heart lodging in her throat. "Oh my God."

Con. It *had* to have been Con. Right? If not . . .

She didn't even want to think about it. Grabbing a handbag, she marched back up to the salon where Flynn and Con were talking and eating.

"Change your mind on the pancakes?" Con asked, moving over to make room for her.

She noticed his khaki-colored, beat-up backpack on the floor . . . big enough to carry what she knew in her gut he had.

She gave him a look as she slid into the booth next to him, but he just replied with a surreptitious squeeze of her leg.

Lizzie was still unhappy about the turn of events when the three of them climbed aboard Flynn's boat. She'd wanted to undertake this job on her own, without any prying eyes and opinions on how it should be done. And, damn it, he was swinging that bag like it contained his dirty underwear, not a priceless artifact.

But they never had a moment alone, so she never got a chance to ask him how he'd gotten into her room to take the scepter, or why.

Con stayed up on the bridge with Flynn until they reached the tricky waters of the Sebastian Inlet, a zigzaggy, white-water, man-made cut in the coastline meant for smaller boats that wanted to get into the wide, calm waters of the Indian River.

This shortcut was convenient, but required some skill to navigate the rocks. Con had plenty of that, standing on the bow of the boat, calling up to the bridge where Flynn was at the helm. Con's instructions and guidance helped them round rocks and whitecaps, a monster hole of a sandbar drop-off that could flip a boat with one bad move, then through the shallows into the river that separated the barrier islands from the mainland.

The whole time, Lizzie watched him, drinking in his attitude, his confidence, his power.

Maybe it was in her blood to be attracted to dark, broody men straddling a bowsprit like a pirate, or maybe it was just that *this* man was a stunning figure of command. A strapping, strong leader who had already demonstrated he'd be as good in bed as he was at the bow.

Her lower half curled with arousal at the thought, the memory of his tongue sliding up her thigh, his warm breath on her skin still fresh enough to be recalled with far too much clarity.

The man obviously got whatever he wanted, whenever he wanted it. And he seemed to want her.

She'd never had a fling with a fellow diver, mostly because her father was on board nearly every boat she'd ever been on. Shipboard romances were as common as finding pieces of eight. They didn't have to mean anything; they didn't have to last. They could just be fun.

He turned his gaze toward her, her whole body responding to the way the wind pressed the T-shirt to his shoulders and how his jeans fit like a dream.

Did he know what she was thinking?

He lifted his sunglasses and revealed the direction of his gaze—locked on the bag next to her.

So he was thinking about the *treasure,* and she was thinking about . . . him.

She shifted her own attention to the water, determined to keep it there until they'd docked at the Sebastian Marina.

A half hour later, they climbed onto the wooden planks after tying up. Flynn was holding his bag with the medallion with a lot greater care than was Con, who flipped the backpack casually over his shoulder.

"What time do we need to be back here, Flynn?" she asked.

"Four o'clock, drop-dead latest," he replied.

"We'll see you back here long before four," Con assured him. "You've got my cell if you need us."

Lizzie let out a soft breath. "How come you get to have a cell phone out in the open and nobody else does?"

"It's in my contract."

"You have a *contract*?"

He just smiled and draped his arm over her shoulders, steering her toward the bait shop. At the door, he put a hand on her arm.

"Wait here, and watch where Flynn goes."

Before she could question or argue, he disappeared inside, and in less than two minutes returned holding keys.

"Has he left the lot yet?"

"No, he's over there, getting into an SUV. Why did you take that scepter from my room?"

"It wasn't safe for you to have it. Let's go." He nudged her to a separate section of the huge lot. "Our ride's over there."

He steered her to a menacing black motorcycle tucked between two trucks, two black helmets clipped to the seat.

"Before we can go to your sister's house," he said as he unlatched the smaller of the helmets, "we've gotta follow Flynn."

Her annoyance, already peaking, ratcheted up about ten degrees. "We are not."

"Yes, we are."

"On *this* thing?"

He shoved the helmet into her hands. "He won't be looking for it, and we'll have much better maneuverability for following. You need help with that? Hurry up, he's about to pull out. Don't worry, it's a great little bike."

"You are *not* going joyriding with the freaking scepter of the king of Portugal and one of the most valuable diamonds in the world on your back!"

"We're not joyriding, Lizzie." He took the helmet out of her hands and eased it over her head. "I want to know where he's taking that medallion, and so do you." He tucked some strands of her hair under the helmet and snapped the chin strap.

"Why do you care?"

"Because you do." He threw a leg over the bike and started it up with a rumble. "You coming?"

She reached for the backpack straps, tugging hard enough to pull him back an inch. "Damn you, Con! You are not hijacking my plans again. I didn't invite you on this trip. Give me this bag. Go follow him to the processing lab if you want, but I'll go call my sister and she'll pick me up, exactly as I'd planned."

"This bag is coming with me, and so are you." He revved the engine and patted the seat behind him. "Climb up, hang on, and I promise we'll get to your sister with time to spare. We have to know what he's up to."

At the sound of squealing tires, she looked up to the street and saw the silver SUV peel out, headed south.

The opposite direction of the Paxton Treasures processing lab.

She slid her leg over the leather and scooted into him, pressing her chest against a priceless treasure and her legs against his rock-hard thighs. "Fine. Go."

"Good girl."

He took off and she held on, and suddenly didn't feel like a very good girl at all.

CHAPTER
ELEVEN

CON MADE UP the delay easily, wending the Kawasaki the Bullet Catchers had arranged to be waiting for him through the light traffic, staying far enough back not to get on Paxton's radar, but close enough not to lose him. Easy, since he stayed on A1A and kept a steady speed.

"We just passed the turnoff to where my sister lives," Lizzie shouted in his ear.

He gave her thigh a solid pat. They'd get there. But if he didn't find out what the hell Paxton was up to, he'd be remiss in his duties.

Paxton took a right when they reached the smattering of stores and restaurants of a tiny beach town, and Con slowed a little. It'd be tougher to follow without being seen, now that they were on side roads, but he could do it.

They weaved through some commercial areas, then backtracked north a few blocks, past several high-end gated communities. As he drove past an oversized manicured entrance flanked by marble slabs bearing the words *St. Richard's Island* in gold, Con saw Paxton's SUV at the gatehouse, his head out the window, speaking with a guard holding a clipboard. At the next intersection, he turned on a side street and stopped.

"What are you doing?" Lizzie asked. "Didn't you see him at that guard gate?"

"Hang on. I'm getting us in," he said, taking out his cell phone and dialing. Lucy said use the resources, and he intended to.

Avery Cole, Lucy's assistant, answered on the first ring. "Hello, Con, what do you need?"

"Information."

"Name it."

Seriously, he could get used to this. "St. Richard's Island, a private development about ten miles south of Vero Beach. Need a resident with a close relative named Elizabeth."

"Hang on," she said.

Behind him, Lizzie released a dismayed breath. "You're kidding, right?"

"The guards to these places are trained to let family members in."

"Family members usually have the same last name," she said. "If they don't, don't you think they'll call the resident and confirm?"

He'd broken into so many ultraposh Florida gated developments, he'd lost count. This technique never failed.

"All right, Con," Avery said. "There's a David Rollins at 546 River Run Road, in St. Richard's. His sister is Elizabeth Fournier, and she lives in Madison, Wisconsin."

"How old is she?"

"Thirty-seven."

"Thanks, Avery. Does Mr. Rollins have kids?"

"Two. Ten and twelve. Jessica and Gabriel. Wife's name is Sarah."

"Perfect. That's all I need, thank you." He revved up the bike, then paused at the intersection for a passing car.

"Aunt Liz," he called over his shoulder. "It's a surprise visit to your brother and his wife, David and Sarah Rollins. You're in from Wisconsin."

"What? How the heck do you know they live there?"

"Just work with me and I'll explain later."

He pulled up to the guardhouse and slowed the engine, earning a wary look from an older, balding man who wore a badge with "Mike" on it.

"This is Elizabeth Fournier, here to see the Rollins family at 546 River Run."

He frowned and read his clipboard. "No one called you in, sir. I'll have to call the house."

"No, wait." Lizzie leaned forward to speak over the engine. "If my brother answers, then the whole surprise is ruined."

The guard looked dubious.

"How about if we showed you some ID, Mike?" Con suggested with a smile. "Liz, do you have your license? It has your maiden name on it, right?"

Behind him, another car pulled up. And behind that, a furniture delivery truck. The guard glanced at the growing line and waved them in. "Go ahead. Hate to ruin a surprise."

Con thanked him and rolled the bike respectfully through the gate as it rose. Luckily, St. Richard's was one big circle, so he headed right and slowly made his way down River Run, looking for the SUV.

"Who did you call?" Lizzie demanded into his ear. "How did you get the names of residents in that place?"

"I have some great connections."

She nudged his shoulder. "No kidding. Who, the CIA?"

"Actually," he said with a smile, "you're not too far off. Look for Flynn's vehicle."

"Is that it?" She indicated a silver Highlander parked in front of the furthermost house.

"I'd say so." He passed slowly, taking in the towering front windows and stately columns at the end of a long drive. He got the address and took one more pass around the circle, but there wasn't much more they could do, unless he wanted to follow Flynn when he left.

What he wanted to do was call Avery with the address, but maybe he'd just text it to her so he didn't invite more questions about his CIA connections.

"He might not come out for hours," she said, impatience in her tone.

"I'd like to see if he even goes to the Paxton Labs."

"If we hurry up and get to my sister, there's still time to go up there before we need to be back at the marina. Please." She gave the bag a gentle nudge. "Riding around with this is making me nervous."

"All right." He pulled out, taking one more look at the entrance to St. Richard's Island, then headed back to the beach highway.

They zipped onto A1A and he opened up the bike, weaving through the little bit of traffic, glimpses of the cobalt blue Atlantic Ocean on their left.

In Vero Beach, she led him to a simple, established neighborhood of ranch homes, mostly built in the fifties and sixties.

"Your younger sister lives here, alone?" Seemed like an awfully quiet street for a twentysomething single girl.

"Oh, she'll tell you how much she hates it. And she'll be moving soon. But she lived here with my dad, and now she's in the process of emptying out his office and organizing all his papers so we can sell both places."

"Both?"

"My dad had another place right on the beach, where he worked," she told him as he slowed down on the street. "That's the house. The blue one on the right."

He pulled into the driveway. "Does your sister dive, too?"

"God, yes. And she's really unhappy that she's not on this dive with me."

"So why isn't she?"

As he brought the bike to a stop in the driveway, Lizzie pulled off her helmet and shook out her curls. "Long story." She scanned the outside of the house. "Boy, she really is holed up."

"What do you mean?"

"No windows open in November? All the blinds closed?" She frowned and took a few steps up the driveway, squinting at the small front porch of the stucco home. "Is that a flyer on the door? That's not like her."

He took her helmet and attached it with his to the bike. "You sure she's here? Maybe she went away for a few days."

"She'd have told me if she were leaving." She slid the advertising flyer from the handle, then pulled out her keys and unlocked the door.

"Hey, Bree," she called out. "It's me."

Con followed her into a dimly lit living area in the front of the house. The shutters were closed tight and the house was warm, as if neither fresh nor conditioned air had been blowing through for a day or two.

Lizzie breezed through the tiny front room/dining area, popping out to a covered patio, then went down the hall to what he assumed were bedrooms. On the other side of the dining room, a tiny kitchen opened up to the lanai and a small pool area decorated with a Tahitian theme, including a thatched roof hanging over a two-person outdoor bar and a kitschy totem pool.

Surprisingly, not a lot of money for a treasure-hunting family. And not a lot of real treasures on display, unless he counted Lizzie's high school graduation picture on the dining-room wall. Next to it was a darker-haired version of Lizzie with similar features and a devilish smile. That must be Bree.

Lizzie headed to the other side of the house. "I'm going to go back into the office and look around."

"What about this?" He unshouldered the backpack and set it on the dining-room table.

"I have a place in the spare bedroom. But let me see if I can figure out where she is, first."

He followed her into a small office, and there the orderliness of the house ended.

"My dad was a mess," she said apologetically. "But this is nothing—you should see his beach house. It's tiny and packed to the gills with crap he's collected over the years. Maybe Bree is over there, getting more stuff."

"She ought to get through this pile first." The floor-to-ceiling shelves bowed under the weight of reference books, files stuffed with papers, journals, magazines, yellowed newspaper clippings, crammed shoeboxes, and pictures on every inch of wall.

"I know, right? That's why she's here and not on the dive. We have to get through all this."

The floor was full of packing boxes, crates, and plastic storage bins, all of it in disarray. On every wall were pictures of boats and coins and jewels and chipped porcelain and dark bronze utensils. Images of dozens of happy faces, almost all with diving masks pulled up, hands stretched out, beaming victorious smiles to show off a recovered treasure. Many were obviously Lizzie's father, flanked by two girls with matching grins.

"So, where's your mom?" he asked.

"She passed away when I was nine," she said, pausing at a picture of a young couple with a toddler. "Here she is, pregnant with Brianna."

"Was she sick?"

"Yeah, very. But we muddled through somehow. I managed to get Brianna through her teens without killing herself." She laughed softly. "No mean feat, with that one."

"*You* managed?"

She shrugged. "My dad was always on a dive, or researching or speaking somewhere. I just stepped in and did the big sister thing." She looked around, zeroing in on the one empty surface, a small typing table. "Wherever she is, she has her laptop. That's strange."

Con noticed the printer silently flashing a yellow light over the empty paper bin. He grabbed a few sheets of blank paper, fed them in, and instantly the machine clicked to life.

"Something's in the printer cue." He read the paper as it fed out of the ink-jet printer. *Delta Airways. Boarding Pass. Brianna Lynn Dare.* "Could she have gone to Lisbon?"

Lizzie laughed. "I seriously doubt that." When she read the paper he held out, she paled a little. "I will kill her if she went to Portugal."

"Why? She's not a child."

Her eyes flashed. "I know, but . . ." She waved her hand, studying the boarding pass. "There has to be an explanation. I'm going to call her."

She slipped her phone from a side pocket of her cargo pants and dialed.

"Not that I think it will go through in Lis—" From down the hall came a digital jingle. "Shit," she murmured, hitting a button. "Why would she do this?"

"She's a grown woman, Lizzie. Is it really out of the realm of possibility that she'd take a trip? Maybe she couldn't reach you."

"Maybe. And nothing's out of the realm of possibility with her. It's just that . . ." She sighed. "She's all I've got. And I've always been a little protective of her. More so since my dad died."

"But she took her laptop," he noted. "Why don't you e-mail her? My phone has Internet service."

She agreed and took his phone, sending a message while he perused the papers on the desk, on the file cabinet, everywhere.

"Alachua High Springs?" he asked, reading out loud from some notes on a yellow pad. "I've been—"

"What is that?" Lizzie put down the phone, drawn to what he was reading. "That's my dad's handwriting," she said softly, her body slumping. "And those must be the notes from his last dive. That's where he died, and the day it happened."

"He was cave diving?"

She gave him a look. "You know the place?"

"I've dived there, up under the Suwannee and Ichetucknee rivers. I spent most of my life over near the Panhandle in Tarpon Springs, not far from there, so, yeah, I know the whole area. Tons of caves." He frowned, studying the map. "When you said he died of nitrogen narcosis, I figured it was a deep SCUBA dive for salvage. This . . ." He indicated the hand-drawn map on the page. "Is a whole different thing. This is more of a thrill-seeker's sport."

"I know, which is why it was strange. He didn't even tell us he was going on this dive, but I figured he didn't want me to worry." She bit her lip. "Which makes me mad as hell, on top of missing him."

She glanced at the notes along the side, describing "underground rooms so big you could drive two tractor-trailers through side by side" with three exclamation points.

"Have you dived these caves?" she asked.

"I have. And this particular one"—he circled the map sketch with one finger—"is very advanced. It's a three-and-a-half-mile labyrinth about three hundred feet deep. That's some serious diving. Was his dive partner a pro?"

"Dylan Houser, a California cave diver. I never even met him during the investigation, but the authorities interviewed him. He was a diver my dad met through his contacts. He was on the surface when my dad died, and, no, they didn't use tethers." She shook her head, dropping the pad on top of a pile of books, and headed out of the room.

Con picked up the printed boarding pass she'd left behind, folded it and slipped it into his pocket, then grabbed the backpack from the dining-room table on the way to the spare bedroom.

The room was small, barely holding a double bed, dresser, chest of drawers, and a small empty aquarium in the corner. Lizzie paused at the door, reached for the bag, and gave him a pointed look.

"Okay. Thank you. Good-bye now."

He laughed softly. "Excuse me?"

"I can't get to the bank on Sunday afternoon, so I'm going to hide this, and I don't want anyone to know where it is. Even you." She put both hands on the bag and gave it a strong pull; he relinquished it.

"Are you crazy? What if someone broke in here and stole it—"

"No one will ever find where I'm hiding it."

Right. "What if there's a fire?"

She looked hard at him. "The bank's closed. We're due back at that marina in an hour. And he *will* leave without us, to make his point. Do you have a better idea, Con?"

He did. He'd have Lucy send someone down here and retrieve it if he had to. "Not this second. Go ahead, hide it."

She backed into the room, and closed and locked the door. Like that little scrap of metal could keep him out. But he didn't need to be in the room to know what she was doing; he could hear her moving around.

He put his ear to the door and picked up the ruffle of some bedding, the brush of someone crawling on carpeted floor, and pictured her crawling under a bed. She liked that hiding place; it was the same thing she did with the scepter.

He pressed his ear to the door and heard a snap, then a zipper too high-pitched to be the backpacks. Something hit wood . . . the scepter? If he had to find it without her, he now knew enough from what he'd heard.

A loud knock on the front door pulled him away from her door. When she didn't emerge and the visitor knocked again, harder, he missed the nuance of the next sound.

"Lizzie," he called. "Someone's here."

"One sec." The zipper sound again, and a snap, then another.

He inched to the door to hear what she was doing, but another sound caught his attention. The lock opening in the front.

Automatically, he reached for his weapon. He advanced down the hall toward the front, listening. Whoever it was made no effort to hide that he or she was there. A female, judging from the sound of heels on tile, moving fast across the living area.

He gave it three seconds, then popped around the corner to surprise her, and got a deafening scream in return.

Behind him, the door to Lizzie's room crashed open and she tore out. "What the hell?"

An older woman with graying hair, huge brown eyes, and impressive lungs stood frozen with her hands balled to her cheeks.

Lizzie shot right past him and almost lost her balance at the sight of the woman.

"Joy!"

The scream stopped. "Oh my. Lizzie. You scared me!"

"No, *he* scared you." She glared at the Glock. "You can put that away. This is a neighbor, Joy Caldwell. What are you doing?" she asked the woman.

She held up a handful of mail. "Getting the mail while your sister's out of town."

"Damn. She really is gone?"

"She went to Lisbon, honey. I don't think she was expecting you to stop by anytime soon. Aren't you out diving?"

Lizzie just shook her head. "Is she alone?"

"I believe so."

"She didn't happen to say why she was going to Portugal, did she?"

Joy shrugged. "I thought it was for fun. She was

awfully darn excited and, well, you know Brianna. Just doing something spontaneous."

"Thanks for the mail, Joy," Lizzie replied, resignation in her voice. "Did she leave an itinerary?"

"I'm sorry, no." The woman's gaze flicked to Con. "Are you a cop or something?"

"Something."

Lizzie gently nudged Joy to the door. "I'll call you if I hear from her, and you do the same. You have my cell phone number, right?"

"I do."

Lizzie closed the door and turned to face Con. "First of all, why in God's name are you armed? And second, do you think your amazing contacts can help me find my sister?"

CHAPTER
TWELVE

FOR ALL THE money this guy must have to be able to buy the medallion, Gerard Dix's winter home in St. Richard's Island wasn't *that* nice. The McMansion couldn't go for more than two or three mil, and the furnishings were right out of the pages of *Southern Living*. Nothing like what Flynn would have if *he* could shell out six figures for a necklace. But ever since his mother had married Judd Paxton and Flynn had been exposed to true wealth, he'd noticed that some of the richest people didn't reveal it to the world. But Dix was happy to part with his money, clearly enamored with the medallion. After he examined it, he disappeared from the spacious pool deck, leaving Flynn alone with a watery iced tea, then he bounded back, beaming, with cash.

"Well done, Flynn. I had a good look inside. It certainly needs a little more treatment and cleaning, but I have no doubt that this is genuine and valuable." He pulled out a seat across from Flynn at the glass-topped poolside table. "You've clearly inherited the salvaging gene."

Flynn's lip practically curled. "Judd's married to my mother, Gerry. No blood or genes shared between us."

"Oh, excuse me. Since you have the same name, I assumed you're his son."

Fucking liar. Everyone in this world knew Flynn was the stepson riding on the coattails of Judd's success. "You do remember our agreement?" Flynn crossed his arms and rested them on the table. "Keep Judd out of this."

"No worries, son. I'm no friend of the man's. He's never wanted to play by our rules."

Those would be the rules of commercial underground. "So true," Flynn agreed. "Judd likes to keep his name front and center, and we . . . don't."

Gerry chuckled. "Isn't that the truth? I hate to say it, but he's a bit of an egotist."

"Ya think?" Flynn rolled his eyes. "He loves nothing more than seeing his name in print, on walls, in books. His motto? 'Underwater treasure diving should be synonymous with the name Paxton.' "

"He's achieved that," Gerry said with a note of admiration. "I admit, now that I know he's not your real father, you seem like less of a . . ."

"What? A traitor? A thief? A person willing to backstab the man who married his mother?"

"No, no, it's just that—"

"That what?" His voice got edgy, as it always did when his stepfather's name was mentioned. "That Judd Paxton's blood son wouldn't screw him in the back?"

Gerry inched back, assessing Flynn. "Frankly, yes. That's what I was thinking. You *are* cheating your father out of money."

Fuck you, Gerry. It was your *money.* Flynn managed a tight smile. This was, after all, a good customer. "He's not in this business for money."

"Coulda fooled me. Judd Paxton is a very wealthy man."

"He's in it for the glory. Notice his name on the museum doors? The grants to universities? The mile-high mountain of press coverage? That's what gets my old man off."

"Your old *step*man."

Flynn's blood bubbled to a low simmer, but he covered the anger by crossing his legs and leaning back. "But he won't have his name on that piece." He slanted his head toward the house where Gerry had taken his treasure. "And I have a feeling there could be more on this dive. A lot more."

"I'm always interested," Gerry said, standing up. "Just give me a call."

Flynn maintained his calm demeanor as they walked to the front of the house, kept his temper in check while they shook hands and said good-bye, then climbed into his SUV, driving slowly around the circle even though he wanted to smash his foot on the pedal. He pulled onto A1A with a remarkable amount of composure, considering that his heart rate soared higher with every moment.

Then he smashed the heel of his hand on the steering wheel so hard it sent pain up his arm. Stealing from his

stepfather wasn't enough. His full-scale piracy only created pity and support for the great and powerful Judd
Paxton. And frankly, being an irritant to the man just
didn't give Flynn the satisfaction he needed anymore.

Judd Paxton had to *suffer* for being an egotistical
prick. For fucking Flynn's mother, and never truly acknowledging Flynn as his son. Judd Paxton needed to
get it where it hurt him the most: his reputation.

Flynn drove back to the marina like a maniac, for-
mulating a plan. If the authorities found out about the
unregistered dive, Judd would merely get his knuckles
rapped and he'd buy his way back into the Florida state
reps' good graces. He'd done *that* often enough.

No, it had to be something bigger. Something more
shocking. Something that would expose the dive and
leave a permanent stain on the name Paxton.

Judd wanted headlines? That's what he'd get.

An ankle holster? Lizzie watched dumbfounded as Con
stashed the gun into a leather contraption around his
ankle. "You want to explain that to me?"

"I'm armed because it's stupid not to be when carrying around an artifact that I have no doubt people
would kill for," he said, straightening his jeans. "And to
answer your other question, yes, I can get confirmation
whether or not your sister was on a plane to Lisbon.
If she's registered in a hotel there, I can probably get a
phone number for you, too."

She wanted to jump all over the first explanation, but
the urge to throw her arms around him for the rest of it
was stronger. She quelled both reactions, watching him

warily as she deposited Brianna's mail on the dining-room table. "How? How can you do that?"

"I told you, I have—"

"Connections. Yes, I know, but . . ." She shook her head, the very first question she ever had about him snaking back into her mind. A question she'd conveniently tamped down as she grew more attracted to him, and more dependent on him. It was time to ask. "Who *are* you?"

He gave her a slight smile. "That's not what you want to know, Lizzie."

"It's exactly what I want to know."

"No." He pulled out one of the dining-room chairs and offered it to her. "What you want to know is what I'm doing on this dive, and why I'm helping you."

She stayed standing, until he put a strong hand on her shoulder and guided her into the chair, as if whatever he was going to tell her would make her lose her balance. Her heart did just that, so she took the seat, while he pulled out the other and sat knee-to-knee.

For a long moment, he didn't speak. He finally said, "There is a reason that I carry a gun and a satellite phone, why I'm willing to help you take and hide treasures from the boat, and why, with a single phone call, I can find out the names of a resident in a development or a list of passengers on a plane."

He waited a beat, while her brain whirred over possibilities.

"It's the same reason," he continued, "that I came after you in the lab when I thought you were stealing, and was able to have a motorcycle waiting when we arrived, and can pick up my phone and find out who lives in the house where Flynn Paxton was visiting."

"Oh my God." She put her hand to her mouth as realization and understanding dawned. "You're an undercover agent for the government."

He said nothing, just looked her right in the eyes and didn't react. Of course he wouldn't. He wasn't allowed to confirm or deny.

That's why he was armed and . . . dangerous.

He worked for the government, probably investigating Paxton's whole operation to stop the siphoning of treasure that was supposed to generate millions in taxes and co-profits for the state.

A thrill exploded in her heart.

"FBI?" she asked.

He shook his head.

"State government? Art crimes? Tax evasion? Police? What is it?"

He just kept his mouth closed and let out a soft breath, obviously pained by the conversation.

"You're not allowed to tell me, are you?"

"Lizzie, I want to." He put his hand on her leg and leaned closer. "I really want to."

"But then . . ." A smile pulled at her mouth. "You'd have to kill me."

"You just need to trust me," he said, not smiling back.

"I do," she said with conviction. It all made so much sense now. Of course he wanted to take over everything and do it his way. Of course he wanted to know where she put the scepter and diamond, and go out of his way to follow Flynn with a priceless medallion.

If he was with the government, he was on *her* side.

"You *know* I don't want to profit from this dive, don't you?" she said quickly. He had to understand her real objectives, especially now. "You know that my goal is to share everything we find in an exhibit that millions of people can enjoy."

"And clear your ancestor's name," he added.

"And the government would want that, too, right?"

He didn't answer, his gaze cutting her.

"You can't say anything, can you?"

"I can say this: We both want the same thing, we just want it for different reasons."

She leaned back, a tsunami of emotions washing over her. Admiration. Relief. Joy, even. And something else. Something like a big, bad, nasty crush.

"You're really one of the good guys," she said softly.

"Not entirely."

She smiled. "Funny time for you to suddenly get humble."

"I don't want you to . . ." He trailed off, at a rare loss for words.

"Tell anyone?" she offered. "I swear I won't."

"Good," he said. "But I also don't want you to think you know everything."

"I'm sure I don't." But she knew enough.

He stood, reaching for her hand. "We need to get back to the marina, as soon as I make a call and get that information you want."

"About my sister?" Gratitude pulled and settled like a lump in her throat. "Thank you, Con."

"It's the least I can do," he said. "Because you're really helping me, too."

He made a call, walking away and speaking softly, reading information from the boarding pass printout. She managed not to follow him or stare like a lovesick puppy, but the sensation that rocked her body wasn't too far from that.

He'd *trusted* her. He hadn't actually broken his . . . code, or whatever they called it. But he never denied her assumption, and that very thing confirmed it.

He'd moved into the office, and she headed back there, taking Brianna's mail with her.

"It's Houser," he said, the name stopping Lizzie cold. "Dylan Houser. Cave diver from California. Just let me know what you can get on the investigation into that drowning last August."

Dad's drowning? She felt the blood drain from her head.

"I hope you don't mind," he said when he turned to her, reading her reaction. "I thought I might be able to get some information on your father's accident."

She tried to swallow but couldn't. "Why?"

"Because it strikes me as odd that a diver as experienced as he was would cave-dive alone."

"You don't think . . . it was . . ." She almost couldn't say the words. "An accident?"

"It's my nature to be suspicious, Lizzie."

And his job. "There's an investigator's report on record—"

"We're going to get it."

Of course "they" were.

He reached a hand to her. "I just want to help you, Lizzie, because you've done a lot to help me."

All the way up A1A to the marina, Lizzie wrapped her arms around Con's powerful body, all her different feelings fusing until she felt like she might combust.

The revelation about Con. The disappearance of Brianna. The resurrection of her father's drowning. The scepter, the dive, the truth . . . *The man in her arms.*

She closed her eyes and rested her chin on his shoulder, none of it making sense, yet suddenly all of it making sense.

He rolled into the marina lot half an hour before their cutoff. As she got off the bike, Lizzie frowned, looking for Flynn's cabin cruiser.

"Didn't we dock in that slip?" she asked, pointing and not seeing the tuna tower of his cabin cruiser.

Con pulled off his helmet. "Did he move the boat?"

They scanned the area, then walked to the dock that handled boats of that size. Nowhere.

"Who ya lookin' for?" The voice came from behind them, a young man. "That big Tiara?"

"Do you work here?" Con asked.

"Yeah, and I came on just when that guy took off in a big, fat hurry. The son of a bitch didn't even pay his docking fee. Said he'd be back tomorrow. But if that prick stiffs us in a half-million-dollar boat, I'll be pissed."

"Tomorrow?" Lizzie blew out the word, disgusted. "I can't believe he did this."

"I can," Con said quickly, walking her away. "He's got to go do damage control immediately. Has to go back to the boat and claim the medallion was taken from him, and come up with a story to tell his stepfather."

"So you think he left us here on purpose, so we couldn't contradict him or question him?"

"More than that, he doesn't want me anywhere near that boat, because he thinks Alita took the medallion and gave it to me. He can pay her off, but not me. The longer I'm away, the better chance he thinks he has of getting me fired."

"Can he?"

"Actually, no." A soft beep got his attention and he pulled out his phone, stepping away and speaking softly. When he returned, he look pleased.

"Don't tell me," she said, forcing her voice to be light. "You got us a boat with one phone call."

He smiled. "No, I have another plan for us tonight." The way he said it sent a slow burn through her.

"And what would that be?"

He put his arm around her, his mouth very close to her ear.

"I've developed one other very specialized skill in my life."

She looked up, getting a little kick from the shared secret and a bigger one from the sheer proximity of his mouth to hers. "Which is?"

"You could call it reclamation. The man who lives at 662 River Run is a known black-market art collector. I think I have to *reclaim* the medallion he illegally purchased today."

She melted right into him with a sigh. "You are something else, Con."

"Yeah." His tone was wry. "I really am."

CHAPTER
THIRTEEN

BY NINE O'CLOCK it was dark, and Con parked the bike behind a row of oleander bushes across the street and a few hundred yards down from the entrance to St. Richard's Island.

Gerry Dix, that wily son of a bitch, was about to get a visit from an old acquaintance. Con had done some work for him years ago, when he'd taken a nineteenth-century chalice from the State Hermitage Museum in St. Petersburg, Russia, and delivered it to Gerry's home in the Hamptons.

Con liked symmetry and balance; stealing from Gerry would bring their relationship as thief and buyer full circle.

Lizzie's assumption that he was a government agent answered most of her questions and created the necessary trust, so he had let it go. If and when she found out the truth, he'd be long gone on the next Bullet Catcher job. Because if he got the medallion back, that could seal the deal, accomplishing the whole mission to guard the treasures, find the thief, and target the traitor.

Flynn Paxton was obviously their thief, and no doubt he was sharing plenty of information with this buyer and others. So when Con turned over the medallion *and* the diamond-topped scepter to the client, that should take some of the sting out of the fact that Paxton's traitor was in his own family.

If Gerry Dix was a creature of habit, getting the medallion would be relatively easy. If not, Con had faced bigger challenges to get even more impressive prizes.

Before he did, he always considered one question.

"What's the worst that could happen?" he asked over his shoulder, curious what Lizzie's response would be.

"They won't fall for my Oscar-worthy performance and we can't get in," she answered.

"That's not the worst. What's the worst that could happen if we *do* get in?"

"The medallion buyer is home and you can't steal it back?"

He shook his head. Even if Dix was home, Con could probably get it, unless the guy was asleep with the thing under his pillow. He'd taken many items from rooms where people slept, though.

"You could get shot?" she suggested.

"I can defend myself. I think the worst that could happen is that the medallion isn't there, and this was a waste of time," he said. "Making this a low risk endeavor."

"Very optimistic. I'm still not sure we're going to get past that guard," Lizzie said.

"We will. That's the easiest barrier we're going to face tonight."

"Can't we just do the same thing we did earlier? They already think I'm Dave's sister and let me in once."

"It's an option, but not my favorite," he said. "What if Dave or Sarah Rollins happened to leave, and the guard asked how the surprise went when his sister showed up this morning?"

"I see your point. They could all be on alert for the scam."

He nodded, watching a beat-up Honda pull in and circle around the entrance, pulling into a small area where a golf cart and a roving security truck were parked.

"But I think we have the changing of the guard now." Yep, the new arrival had a uniform on. "Get ready to roll."

He turned to glance at Lizzie, smiling at how bad she looked with bloodshot eyes from drops of shampoo and her makeup smudged and smeared. "Thanks for taking one for the team."

"Vas your name again, shweetie?" She slurred the words in classic drunk-speak, giving him a loopy smile. " 'Cause you're kinna cute." She winked a red eye at him.

He turned on the engine and headed out onto the road, watching the new guard enter the small gatehouse. He continued to the next intersection, turned around, and drove south, just in time to see the first guard get in his car and drive off. After one more pass, Con pulled in as Lizzie slumped against his back, her face turned away from the guardhouse.

The young man stepped out with his clipboard, and Con leaned forward.

"All right, I think we can do this now— Oh, you're a different guy." Con feigned surprise. "The other guard let us in about fifteen minutes ago, but I had to take her out to the bushes to . . ." He opened his mouth and mimed throwing up, whispering the rest with a thumb pointed to his passenger. "She's in really bad shape."

The guard looked hard at her, trying to see around to the other side of the bike by standing on his toes and not leaving the entrance to the little guardhouse.

"She lives here?"

"That's what she says."

"Who is she?"

"No clue, pal. I just pulled her off a bar stool at Friday's because she was about to be attacked by every horny dude in the place. This is my random act of kindness for the day," he added, rolling his eyes.

"I can't let you in without a name."

He shrugged. "Then she's all yours, buddy. Hope you have an empty trash can, in case she pukes again."

The guard made a face. "Can't you, uh, get her . . ." He cleared his voice. "Miss, can you turn around?"

Con felt her head slowly lift, then plop down in the other direction.

"Hi, honey." She dragged the word out and Con could feel her drunken smile against his back. "Where's Mikey? Did he go home already?"

The guard frowned at Con. "I never saw her before."

"I never saw *you* before," Lizzie said, straining to lift her head and pointing a wobbly finger at him. "And I never saw *him* before." The finger poked at Con's shoulder. "And you never—"

"What's your address?" he asked.

"My address? Umm . . ." She dragged the sound out. "It has a six in it, and the street is River Run." She giggled. "It's all River Run, so that's kinna dumb, huh?"

The guard's frown deepened. "Then how you gonna find your house?"

"I'll know it when I see it. It's my parents' house— and, oh fuck, are they gonna be mad."

"What's your name?" he asked.

"Liz."

"Your last name."

Con said, "I think she said her last name was Dix."

"Maybe I said I like dicks," she said with a drunken tease. She tried to lean closer and almost wobbled off.

"Mr. Dix left an hour ago," the guard said, flipping through papers on a clipboard.

"Thank God!" Lizzie said. "He freakin' hates when I drink."

"I can't imagine why," Con said wryly, sharing a look with the guard. "If you can't let her in, I understand, man. But I'm leavin' her here because, seriously, she's about to fall off the back and *you* can have the freaking lawsuit, not me."

The young guard shook his head and reached for the button that lifted the gate. "Just get her home, and don't tell anyone I did this."

"Thanks. I'll be back if she can't find her house."

The guard nodded, clearly hoping that didn't happen.

"All right, sweetheart, hang on. We're taking you home now, nice and slow." Con moved ahead as the gate was raised for him. "Nice work, Ms. Dare."

She squeezed his waist a little. "And we found out Dix isn't home. That was brilliant."

"Just because he left doesn't mean no one's home," Con warned. "But it's a good piece of information to have."

Along with a lot of other random facts that resided in his memory about Gerry Dix. The guy wasn't married, and his lovers weren't exactly the kind that spent the week with him in his winter home. Knowing his clients' weaknesses had been an important, sometimes life-saving, part of his former job.

Gerry's house was completely dark but for a few small landscaping lights. Con spotted a house under construction two lots away, with two Dumpsters in the unfinished driveway.

He pulled the bike between them, hidden enough so that it wouldn't be seen by someone driving by unless they were looking for it. Still, Lizzie could see the entire property around Dix's house.

"Give me your cell phone, Lizzie." He programmed his number into speed dial as he talked. "Your job, your *only* job"—he added a sharp look—"is to warn me if someone is coming anywhere near that house." He finished the program, tested it, and his cell phone vibrated. "If our target comes home or a guard goes to check the house, you press one and alert me. I will get out however I can, and make my way behind the next house and come up behind you. If you have to move for any reason, circle the lake, then come right back here. If that's the case, press number two on the phone before you do."

He tested that one, and a different rhythm of vibrations buzzed in his pocket.

"What if Dix comes home, goes right in the garage, and you're stuck?"

"I won't be if you press one. That'll alert me."

She drew back, shaking her head. "You really can't just go to the door, flash a badge, and demand he give it to you?"

"And have him alert Flynn Paxton with one phone call?"

"Okay. It's just . . . dangerous."

"You just do what you need to do out here." He wiped some of the makeup under her right eye. "By the way, you're cute when you're drunk."

She grinned. "So maybe I have a second career as an undercover government agent."

"Maybe."

He stepped away from the bike, turning sideways to get between it and the Dumpster as she slid into the driver's seat and peered at the house.

"Con, what if someone's home?" she asked. "Do you have a Plan B?"

It was no problem for him, just a nuisance. "As long as they're asleep, I'm fine."

"And if they're awake?"

Still not really a problem for an accomplished thief. "There'd be a light visible. My gut says Dix is out for the evening." And really stupid about security, considering he was a fine-art collector. "We just have to hope he didn't take his new medallion with him. Stay alert."

He slid out from the cover of the Dumpsters, scanning every visible inch of the house.

These guarded and gated communities were a joke. They had a snotty-faced twentysomething at the entrance and some idiot driving around in a golf cart who was probably jacking off in an empty lot right now. They had shrubbery right up against every window, dozens of easy-access sliding glass doors, alarms that were just as often turned off as they were on, and at least one out of every five left their doors unlocked.

Dix had actually locked the utility room door next to the garage; that was the most common one left open. So Con made a complete pass around the perimeter, looking in every window, checking out the pool, getting the lay of the land for a quick getaway.

He could get in this house six different ways, have the alarm disarmed in less than fifteen seconds, and get to the top ten most common hiding places in under five minutes.

If Gerry Dix had designed this house the way he had the one in the Hamptons, then there would be a vault built into a wine cellar that was invisible to a casual visitor, behind a locked door that Con could pick.

If Gerry didn't want to think too hard when he was in his winter home, then his vault combination would be the same as it was up in the Hamptons, and Con had used one of his favorite tricks to get that combination—he'd left his video phone on the bar where the vault was hidden, politely excused himself while the client opened the vault, and recorded the number in his files when he got home.

The safe combination was Gerry's home phone backward, so he'd had Avery text him Dix's phone number in Vero, and sent up a silent prayer that Gerry was unimaginative and lazy.

Because if he was, this would be a very easy job.

He returned to the utility room door, always an easy one to crack and guaranteed to have an alarm pad within two feet of it, but there was a dead bolt across it and he didn't have time to remove it. He lightly jostled the door, enough to alert a dog.

All was silent.

The back slider would probably be easiest. These kinds of homes never installed a security bar on the sliders. Undersized apartments with nothing of value but a laptop inside? Bars all over the place.

The family room slider was locked, but the dining-room door wasn't, which didn't surprise Con at all. Still, there would be an alarm. He peered in, but couldn't see the digital flash of an alarm pad anywhere. He'd have to move fast, straight to the utility room near the garage.

He slid the glass soundlessly, just enough to lean his head in and listen. If anyone lived, breathed, or walked in this house, he'd hear it.

Silence. A clock ticking. The rhythmic tap of an overhead paddle fan. Meaning Gerry hadn't left town, just the house.

Inside, he moved stealthily toward the kitchen, rounding it to the utility room he'd tried to open before. The keypad was right at the door, flashing red. Armed.

He had a few special tools in his backpack, but all he needed for this was a screwdriver and flashlight. He slipped a flathead out, popped the cover off the pad, and shined his light on the rubber numbers. Only two were slightly depressed, the six and the two. Damn. Most people used four numbers for their alarm, so one or both of these were used twice. He had about five seconds left.

Most people used four numbers, but many people used their address, especially for second homes. He pressed 6-6-2 and the light turned green.

One barrier down.

Outside the utility room, he scanned the layout of the first floor. A huge curved staircase with a wrought-iron rail ran up the center with a living room and dining room on either side. He guessed the office was the only other front room.

No basements in Florida, so a bar or wine closet was usually off the family room. He headed that way, taking in the details of standard high-end décor and slightly musty smell of a house that was barely lived in.

If Dix didn't have a vault in his wine cellar here, then he'd check the master closet or the office for a safe.

The family room was sports themed, with multiple TV screens and a full bar with stools. No sign of an entrance to a wine vault. Con walked around the bar to a door he suspected was a storage closet, opened it and found . . . another door. Metal and bolted.

No need to be neat, since Gerry would know he was robbed ten minutes after he got home. With luck and timing, Con would be long gone from St. Richard's Island by then.

He brought out his gun and fired once, destroying the lock. Behind the door was a floor-to-ceiling safe with a combination lock.

Taking out his phone, he clicked on the text with Gerry's phone number and tried a combination, spinning the wheel easily. Click. Click. Click.

Three cheers for creatures of habit. He opened the walk-in safe, flashed his beam of light, and swore.

There must have been thirty small jewelry cases. Evidently Gerry liked more than just religious artifacts. Kneeling down, he started snapping open the cases, just as his phone vibrated with the warning from Lizzie.

He flipped open two, then heard the rumble of the garage door.

Shit. He had less than three minutes. Two more boxes, one empty, one full of diamonds.

But no Our Lady of Sorrows medallion. The sound of the garage door closing was like trumpets of warning in his ears. He really did *not* want to come face-to-face with Gerry Dix.

He scooped up the remaining boxes, pouring them into a makeshift apron of his T-shirt, and, kicking both doors closed just to buy himself a little more time, bolted toward the slider he'd left open. He didn't bother to reset the alarm, because Gerry had to know by now that it wasn't set.

Just as the kitchen door from the garage opened, Con eased through the slider door and flattened himself against the wall long enough to hear which direction Dix was headed.

To the safe, of course. Probably with a gun in hand, since he saw his alarm had been disarmed.

Holding the boxes in his T-shirt, he ran across the expanse of the pool deck, through the next yard, around the house under construction, straight to the Dumpsters.

"I heard a gunshot!" Lizzie whispered when he got there. "Oh my God, how much did you steal?"

"It's in one of these." He let go of his shirt, and the leather and velvet jewelry cases tumbled to the ground.

Instantly, they were on the ground, opening.

"Holy crap," she exclaimed at a million-dollar necklace.

"Don't get attached, Lizzie, just open. And don't let anything fall on the ground."

On his third try, he had it. "Here it is. Turn around and let me put this in the backpack."

She did, and he tucked the box safely in the pack she wore.

"What about this other stuff, Con? Are we going to just leave it here?"

Ripping off his T-shirt, Con swept all the boxes into it and wrapped it up like a makeshift pouch. "Get on the bike, Lizzie. I'll drive."

"You're *keeping* all that? Con, you can't!"

"Get on the bike, Lizzie, fast!" He hopped on in front of her, the sack of boxes dangling in his left hand, his right turning the key and thumbing the starter button. The bike roared to life. The second he felt her thighs around his and her arms grab hold of him, he rumbled to the road, straight for Dix's house.

Just as they reached the front, the security lights

exploded and every house light glowed simultaneously, bathing them in brightness. Con slowed down just enough to hoist the bag and get some muscle behind his throw, when the front door opened and a rifle aimed right at his head.

Damn. If he was killed the first time he *didn't* steal, he'd be pissed.

"What the hell are you doing?" Dix hollered, lowering the rifle a fraction.

"Returning what I don't want." He tossed the shirt.

The rifle dropped six inches. "Con Xenakis? You son of a bitch—"

The rest was drowned out by the roar of the bike as Con took off. The bike exploded with speed, just missing the wooden gate as it slowly lifted to let them out, then he tilted so far right to get onto A1A, his jeans almost kissed the pavement and Lizzie let out a shriek.

Con righted the bike and tore into traffic, but got stuck at a light. When it finally changed, he barreled along, one eye ahead, one eye in the sideview mirror. "What was he driving?" he asked.

"Big, dark SUV. Maybe a Cadillac."

Gerry Dix was a vindictive son of a bitch, and he'd probably figured out what Con had taken by now. Or maybe he didn't even wait to do inventory.

He glanced into the rearview mirror and saw a black Escalade roaring up the road behind them.

CHAPTER
FOURTEEN

WHEN LIZZIE TURNED around and saw the lights of the SUV, a scream lodged in her throat.

"Hang on," Con called.

She clutched his stomach tighter, squashing her thighs against his. Wind whistled through her helmet and smacked her face every time she leaned around Con's bare back to look in the rearview mirror.

She did anyway. The SUV was gaining on them. He whipped to the left, accelerating to a heart-stopping speed that made her squeeze her eyes shut. The left? *They* were in the left. That meant . . .

Lizzie opened her eyes to confirm they were on the wrong side of the street, headed into oncoming traffic. The lights were a half mile away, but in an instant they'd be hit.

She gripped tighter instead of screaming, and wished to God she'd had a chance to say good-bye to Brianna.

A car whizzed by, the horn blaring. Con flung them around another car, more horns blasting. The bike swayed left and right, braiding the oncoming traffic as if the cars were merely cones in a motorcross route. The cacophony of screeching brakes and furious horns added to the insanity, deafening even over the bellow of the full-speed motorcycle.

She stole a glance to the right. They'd outrun their pursuer by about fifteen car lengths. Con rolled them to the left again, doing another tip-until-you-touch turn that stopped Lizzie's heart, righting them as he turned left again into a side street.

"We're not far from my sister's house," she said, amazed she still had a voice. "We can go there for the night."

The blare of horns and screeching brakes drowned out his answer. She whipped around to see the Escalade doing exactly what they'd done—crossed oncoming traffic to follow them.

Con hit the gas and they launched forward, but the SUV almost caught up. Lizzie turned to see a half-bald man stick his head out the driver's side as he managed to pull up almost next to them.

"Give me the fucking medallion, Xenakis!"

Before she realized what was happening, Con had his gun out, the muscles of his back tensing as he shot twice at the front right tire, then, if it was even possible, increased their speed to what felt like a hundred and careened through the residential neighborhood, eventually working their way back to the highway, where he tilted the bike and took a right.

"I live in the other direction!" she hollered.

"We're not going there."

When he slowed down to the same speed as traffic, Lizzie breathed for the first time, still checking the rearview for that big Escalade.

Finally, he pulled into a 7-Eleven parking lot, rumbling to the back behind the building so they couldn't be seen from the street, his bare chest heaving from the effort.

"What are you doing?" she asked.

"We can't stay here tonight. We've got to get back to that boat before Paxton takes something else, or blames us for this one."

"Tonight?" He didn't really think he could navigate that treacherous inlet at night, did he?

He pulled out his phone and hit one number. She thought she heard a woman's voice answer.

"We need a boat. Fast. Have it at Sebastian Marina, ASAP. Paxton left us stranded and we need to get back on board." There was a pause. "Big enough to get us through the inlet, but something fast."

He gunned the engine again, rolling out.

"The marina's about two blocks from here," she called out, glancing up and down the road for the Escalade.

"Listen to me," he said over his shoulder. "We're going to move fast. We'll ditch this bike in the lot and get to the dock as fast as possible. Not that I expect Dix to come looking for us, but I don't want to take chances."

They parked and he took the backpack from her, then they ran to the dock in silence. One of the marina workers was waiting with a twenty-one-foot twin outboard with a cuddy cabin in the bow, keys in hand.

Wow. When the Feds called, the marina workers jumped.

"That ought to get us through the inlet," he said, taking the keys.

"It'll be rough." Lizzie climbed in, unafraid. "But you can do it."

He gave her a sideways glance, probably surprised at the comment, thanked the dock man, and situated himself at the helm, as bare-chested as a pirate. "I'm going to need you on the bow, Lizzie," he said, aiming the spotlight on the water.

She scrambled around the slender space of deck to climb on top of the cuddy and get into position, holding onto the safety rail as she leaned over to help him navigate.

Boats this size capsized in Sebastian all the time. There was a monster hole formed by the jetty, and the whitecaps ate up little crafts. Their's was only half the size of what Flynn had brought through here earlier, but Con handled the helm with skill, avoiding the worst of the swells, managing the weight when they did hit one.

Still, even her seaworthy stomach rolled a few times as they battled treacherous waves and unexpected rocks.

She stayed on the bow, clinging to the rail, calling out warnings. Every once in a while, she turned to see him fighting the wheel, a gleam of sweat on his muscular chest, his silvery eyes slicing through the water like the hull of his vessel.

When they finally hit open water, she went back to her seat. When Con gunned it, she stopped trying to hide her admiration and just watched him.

Her heart swelled. If only Dad were alive, he would love this guy. This is what he'd always wanted for her. *Get yourself one of the good guys, Lizzie Lou.*

She couldn't get back to that boat fast enough. Tonight, her undercover agent was going under her covers.

Con peered hard into the darkness, glancing at the compass and his GPS. After a while, he was shaking his head.

"What's the matter?" she asked, sitting up.

"The *Gold Digger.*"

She looked over the bow, seeing nothing but a hundred miles of black Atlantic Ocean.

"Are we in the right place?" She stood, bracing her feet and scanning the horizon.

"Precisely."

They looked at each other and said simultaneously, "The boat's gone."

Something was very, very wrong. Solange paced the second floor of the farmhouse, staring out the window, past the windmill to the blackness of the endless sea. Why hadn't he called all day and all night?

Something was wrong. She could just feel it.

"Madame Bettencourt?" a voice called up the stairs to her room.

Her new hire was a grating woman, but the pickings were slim, especially since they were all spooked by Ana's suicide. Gabby, another transplanted American, was one of the few people not related to Ana, not in mourning, and willing to work for Solange. As much as she liked not having a nurse hovering, she wasn't about to live without domestic assistance.

When Solange didn't answer—because she didn't yell in her own home, for heaven's sake—footsteps clomped up the ancient stairs.

"Mrs. B?" God, Solange hated that. And the incessant pounding on her door.

"What is it?" she asked as she opened the door.

"There's someone here to see you."

Solange's stomach tightened. An investigator? So far, not a single question had been asked of her regarding the young woman who threw herself into the sea. But surely someone would look into that death.

"Who is it?"

"Someone named Brianna Dare."

Blood drained from her head, making her dizzy. "What?"

"I know, it's late," Gabby said, obviously misinterpreting Solange's shock. "But she's a nice girl, and she's come all the way from Florida just to see you."

"To see me?" This wasn't good. This couldn't be good at all.

"She said it has something to do with a genealogy project she's working on about the Bettencourt family, and she's sorry it's late, but she just got to the island." Gabby made a solicitous face. "Why don't you talk to her for a minute?"

Why? Because Brianna Dare was the last person on earth she wanted to talk to—except maybe Jaeger.

"Tell her I'll be right down." She dismissed her with a wave, then locked the door, taking a deep breath to think.

She thought better with a drink. Under the sink in her bathroom, she pulled out the bottle of Jameson, poured a healthy amount into a glass, and knocked it back. Then she rinsed with mouthwash and stared at her pale eyes, and the circles beneath them.

The scepter sat for one hundred and fifty years under a stone stair, and no one knew about it. Then Malcolm Dare found out about it, and she'd handled that. Ana saw it, and she'd handled that, too.

Now one of Malcolm's daughters was in on the secret? She hadn't counted on that. Would she have to handle this like she'd handled the others?

This time, she hoped she could do so with a little more finesse.

She opened her wardrobe to choose something that would let this woman know exactly what she was dealing with. Chanel. She dressed, and then, as though she still ruled from a ten-thousand-square-foot penthouse overlooking Manhattan, instead of a three-hundred-year-old converted barn in the Azores, Solange swept across her room and carefully navigated the crooked steps down.

In the parlor—if you could even call the tiny room that—a young woman popped up when Solange entered.

"Mrs. Bettencourt," she said, a wide smile across her pretty features. "Thank you so much for seeing me. I know it's late, but I had a hard time getting here. This place is really out there, isn't it?"

Solange just looked at her, and gave her a withering smile. "What was your name again?"

"Oh, sorry." She held out her hand. "I'm Brianna

Dare. And, honestly, I would have come here in the morning at a more reasonable time, but did you know there's no hotel on this whole island?"

"I know."

"So anyway . . ."

Solange didn't make it easier with small talk. With luck, an icy attitude would scare the girl off. Unfortunately, she looked spunky and curious and not easily scared.

"The reason I'm here," the girl continued, "is that I'm working on a family project involving the genealogy of the Bettencourt family here in the Azores."

"Mmmm."

"You are a Bettencourt, right?"

"By marriage."

"But still, a Bettencourt." The girl tucked her hands into her tight jeans and gave her another winsome smile. "Well, I'm a Dare."

Solange didn't react.

"That name doesn't mean anything to you, does it?"

"Not at all." Solange launched a brow north. "What exactly are you looking for, Ms. Dare?"

"Some answers to a really old mystery. Evidently my great-great-great-plus-more grandfather and your . . . probably about the same grandfather-in-law had a business arrangement that might have never been . . . completed."

Oh, this girl knew far too much. Far, far too much. Who had she told?

Finding out might require her to be a little friendlier. "How interesting," Solange said, finally indicating the settee under the window. "Why don't you have a seat and tell me all about it."

Brianna beamed at the sudden change. "Thank you, I'd love to."

"Something to drink? Some tea or something stronger, perhaps?"

"No, that's not necessary."

Solange settled in a chair, sizing up her opponent. Small, but wiry. Guileless, too. Clearly not expecting . . . danger. "So, tell me, however did you find me?"

"A genealogist in Lisbon helped me. She'd been helping my father, who started this project."

"Oh, did he come with you?"

"No. He passed away a few months ago."

Solange gave a solemn nod. "So sorry." There was probably a special place in hell for people who offered sympathy for a death they caused. But she wasn't worried about hell; it couldn't be much worse than this. "So you came all alone? You traveled here without anyone else?"

"Oh, yes," she said brightly. "But I'll pay for it when my sister finds out."

"She doesn't know?"

"She's very protective, and I thought it was better not to let her know I was taking this adventure. But I don't need to waste your time telling you about my family. It's yours I'm most interested in."

No one knew she was here. "How exactly can I help you?"

"Well, since this home and this property have been in the Bettencourt family for so many generations, I was hoping that you might have some old documents, maybe some paperwork that would detail a business transaction that took place between my ancestor, Aramis Dare, and yours, a man named Carlos Bettencourt, back in the 1860s."

"What kind of documents?"

"I won't really know until I see them. Aramis, I believe, purchased some items in Cuba and brought them by ship to Carlos, here in the Azores. I'm trying to find proof that Aramis was paid for the items."

She smiled. "I would think that whether he did or didn't, a transaction that old would be forgiven and forgotten."

"Oh, I'm not looking for money, Mrs. Bettencourt. I'm just trying to iron out some ancient history. I want to clear my ancestor's name. It's been kind of sullied by this."

"That's it?" She didn't believe it, not for one minute. "You're worried about the reputation of someone who lived a hundred and fifty years ago?"

"It's a little more complicated than that," Brianna said, relaxing a little and leaning back. "You see, my father was a marine archaeologist, and he was very close to uncovering some artifacts involved in the business arrangement."

Artifacts—*plural*. "What kind of artifacts?"

She hesitated, taking a breath. "Some very valuable ones."

"Whom did they belong to?"

"That's what I'm trying to figure out."

"This sounds like it might be more involved than just some documents. Is this something you're working on all by yourself, Ms. Dare?"

"Well, as a matter of fact, my sister is working a salvage dive right now, where the artifacts are believed to be buried undersea."

"Really. Are you in touch with her?"

"Daily."

She tamped down the fury inside. No one should be in touch with *anyone* on that ship. "This is utterly fascinating. I'd love to know more."

"Then you'll help me? Can you search the house, the town, any historical archives for paperwork?"

"I wouldn't want you to get your hopes raised, only to be dashed. The chances of anything surviving all those years is very small, don't you agree?" What had she been told by her own expert? "Paper doesn't survive that long." Unless it's buried in a cold, stone cave. "But I must admit, I'm absolutely captivated by your story."

She hadn't spent nineteen years married to the shrewdest man in America and not learned anything. Keep your enemies close. *Very close*. And then destroy them without leaving a shred of evidence.

"Why don't you stay here with me for a while so we can search together?" Solange suggested. "As you said, there is no hotel in Corvo, so you are at the mercy . . ." She smiled benevolently. "Or the *kindness* of strangers."

Her eyes glistened with gratitude. "Thank you so much, Mrs. Bettencourt."

"Please, call me Solange."

"And I'm Brianna."

Solange reached out a hand. "I've no doubt we'll become good friends."

CHAPTER
FIFTEEN

"I KNOW EXACTLY what happened." Lizzie was wrapped in a wool blanket she'd found in the cuddy cabin, curled into the passenger seat as they trolled the empty waters seeking clues for the missing *Gold Digger*. "We did this the first week on the dive."

"Hid from poachers?" Con asked as he dialed the number he had for the bridge again. "I thought of that. But someone should be answering the radio, even if they moved to escape detection."

"Flynn made us go completely dark that time. The Captain took us about ten miles farther west, and we turned off the engines and lights. Paxton is totally paranoid about being caught."

Con considered calling the Coast Guard, but Judd Paxton would not be pleased with that decision, so he settled for a text to Lucy to see if the Bullet Catchers had been apprised of the move. If they had, though, someone would have alerted him.

In the meantime, they had two choices: wait where

the boat had been, or search for it in the vast blackness
of the Atlantic Ocean.

"My guess is they'll be back in the morning," she
said, tucking deeper into the blanket with a shiver.

"You should go below," he said. "You're going to
freeze up here. I'll watch for them."

"Me?" She fluttered the blanket corner. "*You're* the
one with no shirt."

"I'm fine."

"*I'll* say."

Oh, boy. This might be worse than he thought. He
gave her a half smile, but kept his gaze on the black
horizon. "I think you've caught a case of hero worship."
And a serious misinterpretation of the events.

"Get real, Xenakis." She smiled slyly. "The bare chest
doesn't suck, though."

His half smile grew whole. "No? You wouldn't
give me the time of day, and now . . ." Now that she
thought he was an undercover agent, she was suddenly
a big fan.

"I took two showers with you. That's the time of day
in *my* book."

"Life saving, both times."

She shifted and wrapped the blanket tighter as he
dropped back on to the captain's chair with a frustrated
sigh. "No one is out here, Lizzie."

"Ten miles west, believe me. Try it, you'll find the
Gold Digger."

"All right." He kicked up the engines a little, watching the GPS. "We've got nothing to lose."

He leaned back, one hand on the throttle, not mind-ing the chill of the wind on his skin. But after about a mile, Lizzie stood up.

"Going down to get warm?" he asked.

"Nope." She slipped behind him, opening her blanket like a cape to wrap it around him, snuggling them together.

The welcome heat was almost a shock.

"You have to be cold," she said.

"I've been colder, but thanks."

She leaned her head closer to his, her cheek silky as it brushed his face. "I know. I was there last time you had hypothermia, remember?"

"One of the best recoveries for hypo I ever had."

She laughed softly, the sound transmitting from her chest to his back from the direct, close contact.

"How many times have you had it?"

"In BUD/S training? A few."

"Is that SEAL training? I've heard about it. Was it as hard as they say?"

"No." He laughed. "Way worse."

"What made you decide to be a SEAL? And why did you quit?"

"Those two questions are so far apart, they don't belong in the same conversation."

"Really?" She inched around to see his face. "Tell me."

The chill was gone completely now, replaced by her body warmth and by the slow simmer of arousal that tightened his jeans every time the boat bounced and her breasts moved against his back.

"Start with the first question," he said. He'd end with it, too. "It was the Navy or . . ." Prison. "A tough life."

"You said you grew up in Florida, right?"

"Tarpon Springs, home of the Greek Americans."

She laughed. "Are you from one of those crazy Greek families like in the wedding movie?"

"No." He maybe said it too harshly, because she eased around even more to look at his face.

"What was your family like?"

He shrugged. "Define family."

"The people who raised you?"

"Friends, not family."

"What do you mean?"

"My parents never married," he explained, keeping the unusual tale to a minimum of detail. "My father was in the military and was killed on a black ops-type mission when I was a baby. He'd been some kind of bad-boy rebellion for my mother, I guess, since she was from an old mainline Philadelphia family."

"So what happened?"

"She was really young, barely twenty, and probably really scared. Her family had basically disowned her for having a baby without a husband, and she was pretty lost in Tarpon Springs. No job, a baby, no family. I give her credit for lasting as long as she did."

"What did she do?"

"Her parents eventually came down to get her, but they didn't want the whole package."

She sucked in a breath. "They didn't want you?"

"You'd have to understand what kind of people they were."

"Scum of the earth?"

His laugh was dry. "Proper. Very proper. They suggested adoption but she didn't want to completely lose touch with me, and eventually some friends of my father stepped in and offered to take me. They didn't actually adopt me, but they raised me. Her parents sent money." At her incredulous look, he added, "It wasn't as bad as it sounds."

"What happened to your mother?"

"She's fine. She's had a good life," he said quietly. "She met a guy and got married, and that time, she got it right. He was perfect for her—big money, big family."

"Are you in touch with her?"

"Not much. She has other kids, all grown."

"So what was that family like who took you in?"

"The Demakos family? Very poor. The father lived off the water, paycheck to paycheck. He needed every dime that my mother's father sent."

"Other kids?"

"One. Alix. He was . . ." God, how did he describe Alix? "Crazy, impulsive, and . . . really great to grow up with."

"That sounds an awful lot like my sister," she said, giving him a squeeze. "Are you older, younger? Close?"

"He's dead."

"Oh." She came all the way around him then, getting between him and the console, blocking the western view with her pretty face and sympathetic eyes and too-many personal questions. "What happened to him?"

And this would be the answer to her second question—why he left the SEALs. "He was killed in a training mission."

"Was he a SEAL, too?"

His jaw clenched and he leaned back, focusing on those amber gold eyes. "Yes. We went through training together."

"So you were there when he died?"

If he had been, Alix wouldn't have died. "Not exactly. You know, you are blocking my view. Would you mind moving?"

"One more question."

He put his hands on her shoulders and moved her to the side. "No more questions. I want to find our boat." He pulled the throttle back, looking from side to side, now that they'd traveled about ten more miles. Nothing.

"One more. How'd you learn to steal things like you do?"

For a moment, he considered telling her the truth.

Alix taught me how to take everything that wasn't nailed down, and I got really good at it. So good that I was one of the best thieves in the country. You name it, I've stolen it. Right out of your precious museums.

That'd burst her hero-worship bubble in a hurry. And cool the look of lust in her eyes, and shut that sweet little mouth he imagined kissing every time she got close.

"It's just a talent I have," he finally said.

She wrapped the blanket around his shoulders, moving between his thighs, her chest just below his chin as he sat and she stood. "It's a talent that's come in handy this week."

"Lots of my talents have come in handy this week."

He tightened his thighs around her hips to punctuate that. "And if you don't back off and stop looking at me like that, you're about to find out about a few more."

Her lips lifted in a slow smile. "Threat or promise, X?"

He was already going to be number one on her shit list when she figured out that he not only wasn't her superagent here to save the day, but he was working for her sworn enemy. Could he make her hate him even more by taking what she was offering?

Probably. If he let his body do the thinking.

"You're playing with fire, Lizzie."

"Is that why I'm feeling so hot right now?"

She didn't want to be warned. Didn't want to be told no. Didn't want to know the truth. "You could get burned."

"So could you. Singed." She hissed the last word and added the tiniest rock of her hips toward his.

He was already hard, already pulsing. "I'm asbestos, sweetheart. And you . . ." He snaked his hand through the blanket to her body, fingering the zipper of her hooded jacket. He dragged it slowly south, his knuckles grazing the rise of her chest on the way down. ". . . are not."

"I can handle the heat," she said, arching her back to let the blanket fall to the deck with a soft whoosh. "Like I can handle the cold."

He clicked the zipper at the bottom, then flattened his hand on her stomach, sliding it up over her button-down shirt. Her gaze widened as he spread his palm over her breast, the nipple budding from his touch and the chilly wind.

"Let's just be clear, Lizzie Dare." He popped the first button with ease. "I'm not what or who you think I am."

She lifted one brow in an almost imperceptible nod of permission. "You don't scare me, Con Xenakis."

"I'm not trying to scare you." Next button, open. "I'm undressing you."

She smiled. "You think you're some badass who's going to break my heart or my spirit."

"Never your spirit." Third button, done. Too easy for a thief like him. "It's unbreakable."

She liked that, leaning closer, offering access to that last little button. "You forget I already pegged you as one of the good guys."

He barely blew out a breath, his gaze leveled on the sweet rise of her breasts, the pale flesh pressing against a silky, lacy bra. Blood throbbed in his cock, his throat dry, his fingers itching for the touch he knew he was going to take. All he was about to take.

"Honey, you pegged me wrong." His voice was gruff, raspy, honest.

He pulled her closer, smashing her body into his and standing slowly, his erection prodding her stomach, their gazes locked on each other's mouth.

"I don't think so." Her eyes were dark with arousal, hooded with surrender. "I know exactly who you are."

Then she was a fool.

He pushed her back on the console, pressing his hard-on against her crotch as he spread the blouse open completely.

He lowered his face to her breasts, opening his

mouth over one and closing his hand over the other. He sucked, caressed, licked. Under him, her body pulsed in an instinctive rhythm, soft sounds cooing from her lips each time her hips hit his, the sound drawing him to her mouth and throat and lower to close his lips over her breasts.

She pulled him right into her, wrapping her legs around him and rolling up and down his erection.

He finally broke the kiss, pulling her to her feet before he stripped her bra off right there.

"Just know that you were warned," he said, twisting the key to turn the engines off. "Go below. I'm going to anchor the boat here."

She searched his face, unsure. "You're not going to change your mind, are you?"

He could. He should. This was his chance to be the man she thought he was, a chance to demonstrate the code of honor that turned her on so much. A chance to do the right goddamned thing, instead of the easy, irresponsible, *wrong* goddamned thing.

Would he take it?

"Not a chance."

Lizzie stripped to her bra and underpants, quaking with arousal as she rolled onto the lumpy triangular cushion shoved into the bow of the cuddy. The space was no more than a four-foot-wide envelope, barely big enough for both of them next to each other or on top of each other.

Which they were about to be.

She heard him winching the anchor in place, moving

from bow to stern and back, then thudding down the three steps to the darkened cabin. She tucked into the blanket she'd brought down, wet and warm and ready for him.

He barely fit in the tiny space, depositing the backpack on the floor, his hot gaze searing her as he stripped off his jeans. She watched, mesmerized as his shaft released, stiff and dark, glistening at the top.

She wanted him to talk, to say something sweet or funny.

But he didn't say a word as he crawled toward her.

And maybe that was better. She'd had enough of his cautions. She knew what she was doing—having sex with a man she found staggeringly attractive on every level.

Could she get hurt? Hell, yeah. A rogue wave could come up from nowhere and flip this boat, too.

Still silent, he reached down to his bag and dug in the front pocket, pulling out a foil-wrapped condom.

She couldn't help smiling. "And you think you're so bad."

His gaze grew knifelike, slicing her with purpose. He started to pull down the blanket, exposing her breasts, running a finger over the lace of her bra, leaving a fiery trail in its wake. "I'm not thinking. I'm feeling."

"Mmmm." She bowed her back, inviting more. "Feels good."

He took the blanket all the way down, his gaze following. As it reached her hips she wrapped her hand around his neck, pulling him closer, aching for his mouth on hers.

But he resisted. He ran a slow finger over the peak of her breast, slipping into the front snap and opening it easily, letting the silk slide away.

His jaw slackened as he admired her, thumbing one nipple gently, the touch burning and making her hips rise and fall instinctively.

"You're beautiful," he said softly, sending a thousand goose bumps over her.

She dragged her hand from his neck to his chest, fondling him the same way, tweaking his hardened nipple. "So are you."

His response was a rueful smile, then he leaned in and kissed her. Lifting himself again, he shifted his attention back to her body. When his gaze lingered over her hips, she ran her finger over the lace of the pink panties, inviting him to do the same.

He covered her hand, and she pulled it away so that his palm pressed on her mound, the silk already moist. He stared at his fingers splayed from hipbone to hipbone, and her thighs spread in response to the heat in his eyes.

He kissed her mouth as he slid his hand into her panties, his fingers large and hot on her swollen flesh. She captured his tongue deep into her mouth, and rocked to tempt his fingers to do the same in her body.

He did, then inserted another, stroking her, making her clench around him, thrumming with need. What shreds of control she had left disappeared as she kissed him, their tongues tangled, their teeth tapping, his hands taking ownership inside and out.

Sweat tingled her skin while he kissed her throat,

licked and nipped down to her breasts, her stomach, gliding his erection out of her hand as he repositioned himself to taste every inch of her. He spread her legs, sliding down to wedge into the tiny floor space at the foot of the cushion.

He pulled at the panties, and she bent her knees until they bumped the ceiling, laughing as they worked to get off her last piece of clothing.

Finally he buried his face in the center of her, inhaling with a moan of appreciation, then sucking softly on her throbbing clitoris. Heat crackled over her, jolting her senses, fracturing her nerves.

She lifted her hips and he covered her with his mouth, licking and flicking his tongue over her flesh, making her moan in delight, digging her fingers into his shoulders as she got closer . . . and closer . . . finally falling over the edge as an orgasm surged.

He held her hips and kissed his way back, whispering her name and senseless words until he grabbed the condom. He tried to bite it, tearing ineffectually, his expression dark and consumed.

"Let me," she offered, taking it from him to put it on, stroking him until he was completely swollen and stiff. "Please."

He eased inside her, filling her, huge and solid and wholly masculine. All the way in . . . almost all the way out. Slowly at first, then faster, steadier and harder.

With each thrust, each pulse, each deep connection, he lost more and more control. Her senses smashed together. The sight of his face about to come, his eyes closed, ecstasy on his features. The smell of sex, mixed with the erotic panting of their shallow, excited breaths. The taste of his kiss, the feel of his body.

And finally, he came with so much force it overwhelmed her, driving into her with relentless, pounding, full-body strokes accompanied by a long groan of gratification.

Then all was quiet. Still. Sweltering. Sweet. The only thing moving was the insane beat of their hearts.

"You were right," she whispered in his ear. "I *was* playing with fire."

He turned, his eyes dark. "I tried to warn you."

She just smiled. "That's not what you were warning me about. You think I'm going to fall for you and you're not the man for me."

"I'm not."

She stroked his hair, his cheek, his lips. "Why don't you let me be the judge of that?"

"Because your judgment is skewed. You think I'm something that I'm not."

She snuggled in closer, loving the scent of him, the feel of his rock-hard body, the warmth of his skin. "You just don't know yourself that well."

"That, my dear, is where you're wrong."

The way he said it sent a chill up her spine. "A man in your job, with your background? How bad can you be?"

"Bad."

Lizzie sighed into his neck, the sound of satisfaction and resignation. He had to tell her the truth soon. After what they'd just done, he couldn't let her find out what he was doing by accident.

He'd tell her before the sun came up, before they got back on the *Gold Digger*. Before she uttered another mistaken syllable about him.

"Is that your phone?"

He rolled over as his phone vibrated, reaching for it next to the ankle holster, gun, and jeans. He didn't have to check the ID; the tone told him it was his boss. "Hey, Luce."

"Where are you?"

"Floating around the Atlantic looking for the missing *Gold Digger*."

"It's not missing anymore. It's in Port St. Lucie, under Coast Guard investigation, as is every single person on board."

"What? Why?"

"Standard procedure when there's a death connected to a vessel at sea."

A *death*? He moved away from Lizzie's warm body. "What happened?"

"One of the divers, Alita Holloway, died during a dive. When the captain called in the death to the Coast Guard, they had him bring the vessel into port immediately to pronounce her. The FBI has already been notified."

"What happened to her?"

"Carbon monoxide poisoning through the air compressor."

"That was no accident. The same thing happened to me. Why are we just finding this out now?"

Lizzie sat up, curious.

"No one called Judd Paxton until a half hour ago.

They were too concerned with calling the Coast Guard command center and following regs."

"Was Flynn Paxton on board?"

"He arrived an hour before the accident."

Con blew out a disgusted breath. Of course. Flynn thought Alita stole the medallion and he killed her. No wonder he'd ditched them on the mainland.

"We'll go to the investigation now," he said. "We have critical information and I can tell you . . ." He looked at Lizzie, hesitating to say Judd Paxton's name. "The client isn't going to like it."

"Why not?"

"Because Flynn Paxton is stealing the treasures as they're brought up and selling them on the black market. We caught him red-handed. More important, Alita Holloway was not only his lover, but she was also in on the take. And he thinks she betrayed him with the medallion that I recovered a few hours ago. We've got motive and opportunity, and I'm sure he had the means to take the air-intake filters off the compressor."

Lizzie gasped softly, but he ignored it.

"You need to give every bit of this to the Coast Guard and FBI."

"Will do. Right now. When are you going to tell our client?"

"We both are," she said. "I'll fly in for a meeting down there tomorrow."

He unconsciously closed his fingers around Lizzie's hand, her skin still warm from the full-body rush he'd given her.

"Once you do that," Lucy continued, "this assignment is complete. The dive is over. Judd is prepared to file an official claim with the state, and initiate a standard search and recovery of *El Falcone* at the start of the next diving season."

Con threaded his fingers through Lizzie's and gave her a long look. "Anything else, Luce?"

"You will return any treasure you've recovered and helped to hide. It rightfully belongs to our client." There was no arguing with that voice. "After the meeting, we'll discuss your next assignment as a Bullet Catcher."

He didn't answer, still holding Lizzie's hand and gaze. He lifted their hands and pressed his fingertips to her cheeks, getting a warm, if slightly confused, smile from her.

His heart cracked a little. He'd tried to warn her . . . but not very hard.

"You do want to continue working for the Bullet Catchers, don't you, Con?"

"Yes," he said quietly, holding Lizzie's gaze as he placed a kiss on her knuckles.

"Then explain to her who you are, what you've been doing, and get the scepter and diamond back as you planned to from the beginning. That shouldn't be too difficult, right?"

"Not at all."

"And Con?"

"Yes?"

"Excellent work on this assignment. You've got all the right stuff."

"Thanks, Luce." He hung up, felt a gentle squeeze on his hand, and closed his eyes. That touch was the last act or word of affection he'd ever get from Lizzie Dare.

Because she was about to find out that on top of everything else, he was a liar, a traitor, a user, and, of course, a thief.

He'd *tried* to warn her.

CHAPTER
SIXTEEN

WHOEVER WAS ON the phone and whatever she'd said to Con, everything had changed. His expression, his body language—the whole aura of pleasure had evaporated from the tiny cuddy.

And she'd picked up enough of the conversation to know it was bad, bad news.

"Just tell me," she said, seeing the pain on his face. "I can handle it."

He closed his hand tighter over hers. "Alita is dead."

Lizzie tried to suck in a breath. "What?"

"Carbon monoxide poisoning on her dive this afternoon. The Coast Guard ordered the vessel into port to investigate the diving death, and they're down in St. Lucie. The FBI's been called in. And, yes, it happened an hour after that little weasel got back."

"Flynn killed her. He thinks she gave the medallion to you."

"That'd be my guess."

A shock wave rolled over her.

To investigate the diving death.

Those words were all too familiar.

"We have to get down to the port to talk to the investigators and tell them everything, including what happened on our night dive," Con said.

She nodded, her head finally clearing. "Who called you?"

He hesitated just one second too long. "My boss."

"Your boss." She waited for an explanation that didn't come. "From . . . where? Aren't you going to tell me? Even now?"

He said nothing, grabbing her underwear and shirt and handing them to her. "We have to go. Now."

She took the items, but didn't move. "Con? Tell me."

"Lizzie, a woman is dead. We have a lot of information that could help make sure that the right—"

"That's not what I mean! You talked about a client. Who do you work for?"

"Judd Paxton."

"What?" The word was more of a croak than a question.

"Judd Paxton is my client." His voice was low, calm, deadly. "The woman on the phone was my boss. She runs a security and investigation firm called the Bullet Catchers. Judd Paxton hired her to place an undercover representative on the boat to track and secure the treasures, and discover who on the crew was tampering and stealing them."

She blinked, speechless. In her chest, something shattered. Her heart, no doubt. Her pride. Her faith in mankind.

As he ducked out of the cabin she lunged at him, seizing his arm to yank him around.

"You liar! You bastard! You helped me under false pretenses, taking everything I've told you right back to Judd Paxton." Rage caught in her throat, stealing her breath. "You slept with me, letting me think you were some kind of . . . of . . . hero."

"I never told you that. I never, *ever* said those words."

"I did, and you didn't correct me."

"I didn't confirm or deny. You went off on some kind of—of fantasy."

"And you let me."

"I didn't—"

"You didn't exactly put your hand over my mouth, shut me up, and say, 'Hey, Lizzie. I work for the enemy.' "

He turned, put his hands on either side of the opening, and hoisted himself up to the deck. She stayed kneeling on the cushions where they'd just made love, clutching the underwear that she'd just begged him to take off her.

What an idiot! She smacked the cushion so hard a jolt ran up her arm, and then remembered Alita. Mourning and disbelief replaced anger, making her ache, making her relive the loss of her father.

And suddenly she missed her sister so desperately, it hurt more than anything else.

Shaking a little, she started to get dressed. If she was feeling sorry for anyone, it should be for Alita. She could save her own pity party until Flynn Paxton was in jail.

The reality of that hit her again as the engines

started and the boat took off, knocking her backward. Swearing as she stabbed her arms into her sleeves, she fumbled with the buttons he'd flicked off with ease, then yanked on her hoodie.

This would all take Judd Paxton down a peg or two. Now he'd have to come clean about salvaging *El Falcone* and—

Oh God. The scepter and diamond. Con knew where they were!

She turned to his backpack. The engine noise covered the sound of the zipper as she opened it and stuck her hand in, rooting around for the velvet box that held the medallion. She found it and pulled it out. This medallion belonged to her—not that bastard Judd Paxton.

She opened the lid to hide the treasure in her pocket—

It was gone.

She snapped it closed and launched herself toward the deck, yanking herself through the opening to glare at Con.

"Where is it?" she demanded, her pulse soaring. "Where did you put my medallion, you lying thief!"

He stared straight ahead. "It belongs to Mr. Paxton. He financed the salvage effort and he will file a legitimate claim with the state for it."

She hated him. Right down to the bone, she hated him. "You're going to give him the scepter and the diamond, aren't you?"

"Yes."

"Over my dead body."

He turned to look at her. "If you're not careful and

we don't get Flynn Paxton into the hands of the authorities, you might be right about that."

She threw herself on the passenger seat, wrapped her arms around her knees, and refused to respond. He might have the medallion, but he'd never, *ever* get the scepter or diamond. She swore it on her father's grave, even if she had to throw it back into the sea.

Judd Paxton would never get his hands on her treasures, and neither would Constantine Xenakis.

The Coast Guard investigated the boat, but the FBI was handling the people. The federal agent assigned to the case was kind enough to give Con his FBI sweatshirt, and Con repaid him with a two-and-a-half-hour interview, turned over the medallion, and gave him enough information to build a compelling case, plus zero in on a black-market collector as a side bene. By the time he finished, agents had already been dispatched to detain and reinterrogate Flynn Paxton, and he assumed someone would be watching Gerry Dix, too.

At the end of his interview, with dawn on the horizon, Con had walked through the *Gold Digger*, offering detailed bits of information to the investigators and showing them the tampered air intakes. None of the other crewmembers were still there, including Lizzie. Especially Lizzie.

She'd been stone, cold silent on the ride back. The water in her eyes as she stared ahead could just have been from the cold air, but he suspected the impact of a crewmate's death and the shocker news he'd dropped on her might have drawn a few tears.

Which made what he had to do before that afternoon's meeting with Paxton, and possibly Lucy, even more difficult. When he finished his interview he'd learned that her interrogation had ended well before his. And she'd obviously driven home, since this had been the port of departure for the *Gold Digger*.

One of the agents offered to give him a ride up to Sebastian to get his bike, which he took. He figured Lizzie never mentioned the scepter and diamond in her interviews with the FBI, and neither had he. They weren't part of the investigation; no one on the boat knew they existed yet.

As the sun rose to his left over the ocean, he rolled back down the beach highway, following the route to her sister's house, laying out a mental plan for how to convince her to hand it over.

He wouldn't use force, and he sure as hell couldn't seduce them out of her.

Maybe she wouldn't be home yet, and he could just steal them.

He rumbled down the side street to the stucco ranch house that sat among palms and live oak trees, and tensed at the sight of a Scion in the driveway. He couldn't steal the goods, then.

At least he'd get to see her one more time. Parking the bike and bracing for a fight, he went straight to the front door and knocked.

Nothing.

He headed down one side of the house, peeking in windows, seeing no sign of life, then walked around to the back patio. The sliders were locked, as was every window. He pounded on the glass, peered into the dark kitchen, and began to think about a new plan.

Breaking in.

A few minutes later, he climbed through the kitchen window and over the counter to land silently on his feet.

"Lizzie?"

There was only silence, one that only a person with hearing like his could sense. Not a breath, a scuff of a foot, nothing.

Peering into the shadows, he walked through the tiny living room and paused at the dining room, listening. He peeked into the office, but it was still and dark.

"Lizzie!" His voice bounced through the empty house.

Frustration built, along with dread that she'd beaten him at his game, and he marched straight back to her bedroom. He twisted the brass knob, but it didn't turn.

She'd locked herself in her room with the treasure?

"Lizzie!" He pounded once and pressed his ear to the wood, listening for any sound. Nothing.

The room was vacant, or the person in it wasn't breathing.

Her car was in the driveway. The house was silent. Maybe they hadn't gotten Flynn in custody yet . . .

With one mighty shove of his shoulder, he splintered the door open. It popped wide and slammed against the wall.

Empty. Something damn close to a rush of relief rolled through him. Better she was gone than dead.

He opened the closet, then turned to the antique bed, high enough off the ground that she could easily have crawled under there.

He lifted the skirt, peered into the shadows.

Flattening himself on the floor, he shimmied in, able to turn partially on his side before his shoulder hit one of the wooden slats that held the box spring in place. Everything looked untouched, just a normal box spring—but he was sure of what he'd heard. When he maneuvered onto his back, his hands ran over some grit, a few pieces like rock. Digging into the carpet, he grasped a small chunk and examined it.

Purplish. Sandy. Coral.

He pressed his hands slowly over every inch of the box spring and slats to find some kind of hiding place. Then he realized that most box springs were covered with sheer gauze, leaving the inner springs visible.

But this one had a quilted fabric sewn on it, so well done that it looked perfectly normal. He started palming every square of the material until he found it.

A snap, sewn in to be invisible. He yanked at it, opening it, then another. Between the two snaps was a long nylon zipper. Exactly the high-pitched zip he'd heard when he'd listened outside the room.

He slowly dragged it open, half ready for the scepter and diamond to fall down on his chest.

But nothing fell. Behind the zipper was a large metal holding area, like a safe with no door. He reached all the way in to the back, then ran his hand from one side to the other.

Completely empty.

Forty minutes later, he was parked in the lot outside the Paxton Treasures Salvage Museum, ten or so miles north of the development he'd robbed the day before, when a limo pulled in, taking up three of the four spaces.

It was either Paxton, Lucy, or both. Climbing off the bike, Con ambled over as the driver came out, nodded to him, and opened the back door.

"Go ahead. She's waiting."

He slid into the cool car, squinting into the tinted-window dimness to see Lucy in the far back, her legs crossed in pale silk pants, her one foot quietly tapping a three-inch stiletto, a phone at her ear, her dark, Asian-tilted eyes on Con from the second he dipped into the car and took the seat across from her.

She held up one finger. "Judd, I realize this is a terrible blow to you and your wife."

So he'd get to hear the client's reaction firsthand.

"You wanted to know the truth, and now you do," Lucy continued, giving Con a long look.

"I'll see you in a few minutes, then," Lucy said, snapping her phone closed, her eyes narrowed into ebony slits as she shook back thick, shoulder-length black hair. "Do you have the scepter and diamond?"

"No. Does Judd think I do?"

"I never mentioned them, in the off chance that you failed."

"I just don't have them *yet*."

"Then when?"

He rubbed his hands over his face, exhausted, frustrated, disgusted. "Soon."

"Do better than that."

"Very soon?" He shot her a smile, but didn't get one in return. "I'll find her, Lucy."

"I'm not interested in your finding her. I want the scepter and diamond that belong to my client."

"She has them. And she can't go too far. I'll get them. Today."

"You better." She leaned forward, her expression clear. "Or I will assume you stole the treasure."

His jaw dropped open. "What?"

"Your track record doesn't support any other theory."

"Fuck my track record, Lucy." He slapped his hands on the leather seat. "I didn't take them, just like I didn't keep the medallion, which would have been very easy to do."

"Give me your bag."

He burned her with a look, venom boiling in his veins as he tossed it to her. "Suit yourself. The FBI has the medallion, and you won't find anything in there but tools of my trade."

She opened the pouch and rifled through his personal items, then the rest of the bag. "Consider it a test," she said. "Produce the scepter and diamond, and I'll know what you're made of. If not, I'll also know what you're made of. The former is a Bullet Catcher. The latter . . . a fake."

The venom turned cold and he just stared at her, vaguely aware of another car pulling into the lot.

"Here's Judd. I think I'll handle him alone." She set the bag on the floor between them. "I'm sure you'll need some of the things in there to work your magic. For instance, the pack of condoms. I see there's one missing already."

She didn't look at him as she glided out of the car, leaving him with the knowledge that he only had one possible course of action. He had to screw Lizzie Dare again, in more ways than one, and prove without a shadow of a doubt that he wasn't the man she thought he was.

CHAPTER
SEVENTEEN

JET LAG MUST have hit her hard. Brianna turned on the lumpy down mattress, blinking against the sunshine that warmed the third-floor bedroom of the farmhouse. From the looks of the light, it was darn near afternoon in the Azores.

Good Lord, how late had she slept? She pushed up on her elbows, squinting into the brightness to make out the view of an ancient windmill through the dusty panes of glass. Far, far from home and not a soul knew she was there.

The adventurous thrill that gave her was tempered by a splash of guilt. At some point she'd have to tell Lizzie where she'd gone, but right now . . .

She stretched, wiggled her toes under the puffy down comforter, and drank in the heart-stopper of an ocean view.

Mrs. Bettencourt had been chilly at first, but then she warmed to the mission and promised to help today. She did have a library—all these old houses did—and maybe the final piece of proof that they wanted would be there.

In the meantime, Lizzie could explore and sightsee. Not that there was a whole lot to see. Too bad Carlos Bettencourt wasn't from Monaco, or somewhere slightly more exotic than godforsaken little Corvo.

Still, she was free and unencumbered and doing her part for Dad, instead of just sifting through the mountain of papers that just made her miss him more.

"Ms. Dare?" The call was accompanied by a soft tap on her door. "It's Gabby, with coffee. Our kind of coffee, American."

"Just a second." Brianna threw off the fluffy comforter and went to the door in her thigh-high T-shirt. "Oh, you're a lifesaver, Gabby. I crave my caffeine fix."

The woman, easily five foot nine and the size of a truck, nodded and barreled into the room, setting a tray on the ancient dresser. "No need to thank me, hon. The *madame*,"—she said in an affected British accent to drag out the word—"would have my head if I didn't."

Brianna smiled, moving some personal items on the dresser to make sure Gabby had room for the tray. "She seems like she might be . . ." A total bitch. "Tough to work for."

The other woman shrugged. "I'm just stepping in for a few days because she's desperate and I can gouge her for extra cash. Not that I'm trying to exploit the circumstances, but the opportunity was too good to pass up."

"What circumstances?"

"She didn't tell you? You haven't heard?"

Brianna shook her head. "Heard what?"

"About her nurse, Ana. She liked to call her a house-keeper, but the whole island knew that Ana was a nurse hired by Mrs. B's husband to keep an eye on her."

Brianna looked up from the coffee she poured, intrigued. "What happened? And why does she need someone to keep an eye on her?"

Gabby pointed to her temple and made the universal twirl for nutso. "She's a little . . ."

"Off her rocker?"

Gabby smiled. "That'd probably be the medical term for it."

She didn't strike Brianna as crazy, but who knew? "What happened to Ana?"

Gabby made a face. "It's so sad. She killed herself."

"That *is* sad."

"Right there." She pointed to the gray stone wind-mill perched at the cliff's edge, the rotors circling rhythmically. "Threw herself right over the cliff."

Brianna's eyes flew open. "Oh my God. When?"

"A few days ago."

"Seriously?" A chill shot the hairs on the back of her head to a stand. "How old was she?"

"Twenty-six."

Brianna's heart turned over. *My age.* She shifted her gaze to the windmill, suddenly more ominous than picturesque. "That is so, so tragic. Did you know her?"

"Everybody knows everybody in Corvo. There're like three hundred and fifty people in the whole place, all of them related somehow, going back two centuries. The whole island is devastated."

Brianna sipped, studying the sturdy woman who looked as though she belonged on a farm in Iowa. "How did you end up here?"

"Well, for one thing, I didn't 'end' up here; I'm leaving as soon as this job for Mrs. B is over. I was about to leave when I heard about it. But to answer your question, I've been traveling around Europe for a year, after a miserable divorce from a cheating . . . Never mind, it's a cliché. I've been here in Corvo for about two months, 'cause I think it's one of the prettiest places I've ever seen. I was just about to head off to Spain when I heard about Ana, and figured I could scare up some cash working for this lady who apparently never made her own bed in her life."

"Wow, it sounds like a fun adventure."

Gabby laughed, fluffing the comforter into place. "I had to get out of Indiana, that's for sure. When my husband left I was all weepy and miserable, with nothing but half of the cash from selling our split level. Then, one of my friends gave me this book about a lady who went and lived in Italy and India, trying to find herself after a divorce. I thought, why not? I'm fifty and I've never been east of Pittsburgh. So here I am."

Brianna gave her a warm smile. "I love adventurous spirits."

"How 'bout you? Is that research project the only thing that brings you to our lovely rock in the ocean?"

"Yes."

"How is Mrs. B involved?"

"Her genealogy is involved, and I was hoping to have access to her library. She said there's one in the house."

"I don't know if I'd exactly call it a library, but there is a room with some books."

"How did Mrs. B end up here?" With a nurse, no less.

"There are a lot of rumors about that, but I've become friendly with a cousin of a friend of the man who was Ana's fiancé . . ." She laughed at how that sounded. "Trust me, you live here long enough and you know everyone. Anyway, evidently her husband is some big-time Wall Street guy whose family has owned this property forever. She apparently tried to kill herself more than once, so he sent her here."

"Like, he shipped her off and exiled her? Without offering psychiatric help or counseling?"

Gabby held out her hands in a "who knows?" gesture. "They're off-the-charts rich and he's got a big-time reputation. Maybe she preferred this to an institution."

"She doesn't strike me as that whacko."

"She's whacko enough to have tried to kill herself a couple of times since she got here."

"Whoa." What was this place, Suicide Island? "How?"

"I don't know for sure, but I heard Ana was really good with her. That's why it's such a shame . . ."

Brianna nodded, a wisp of sadness curling through her. It *was* a shame. Life, whether you ended it yourself, or a broken regulator in a cave dive did it for you, could be short. "Gabby, do you know if there's any Internet access here? I really need to e-mail somebody at home."

"It's tricky, but Sousa's has a computer and they can get satellite Internet. That's the one and only restaurant in town, and I'm living in one of two rooms above it. It's spotty, but it's your only chance without taking a ferry to a bigger island. Terceira has all that."

Brianna stood and looked out the window, her gaze drawn to the three-bladed windmill. "Maybe I'll go into the village later. I just want to see what Mrs. Bettencourt has planned for me."

"Oh, honey, I wouldn't go into town today. It's Ana's funeral and the place is completely shut down."

"Oh, okay." Brianna shook her head, imagining someone throwing herself into the water. "How bad could life be on this little island, that you'd want to end it?"

"That's just it." Gabby snapped the pillowcases tight and smoothed them as she followed Brianna's gaze. "Nothing was wrong with her life. She had a nice young man, was going to get married, came from a wonderful family, seemed completely happy."

Brianna turned, cold despite the warm sunshine. "Really? Did she leave a note?"

"No. But why else would someone climb up to that thing? She sure didn't go up to work the machinery."

"Does Mrs. Bettencourt know what happened to her? Maybe it was an accident."

"She said the girl spent the day crying. And her mother did pass, but well over a year ago."

"Oh. Grief can make people do very strange things," Brianna said. She'd ached so badly when Dad died—but she'd never considered suicide. Of course, she had Lizzie.

Guilt twisted in her again. "Are you sure I can't get

into the restaurant today? I really want to send my sister a message."

"Tell you what, I'll send your message for you. What's her e-mail?"

"That would be wonderful." Brianna grabbed her handbag and a small notebook, tearing off a page to write down Lizzie's e-mail. "Just tell her I'm fine and that I'm . . . working on Aramis. She'll understand."

"Aramis?"

She wrote the name on the paper. "Yeah. Just let her know I'm safe and that I'll be in touch with her as soon as I can. And tell her I love her."

Gabby took the paper and nodded. "Happy to help you."

When she left, Brianna finished her coffee and stared at the windmill. Death that didn't make sense was so hard to accept.

She closed her eyes and said a little prayer for the girl, then got dressed to go meet with eccentric, if nutso, Solange Bettencourt.

It would take a while for Con Xenakis to find her here. Safe in that knowledge, and in the fact that she could get the scepter to her safe-deposit box in just a few hours, Lizzie walked through the minuscule rooms that Dad had called his workplace. Less than a thousand square feet, the five-room beach house had survived numerous hurricanes. At his office door, she almost laughed. Hurricanes outside *and* in.

Brianna had tried, but they'd need a bulldozer to clean out the man-made mountain in Dad's office.

Inhaling the whisper of Old Spice that lingered in the air, she stepped into the office, imagined him turning in the old desk chair and beckoning to her: *Lizzie Lou, look at you.*

She swallowed a lump in her throat. "Yeah, look at me, Dad. Duped by a hot guy. You'd be so proud."

She dropped into his chair and clicked on the computer, praying Brianna had replied to the e-mail she'd sent from Con's phone. While she waited for the system to come to life, she fluttered through the papers. All of the pertinent stuff was gone; just old notes and Christmas cards from diving friends remained.

She clicked on the Internet browser bar, getting a list of the last sites visited. She recognized most of them, but not the top site—something about genealogy. Out of curiosity she clicked on it, and scrolled down the home page to a flashing link.

Welcome back, MDare, you have private e-mail waiting in the forum. Please read.

She hesitated for a minute, her finger over the mouse. Should she go there? Did this person not know that her father had died?

Possibly not. A treasure forum would know. But genealogy? She clicked on the link.

MDare—I have the information you are seeking for Carlos Bettencourt, circa 1860. Please respond by private e-mail mrdbgenserv@gmail.com.

She was tempted to just let it go, but that wasn't right.

She hit reply and typed, *Thank you for contacting MDare. I'm his daughter and am sorry to inform you that he has passed away. Can you forward the information to me at the following e-mail address?* She added her own e-mail and tapped Send, then opened up the program for her own mail—which did not include a message from her sister.

She wrote another note, pleading with Brianna to write. Just as she hit Send, the ding of incoming mail sounded.

From mrdbgenserv@gmail.com. Wow, that was fast.

I've already given the information to your sister when I met her in Lisbon. I believe she's going straight to the source in Corvo now. Maria Rossos Della Buonofuentes.

Corvo? Where was that? Lizzie grabbed the mouse to hit Google, but froze at the sound of a car engine slowing outside the house.

Damn.

Could he have found her already? He didn't know where this house was, and even his almighty connections wouldn't be able to find a house that was in her mother's maiden name, which he didn't know.

Still, she wrapped her arms around her waist as she headed to the living room. The bungalow was at the end of a dead-end street in a little-known section of Vero Beach. There were only two other houses on the street, and traffic was extremely rare.

She peeked through the window, seeing only the overgrown shrubbery smashed against it. They had to hire someone to hack it away before the jungle overtook the house.

A car door slammed on the street.

But he drove a bike. She let out a little breath, still braced for his deep voice calling her name. *Lizzie! I know you're—*

"Lizzie, honey, are you there?"

"Sam!" The voice of a friend was so welcome, she threw the door all the way open and practically hugged him. "How did you know I was here?"

"I know you pretty well, Lizzie," he said with a smile. "You shouldn't come over and roll around in memories, honey."

She invited him in, shrugging. "I didn't want to go up to my apartment in Cocoa just yet." Con would look there for her next, no doubt.

"So you came to your refuge."

Smiling, she conceded with a nod. "How's Charlotte doing?"

"She's upset about Alita, and all the questioning. Sorry that the dive is over. Worried about you. She sent me here to fetch you and bring you to our house." Sam surveyed her face and uncombed hair. "You look like you could use some TLC."

"I'm just exhausted. It's been a helluva night and morning."

Sam glanced around. "Where's Brianna?"

She settled on one of the two rickety bar stools and rested her elbow on the yellow countertop. "Europe."

He drew back. "Really? Where?"

"Lisbon, I think."

"You think? She didn't tell you?"

Lizzie shook her head. "And probably for good reason. I'm too protective, I know that."

"Did she go with friends?"

"I really have no idea. I have a feeling she's following some genealogical lead that my father was tracking for . . ." She hesitated, torn. "A project he was working on. She's gone somewhere called Corvo."

Sam practically fell off the stool. "The island in the Azores? Brianna went there?"

"I don't know. Maybe. I had an e-mail from a genealogist my father was in touch with, and she said she'd given my sister what he needed when she saw her the other day in Lisbon, then she said something about Bree taking it to Corvo."

Sam looked as dismayed as she felt. "Never been there myself, but from what I know it's tiny, the farthest of the Azores, about a thousand miles from Portugal. That ought to please the adventuress in Brianna's soul."

A thousand miles from Portugal? "That's the middle of the Atlantic Ocean." Her heart swelled with worry. "I really need to find her."

"Why don't you get some help from Con? He seemed like a resourceful guy, and . . ." Sam gave her a sly smile. "Char told me you two were pretty close."

"Everyone makes mistakes," Lizzie said, popping off the stool at the soft ding of an e-mail from the office.

"Oh? Why was he a mistake?"

Because he was a lying, thieving, underhanded, undercover cheating bastard who works for Judd Paxton.

"I just . . . misjudged him," she said, purposefully vague as she headed to the office, praying the e-mail was from Bree.

Sam followed. "He seemed pretty upstanding to me."

"He seemed like a *lot* of things he wasn't."

She bent over the keyboard and clicked, clenching a fist in hope, but it was an advertisement from Office

Depot. Disappointment punched her, and she dropped into the chair with a sigh.

"Honey, why don't you come and stay with us for a while? This place is too depressing for you. All those shrubs smashed against the windows make it dark and dreary in here, along with the memories that are dragging you down. Char and I have plenty of room."

It was only a matter of time until Con figured out her mother's maiden name, and his research team at the Bullet Catchers tracked her down.

And once he found her, he'd find the scepter.

If she left the house empty, he'd tear it apart until he got what he wanted.

Then all the answers came to her.

"Sam, I need to trust you with the biggest secret you can imagine. The one thing that mattered most to my father in the whole world."

Sam raised an eyebrow. *"El Falcone?"*

"You know about that?"

"Lizzie, I was very close friends with your father. Of course he talked about his search."

"Did you realize that we were diving on *El Falcone?*"

He gave her leg a squeeze. "Why do you think we invited you? We wanted you to be there when the recoveries were made. I knew how much it mattered to Malcolm, and how much he'd want a family member there."

"You knew and didn't tell me?"

"Charlotte thought it best not to tell you until we knew for sure. Now it's all kind of moot, isn't it?"

It was *so* not moot. "How did you know?"

"Malcolm showed me his map and told me his conjecture. When I heard where this dive was, and that it was supersecret and taking place off-season, I figured that once again, Judd Paxton was one step ahead of everyone else in the treasure world."

"You should have told me. It would have been a lot easier if I knew you'd known."

"Well, I listened to my wife on that one. When that Our Lady of Sorrows medallion came up, I was pretty sure, but then all hell broke loose with Alita's . . ." His voice trailed off. "What would have been easier?"

"Bringing up the scepter."

He frowned in confusion.

"And the diamond that was in it," she added softly.

Sam's eyes popped open. "*Excuse* me?"

"Come with me." Lizzie tugged him up and back to the kitchen, popping open the freezer and shoving ice trays and frozen pizzas out of the way.

"Char will die if you put it in the freezer," he said.

"Just temporarily. I'm taking it to my safe-deposit box later." But would Con track it down, and somehow figure out how to get it from the bank? The man—and his company—seemed to be capable of anything.

She reached for the butcher paper she'd wrapped it in, pulled it out, and handed the package to a stunned, visibly pale Sam. "I found it the second day and sneaked it off the boat."

"How?"

She grinned. "Blondes find the gold, Sam."

He laughed, still bewildered. "Can I see it?"

She had a better idea. "Can you keep it? is the question. I think it's dangerous, and obviously valuable. And I'll warn you, Con Xenakis is looking for it. That's why I'm hiding here—he doesn't know about this house. But like you said, he's resourceful. By the time he figures it out, I want to be gone."

"Gone where?"

The rightness of her decision settled around her like a warm blanket, making her smile. "To find my sister."

"Can you leave in the middle of this investigation?" he asked. "The FBI agent instructed us to stay."

"They already have Alita's killer."

He almost dropped the scepter. "Lizzie, if you drop one more bomb on me, I'll have a heart attack. How do you know this?"

"Long story, but Flynn and Alita were having a fling. He was stealing treasure and she was helping him. We think he killed her."

"We?"

She felt a soft flush. "Con and me."

"So are you working with this guy, or do you hate him?"

"I hate him," she said definitively. "And the FBI agent told me I could leave town for an emergency. I call finding my sister an emergency if I can be reached. If you have this, I can go knowing it's in safe hands."

"Of course, but what if Con comes looking for it? He might suspect you gave it to me."

"Hide it. And don't tell anyone, not even Charlotte. That way she won't be lying when she denies everything."

Sam pulled the scepter closer. "You have my word it'll be safe."

"Good. Because when Paxton files the claim for the shipwreck, I don't want this to get lumped in with everything else. My hope is that someone will recover the mate, and then I'll go public and shame him into putting them into a museum, instead of selling to a collector. And when I do, the real story of my ancestor will be told."

Sam beamed. "Your father would be so proud, Lizzie."

Lizzie hugged him, the butcher paper crunching between them. "Thank you, Sam."

"So, now what? You're off to Europe?"

"I'll let you know. Hopefully I'll hear from Brianna first, before I go."

"Hopefully," he agreed.

After Sam left with the treasure, Lizzie went back to the office, feeling better than she had in hours. She checked her e-mail, and then started clicking around the airlines for flights. There was nothing under a couple thousand, and even if she paid that, she couldn't get on a flight for two days.

The day and her decisions hit her hard and, yawning with exhaustion, she climbed onto the bed in the tiny back room. Curling on top of the spread, she tucked her knees into her chest and closed her eyes, asleep before her next thought formed.

The pressure on her foot almost pulled her out of sleep, but it wasn't enough. Her head was heavy, her limbs aching with fatigue. She instinctively shook her foot, a million miles from consciousness, but the pressure just got heavier.

She fought to wake, but sleep won, keeping her eyes glued and her body still.

And that cold weight on her leg . . .

In her dream, she imagined it was Con. He'd slipped into her room, looking for more . . .

Reality punched. Awareness squeezed. And Lizzie jerked up, yanking her leg free and flipping over . . . and stared, a strange moan of horror coming out of her mouth.

Two and a half feet of slithering black, red, and yellow stripes. As soon as she jerked, the snake did, too, circling into itself and lifting its head to her with a long, threatening hiss.

Fighting for calm, and losing, she inched her legs away, staring at the distinct bands of color.

Red touch yellow, deadly fellow. Red touch black, okay Jack. The rhyme taught to every Florida child screamed in her head. Shaking, she inched back to the headboard as slowly as possible, staring at the snake. Each red band was lined with yellow.

Her throat closed out a scream, her chest bursting with an unreleased breath.

The snake slithered closer.

Damn! All that brush around the house was like an open invitation to snakes.

Could she vault off the bed fast enough?

The snake hissed again.

She pulled her legs up and stood, just as the snake lunged.

She flattened herself to the wall and screamed, knowing it was probably the last sound she'd ever make.

CHAPTER
EIGHTEEN

THE MOTORCYCLE ENGINE would alert Lizzie that he'd found her, so Con parked it at the corner and walked to the cul de sac that ended at the beach. The other homes were visible from the street, but her house was buried in a jungle of green.

As he reached the edge of the property, he froze at the sound of a muffled scream. He instantly launched forward. Ripping at the overgrown shrubbery that blocked his way, he ignored the jagged thorns that cut his face and arms. At the back he racked the slide of his Glock, automatically ducking at the windows so he wasn't seen by her attacker.

Silence. No talking, no struggle. Whoever had her was quiet.

Or had killed her already.

Crouched low, weapon drawn, he peered in a window and saw an empty office. It had to be the next room; the window was ten feet away. He swiftly worked his way over and maneuvered into position to see, but blinds blocked his view.

Lizzie screamed again, bloodcurdling and helpless. The window was closed and wouldn't move when he shoved it, so with one solid thwack of his gun he shattered the glass. He ripped at the blinds so hard they cracked right out of the wall, and he thrust his gun through the broken pane.

Lizzie stood on the bed, flattened against the wall, wailing as she divided her terrified gaze from the window to the bed. The head of a deadly coral snake rose above the mattress and hissed.

"Hang on, Lizzie— I got him."

He pulled the trigger, exploding the snake's head.

Then he swiftly smashed the other panes and threw himself against the wooden frame, cracking it with his weight and vaulting headfirst into the room with a roll.

As he stood, Lizzie collapsed. He pulled her into his arms, a quivering, trembling, boneless mess, and carried her from the room. He laid her on the living room sofa, then knelt down next to her, stroking her hair off her pale, tear-dampened face.

His own heart hammered with an adrenaline pump and the thought that she had been inches from death. He couldn't resist a kiss on her forehead, and she didn't stop him.

Her eyes shuttered with a sigh as the shock wore off. "If you hadn't come, I . . . I . . ." Realization hit her. "What the hell are you doing here?"

He smiled. "You're welcome."

"Thank you—and I mean it. But we're finished. Everything is over, done. I've given my report to the Coast

Guard and Paxton's closed the salvage site. We're done with each other."

Not quite yet, Lizzie. "I can't just leave you like that."

She surveyed his face, doubt all over hers. "Yes, you can. You were bought and paid for by the man I was working to destroy. There's the door. Use it. Just . . . make sure there are no more snakes on your way out."

"You're right about one thing: the job is over. I'm not here on behalf of Paxton or anyone else. I found you because I wanted to see you again."

For a flicker of an instant, she believed him, he could tell. It dissolved as quickly as it came. "I don't have it."

"That's not why I'm here."

She skewered him with a look.

"Not the only reason," he admitted, stroking her hair. "I really wanted to see you again." That was true.

"I don't have what you want," she repeated.

But she knew where it was. "I understand that." He smiled, rubbing the pad of his thumb on her cheek, liking the sensation and the fact that she didn't jerk him away. "Where is it?"

"None of your business."

It was the only business he had. "Lizzie, you realize you're not safe, don't you?"

A crease deepened between her eyebrows as her frown intensified. "What do you mean? Isn't Paxton in custody?"

"I don't know for certain. But how did that snake get in, with all the closed windows?"

"You think someone planted it here? To scare me?"

"To kill you. Were you on the bed?"

"I went to rest, to take a nap after . . ." She shook her head. "No, it's preposterous. No one wants to kill me."

"Who knows you have that scepter?"

"For one thing, I don't have it. And don't bother to ask, pal, 'cause I'm not telling you. And I'll be safe enough when I leave."

"Where are you going?"

She started to say, then stopped. "You don't need to know."

"Tell me." And then he would go with her. It was the only way to get the scepter. Stay with her morning, noon, and night. "When are you leaving?"

"When are *you* leaving is the question." She tried to wiggle her wrists out of his grasp.

"You don't really want me to."

She snorted softly. "You have some ego. I don't like you, okay? Can I be any clearer? Sleeping with you was a mistake, and trusting you was an even bigger one."

He leaned forward, close to her mouth. "It wasn't a mistake. It was amazing." He brushed her lips, but she pushed away.

"It was an amazing *mistake*. And one I don't intend to make again. So go call Judd and tell him I don't have the scepter or diamond."

"He doesn't know you found them."

"You didn't tell him? Your *client*?" She plastered some disgust on the word. "Why not?"

He put his hands on her shoulders and looked her directly in the eye. "Because it belongs to your family."

"Yeah—I'm really buyin' that, Con Man."

"I'm serious. And my connections can help you. My assignment is over, but my company has a research and investigation division that would knock your socks off. How do you think I found this house so quickly?"

She sighed. "I knew you would. I couldn't get out of here fast enough."

"Listen——I put my resources on the history trail, and they've already uncovered information you'll want to know about Aramis Dare."

She tried to look disinterested, and failed. "What information?"

"What looks like proof that Aramis Dare was never paid for the bounty that he carried to Portugal in 1861."

"What kind of proof?"

"Data from a library in Havana."

"Oh, right——"

He held up a hand to quiet her. "I can give it to you. One of the other men who works for the company spends a lot of time in Cuba on assignment, and his wife is an investigative specialist. She's been doing some digging; has access to old documents that the government has kept under lock and key."

She eyed him. "What did you find?"

"Where are you going?"

"Are you trying to buy that out of me with some shady promise of information? Forget it." She pushed herself up.

"You have a fax machine? I'll have it sent here in ten minutes."

For a second, she almost relented. "You're a lying son of a bitch, and I don't need your help."

"Yes, you do," he told her. "Because it will be a road map for you in Portugal. It leads right to a little island called Corvo."

Her jaw dropped. "Corvo?"

"In the Azores. Heard of it?"

"I know where it is." She pushed off the sofa, getting away from him.

"Where are you going?"

"To make reservations. For one. I don't care what it costs, I'm going. And you're not."

"I'll just follow you there."

He heard her blow out a breath as the computer keys started clicking. He gave her a few minutes, checking out the security of the place, noting that every window and door were locked except the broken one in the bedroom.

He ended up in the office doorway, watching her type, hearing her moan every time a fare came up. On top of a shelf he saw a fax machine and leaned over to get the number.

"It's going to cost me a freaking fortune," she mumbled.

"I have access to a private jet." He sent the text.

She slid a look over her shoulder. "Of course you do."

"Not only do we not know how or when or why someone got in here to plant the venomous snake in your room, but we also don't know *who*. And until we do . . ."

He walked over and put protective hands on her

shoulders, glancing at the long list of flights from Atlanta to Lisbon, all with four-digit price tags and dates three days in the future. "You're not safe. I think I've proven that I can watch your back."

A soft ding of an incoming e-mail got her to tap the mouse, revealing a new one from gabbyone@gmail.com. She read the subject line out loud: *'A message from your sister.'* Finally!"

"*'My name is Gabrielle Roberts and I'm working in a home where your sister is staying on the island of Corvo.'*"

She stopped to look up at him.

"All roads lead to Corvo," he said quietly, his gaze on the e-mail.

"*'She doesn't have e-mail or phone but asked that I write to let you know she's fine. She asked me to tell you she's working on Aramis.'*"

"And they also lead to Aramis," she replied.

"Read the P.S., Lizzie."

"*'She really misses you. This is not part of her message to you,'*" she read softly, "*'but it's a lonely island for an American.'*"

Behind him, the fax rang. While she reread the e-mail, Con retrieved the papers coming from the Bullet Catchers headquarters. Wordlessly, he took the three pages of notes and the manifest list and placed them on the keyboard in front of her.

"Do you really want to wait three days and spend two thousand dollars to get to Lisbon, then to Terceira, then to Corvo, when I can have you on a private jet, having dinner with your sister tomorrow night?" He reached down and fluttered the papers. "You two have an awful lot to talk about."

Her shoulders sagged in resignation. "You win, Con."

He leaned closer, put his mouth on her ear, and did what he'd been dying to do since he'd found her. He kissed her, feeling her body tense at the contact. "We both do."

Chapter
NINETEEN

"This is the last place on earth I'd expect to find my sister," Lizzie said as the Gulfstream jet banked over jagged volcanic rocks and a whitecapped sea. "I mean, she likes adventure, but she also likes clubs, restaurants, shops, and . . . people."

"Then there must be a very compelling reason for her to be here." In a matching buttery leather recliner directly across from her, Con ignored the view, his gaze on her. As it had been for the seven-hour flight across the Atlantic and most of the past twenty-four hours.

Lizzie tried to avoid his steel-blue stare, but it was impossible—and, like everything else about him, unnerving. True to his word, Con had been nothing but protective and helpful for the past twenty-four hours. And still as attractive as he was before she knew his connection to Judd Paxton, damn it.

But he couldn't take that treasure from her, and he sure could help her. So she put up with the misery of having to be so close to him and tried not to be attracted.

She forced herself to look out the window again, drinking in the shocking beauty of a rolling hillside dotted with snow-white stucco buildings, every single one topped in precisely the same coral-colored barrel-tile roof.

The runway started and ended with water, guaranteeing a white-knuckled landing for even the most seasoned traveler. Bree probably loved it.

Lizzie fingered the papers again. Her sister couldn't have had this information, so what did she know that caused her to leave Lisbon?

"You are absolutely positive she flew into this place?" Lizzie asked again.

"When we land, the customs officer has been briefed to show us the records, if that will make you feel any better."

It would. Frankly, everything he could do made her feel better. The stuff he had access to was like something out of the movies. Not only could he confirm Brianna's travel plans—offering proof that she'd flown to Lisbon, then to Terceira, another island in the Azores archipelago, and finally to Corvo—he also produced the identity of one Gabrielle Roberts.

The woman who'd written to Lizzie was a fifty-year-old divorcée from Indianapolis who'd been traveling around Europe and was staying in Corvo, adding credence to the e-mail. Then, like magic, he had them on a luxurious private jet, zipping directly to the island, cutting out days of travel time for her.

And best of all, he'd given her the manifest of *El Falcone*.

She still couldn't believe the document was real. But there it was, on her lap where it had been for most of the flight, a scanned image of the original manifest of *El Falcone*, a stunning find from a library in Havana.

The same library where her father had gone on that Cuban trip, she was certain. Did he have this manifest before he died?

"This document confirms everything my father theorized. That although *El Falcone* was not registered with any country, Captain Dare had paid for almost all the items it carried and had lined up buyers for each—making him not a pirate, but a profiteer."

"And one of those buyers was in the Azores."

She nodded. "Carlos Bettencourt. The CB from the notes, no doubt. This had to be what brought Brianna here. Because if she can prove this Carlos didn't pay for his scepters, then Aramis was no thief."

"How could she prove that?" Con countered.

The landing gear touched the edge of the runway with a slight jolt. "I think we're about to find out. And if she has, then the scepters belong to Captain Dare and his descendants. Not"—she narrowed her eyes at him—"Judd Paxton."

"Let's just find your sister and take it one step at a time."

After they got through customs, they left their bags with their pilot and flight attendant to check out Vila Nova do Corvo. The only village on the island, it couldn't be more than a square mile of charmingly dilapidated houses built right on top of one another along a few cobblestone streets, a large Catholic church at its center.

"We could walk this from end to end in an hour," Lizzie said as they crossed the street from the airport to the village tucked into the foothills of the mountainous island.

"According to our friend in customs, the rest of Corvo is fields, rocks, farms, and lakes. I say we head to wherever people eat and drink. There are only four hundred residents. One of them will know any visiting Americans."

She curled her fingers into his, a jumble of emotions fighting for space in her chest. "I still hate you."

He gave her fingers a squeeze. "I know."

"But I'm very grateful that you've done this for me."

A donkey-drawn cart of fruit and flowers rumbled by, and Con snagged a violet azalea from a bucket in the back, then handed it to her, tickling her chin with the petals. "Forgive me."

"No." She took the flower, unable to keep the smile off her face.

He just laughed softly, guiding them up the cobblestone street where a few older women in wheat-colored bonnets and long, dark dresses were coming toward them, talking in Portuguese.

One of them looked up and smiled. *"Bem vindos,"* she said, lifting the edge of her hat to reveal twinkling blue eyes. *"Turistas?"*

"Do you speak English?" Con asked her.

Three of them looked at a fourth. *"Fale inglês*, Marta."

A younger girl stepped forward from the back of the group, her eyes so much like the first woman's, they could be mother and daughter.

"I speak a little," she said softly, her gaze on Lizzie and not Con. "What do you look for?"

"An American woman," Lizzie said. "Another visitor. Brianna Dare."

She shook her head and lifted a shoulder. "Is she related to Corvo?"

Lizzie took the question to mean does she have relatives there. "No, but perhaps you know Gabrielle Roberts. Another American who has been staying here."

The girl's blank look suddenly changed. "Gabby?" She held her hand up several inches above her head, as if to indicate height. "Tall Gabby? For certain I know her. She is often to be found at Sousa." She pointed. "On Rua das Pedras. There is room to rent there."

The English was choppy but clear. "Sousa is a hotel?"

"No hotel in Corvo," she said, shaking her head. "Sousa is . . ." She made a gesture of eating.

"A restaurant?" Lizzie supplied.

"*Sim.* Restaurant. But no sign on wall. Look for tables by the church."

"*Obrigado*," Lizzie said, handing her the flower. "Thank you."

The walk to the Spanish-style cathedral took five minutes. Every building in the vicinity looked like a private home, until they circled to the front and saw two tables set for dining outside a windowless three-story house.

Con tapped on a whitewashed door and it opened,

revealing a tiny restaurant with a brick oven in the middle. A woman, also dressed in the dark garb of the locals, turned to greet them, the tangy scent of her cooking wafting toward them.

"Hello," Con said from the low-slung door frame, still holding Lizzie's hand. "Is this Sousa?"

She just nodded, looking from one to the other. "Eat outside?" she asked.

"Actually, we're looking for Gabby Roberts. Do you know her?"

"Gabby?" She held up a finger, then slowly walked to the back, opening a door and disappearing up a set of stairs. A minute later she reappeared, followed by a tall, middle-aged woman whose easy, familiar smile pegged her instantly as an American.

"I'm Gabby," she said, reaching out a hand to Lizzie. "The tourists always find me."

Lizzie shook her hand. "Not tourists, I'm Elizabeth Dare. You e-mailed me about my sister."

Gabby's jaw loosened in surprise. "Good heavens, you got here fast."

"Can you tell me where to find Brianna?"

"Of course. She's up at the Bettencourt farm."

"Bettencourt?" Excitement zinged through Lizzie at the name of Aramis Dare's buyer.

"Up the hill—there's only one road."

"Who lives there?"

"The lady's name is Solange Bettencourt, from New York City. Look up fish out of water, and you should find a real nice picture of her." She laughed a little. "I haven't been up there since I sent you the e-mail 'cause

Mrs. B called and told me your sister was going to be helping her out with the cooking and stuff. You should find her up there."

She'd come here to *work* for this woman? That was a stretch Lizzie couldn't even imagine.

"How do we find the farm?" Con asked. "Do we need a car?"

"You could hitchhike up the hill. Any one of the thirty people around who have a car will give you a lift. That's how I get there, or I borrow the Sousa's scooter."

"Can we borrow it?" Lizzie asked. "I'm really anxious to see her."

Gabby nodded. "She's going to be happy to see you, too, I think."

Lizzie pictured the copy of the manifest she'd brought to show her sister. "I think so, too."

Solange had kept Brianna Dare waiting for more than half the day, then let her into the attic "library" to read some innocuous paperwork about the Bettencourt family tree. Nothing that could support her ridiculous theory that Carlos Bettencourt hadn't paid for the delivery of treasures he'd ordered. The girl's ancestor was a pirate, and Solange's was practically Portuguese nobility.

Not that she cared about that nearly as much as this girl did. She was too, too close. Still, nothing she could find or produce would be as powerful as the fact that the scepter was on Bettencourt property today—and the other would be here soon.

All the wheels had been set into motion to retrieve

the mate, and the discovery would make Jaeger sick with remorse. *Then* he'd bring her home.

After the library, Solange brought the girl to the kitchen, suggesting she do a little cooking since Gabby was gone for a few days, then left her there to get the scheduled call.

The satellite phone rang right on time, but Solange hesitated when the ID wasn't a number she recognized. She answered tentatively, and the familiar voice's first words shook her.

"The dive is over."

"What do you *mean*, it's over?" she asked in a hushed whisper as she closed the door to her upstairs room. "How can it be over?"

"One of the divers was killed in an accident. The Coast Guard brought the FBI in, and Judd's filed an official claim, so the site can't be salvaged until next season. We're done for now, Solange."

Fury slammed her. "You didn't find it!"

"No, I didn't."

"That's what I've paid you to do!"

"We still have next summer. Of course, it'll be harder when the dive's not secret."

And Judd Paxton would be even more motivated by her husband's desire to own both of those scepters.

"Brianna Dare is sitting in my kitchen right this minute," she said, measuring every word for the most impact. "She and her sister have done a tremendous amount of research. It's only a matter of time until they know all that Malcolm Dare knew."

"We can handle that."

Did she really want this many deaths on her conscience? Was vengeance worth that price?

"I can't . . ." *Afford another accidental death on my farm*. But she didn't want him to know about Ana. ". . . do anything, except slow this girl down. What are you going to do about that one?"

"I haven't decided yet."

"Well, you better do something, and fast."

"No one knows Brianna Dare is there," he said, his voice rich with implication.

"She flew to Corvo, and to Terceira from Lisbon. The authorities could track her."

"Does anyone know she's at your house?"

She knew exactly where he was going with this. "Just a housekeeper."

"And would she question it if you told her your houseguest left?"

"Probably not."

"Then you need to stop her, Solange."

Her stomach rolled at the thought. Getting rid of Ana had been a momentary act of madness and fear. What he was suggesting was premeditated.

"I don't know . . . how."

"Figure it out," he ordered.

"Excuse me?" she shot back. "The last time I checked, you worked for *me*."

"I'm offering you counsel," he said, softening his tone. "No one knows she's there at your farm, but that could change any minute. You have to get rid of her— and Solange, you have to hide the body. Destroy it and any evidence."

Her throat tightened at the thought. "They'll track her here eventually."

"And you'll say she came and went, without any explanation of why she wanted to leave. It makes sense that her father's research would lead her to you ultimately, but by the time the next diving season starts, this will be ancient history. And I promise you, you *will* end up with the matching pair of the Bombay Blues, the owner of one of the greatest artifacts in the world."

Jaeger would explode with envy. He'd realize how resourceful she was, how talented. And how he should never have let her leave. He'd love her again.

"Do you really think I have to . . ." *Kill again.*

"Yes, you do. And you must be very thorough and neat."

It didn't sound very neat to her. It sounded . . . sickening.

"I really have no idea how to kill a person and destroy the evidence."

"Use your imagination."

Her gaze flicked to the windmill that blocked her view. "I will."

She finished the call, sipped some sustenance, and headed back to the kitchen to convince Brianna Dare to tour the windmill.

"Everything of real interest in this place is in the windmill," Solange said as they walked toward the structure, the soft whoosh of the sweeps getting louder as they got closer. "This windmill was around when your Aramis and my Carlos were alive. Think about that, Brianna."

"Amazing," the girl replied, clearly not that interested. If she knew what was hidden there, she'd be much more enthusiastic.

The secret made Solange smile. "I considered taking it down because it blocks the view." Solange opened the door to the first level, where the sound changed to a constant groaning, creaking, moaning noise caused by the massive wooden mechanism that took up most of the wide, round structure. "But then I had a change of heart."

"Why?"

"Apparently there are only a few windmills of this type left on Corvo, with those three sweeps and that big center wheel that can make them turn in either direction. These are found nowhere else in the whole world."

"Fascinating."

"Oh, but it is," Solange said. "This is the main floor—the meal floor, they called it." She waved a hand across the dimly lit area, pointing to the huge wheel that lay on its side, turning noisily around a fat wooden tube where grain once poured down, ground by the maceration of the wheels and cogs and gears on the level above them.

"It was used to make flour," she continued, chattering faster as her nerves tightened at what she was about to do. "I suppose I could convert it to a power-producing windmill, but I just like the old-fashioned kind of electricity. The kind you get from the wall."

"Oh, I see." Poor Brianna could hardly hide her disinterest.

"The stairs are the best part," she said, nudging Brianna toward the opening to the long set of circular stairs that curved around and up to the top floor.

"They feel kind of medieval," Brianna commented, starting the climb.

"Don't they, though?" Solange agreed. After the fourth step, the wall blocked their view into the gears. "All the way up, you can peek through those slats to the mechanism in the middle. See?" After a moment, they reached the first opening and Brianna peered out.

"Whoa. That's kind of . . . intense."

What was intense was right under her feet. She was inches from the treasures she sought and had no idea. What else could be hidden under the stairs?

A body, perhaps.

A shiver ran down Solange's spine. Could she actually do this?

She had to. "Look at that, Brianna," Solange said, pausing at an opening. "That is the great spur wheel."

This wheel stood on its side, unlike the one at the bottom. Its massive, sinister-looking wooden teeth meshed with three other cogs, all sharp enough to macerate stone into sand.

Brianna stopped and stared, the groan of the wheel almost deafening at this point.

"If you don't use it for power or milling, why is it running?"

"Oh, it never stops," Solange said. "The wind in the Azores never, ever stops."

"You mean you can't stop the mill at all, ever?"

"There's a brake somewhere, I believe." Solange put

her foot on the very stone where she'd hidden the scepter. "Come on—the top is the best part."

The stairs ended at a small door, not five feet high.

"You'll need to crouch a little to get in," Solange warned. "But go ahead. It's worth it."

Brianna entered and let out a gasp of surprise. "Wow, this could be dangerous."

Yes, it could. A two-foot-deep ledge circled the inside of the windmill, open all along one side to where someone could easily tumble right into the grinding mechanism.

Solange looked at it, and imagined that happening.

Brianna put her hand on the wall, bracing herself and peering over to look at the wheel. "That's not for the faint of heart," she said, but didn't appear worried. "Why don't you put a railing up or something? If someone falls in there, you'd have a helluva lawsuit on your hands."

"No one ever comes up here," she said.

"Well, apparently your nurse came up here recently."

Solange gave her a hard look. "She wasn't my nurse. She was my housekeeper. And a very disturbed and sad young lady, I might add."

"Really?" The note of accusation in her voice was unmistakable.

"Really." Where had she heard anything about it? Gabby? She *knew* bringing that woman up here had been a mistake. If they'd talked about Ana . . .

"So is this door where the windmill blades are?" Brianna reached for the door to the balcony and sweeps, but Solange stopped her.

"That's *really* not for the faint of heart," she said.

"Don't worry, I'm not." She twisted the knob and opened the door, almost stumbling backward at the unexpected gust of air. "Whoa."

If she stepped out there, it would be so much easier. But inexplicable. Another fall from the windmill down the cliffs? Besides, she couldn't risk a body as evidence.

The windmill sweeps roared outside, the steady, thumping rhythm filling the structure.

Brianna used her right hand to brace herself, her face away from Solange as she fought not to look down. "This is such a cool view. But, wow, I can't even imagine what drove that girl to throw herself off of here." Again, the note of . . . doubt.

She was about to find out exactly what drove her.

Solange slipped her hand into the pocket of her pleated skirt, her fingers closing over the revolver. With her thumb, she pulled back the hammer.

At the distinct sound, Brianna whipped around just as Solange pulled out the gun. She gasped in shock. "What the hell?"

"You're going to do exactly as I say."

The blood drained from Brianna's face, no words coming out of her open mouth.

Solange's mind whirred. If she fired, the recoil could knock her over, or at least off balance enough to give this wily and strong young woman the upper hand. The wind was still blowing in from the slightly open door.

She took a careful step back, trying to figure out the best way to choreograph this.

"What is your problem, lady?" Brianna's voice was

shaky, but anger was already taking over fear. Solange had little time.

"You are my problem, I'm afraid."

"What?" She scowled, but then her face softened. "Look, Mrs. Bettencourt, you're not well. You need to put that gun down and let us both get out of this place."

"Actually, I'm fine." She aimed at Brianna's heart, bracing herself against the wall for more balance.

"Please." Brianna tried to swallow, her gaze moving from Solange's face to the gun and back, her lip beginning to quiver. "I can help you. Put the gun down and we'll talk. You need help."

Solange scowled. "I don't need anything." Except the nerve to murder in cold blood. Again. She tightened her finger on the trigger and Brianna's eyes widened.

"What do you want?" Brianna asked. "I haven't done anything! Why could you possibly want to kill me?"

"I don't." Once the words were out, Solange regretted them. She'd just given away some power, and that was never a good thing.

Instantly, Brianna's face changed. She started to back up toward the door, nudging it.

"Don't," Solange said sharply. She couldn't risk someone else going over the edge. "Don't go out there unless you want to fall."

"Like Ana did?" she shot back. "You killed her, didn't you? You freaking psychopath—you killed her!"

"Stop it!" She waved the gun. "Shut up."

But Brianna kicked the door open enough for a powerful gust to blow in, stepping toward the balcony.

Outside, a motor scooter climbing up the hill caught Solange's eye.

Oh, Lord, this was not good. Tourists always stopped and took pictures of the windmill. If they saw a body fall, she'd be forced to explain *another* death over the cliff.

Brianna turned to follow her gaze and Solange grabbed her arm, yanking her back into the windmill with so much force they damn near both went over the ledge.

"Hey!" Brianna lunged at Solange to knock the gun away.

She squeezed the trigger and the shot exploded through the stone mill.

Instantly Brianna froze, her eyes wide in stunned disbelief, her hands clamping to her shoulder as her legs gave way. She buckled to her knees, a gasp catching in her throat as she hit the stone, blood seeping through her fingers.

In the distance, Solange heard the soft whine of the motor scooter, closer now. She didn't dare fire another shot.

Brianna moaned in misery, folded in half now, her face to the ground, her body perilously close to the ledge where the gears turned. In there, the giant cogs would crush her, breaking every bone in her body. She couldn't possibly be strong enough to hold them in place, especially wounded.

But if she bled on the gears then Solange would have to clean them off, and she didn't want to even think about that. The motor scooter grew louder, nearing the house. Damn it!

Just as she lifted the gun to take the chance and finish the girl off, Brianna slumped completely, inches from the edge.

Voices rose from below as the engine quieted. Solange bent over, trying to see if Brianna was still breathing, but couldn't tell.

She had to take the chance and leave her here long enough to get rid of the bothersome tourists. Then, she'd come back and finish the job of killing Brianna Dare and hiding her body.

CHAPTER
TWENTY

CON GAVE LIZZIE a hand off the bike, looking around at the picturesque farmland rolling toward a stone windmill perched on a cliff above the sea.

"Pretty," Lizzie said, turning to follow his gaze. In the distance, a few boats dotted the water between Corvo and the slightly larger Flores, but then it was clear for the thousands of miles straight out to North America.

"Pretty deserted," he replied.

"I know," she agreed, turning to the stucco farmhouse. "I was kind of hoping Bree would come running out to hug me."

The whole place was silent but for the steady thump of the windmill sweeps and the distant pounding of the surf. Other than that, Con heard no signs of life at all.

Lizzie bounded toward the door, and he caught up with her in one stride.

"Easy, there." He moved her a little behind him. "Let me go first. We have no idea what we're going to find."

"My sister, I hope."

"You never know."

She gave him a tentative glance, then let him stand in front as he knocked on the door.

"Can I help you?" The voice came across the open field, sharp and strident. Exiting the windmill, a woman strode toward them like she was modeling on a runway, shoulders square, head held high, with an air of authority and haughtiness that was laughably out of place on a farm in the Azores.

This was no country woman.

"I hope you can," Con replied, walking toward her and automatically blocking Lizzie. "We're looking for a houseguest of yours. Brianna Dare."

She slowed her step, an imperceptible change in her body taking her from in control to on guard.

"Are you Mrs. Bettencourt?" he asked when she didn't respond.

As she got closer, he took in the cheekbones, square jaw, and pricey clothes, a jarring contradiction to the rugged stone windmill behind her. Blond hair with darker roots was pulled back in a hasty ponytail.

"Yes, I am," she finally said. She stood with her hands in the side pockets of a full skirt that covered her knees, tense enough that he suspected her fists were balled in those pleats.

"My name's Con Xenakis. This is Elizabeth Dare. We're looking for her sister, who we understand is staying with you."

She kept her gaze on Con, slowly shaking her head and looking confused. Then her eyes widened and the closest thing to a smile he'd seen yet pulled at her hollow cheeks.

"Brianna! The girl from America who was here yesterday?"

"Was?" Lizzie stepped forward. "She's gone?"

"Oh, I'm afraid so. Early this morning on the first ferry to Flores." She looked at her watch and then glanced toward the water, where a boat chugged toward the other island. "And it looks like you've missed the afternoon ferry. I wish I could help you."

"Maybe you can," Con said. "We're looking for the same genealogical information. Could you tell us what you told her?"

She shrugged. "I didn't tell her anything. I'm only a Bettencourt by marriage. I live here alone and have no access to any of the family information. Maybe the church in the village? That's what I told her. Sorry."

She stepped forward, nodding like a queen dismissing the messenger.

Con stepped sideways and blocked her. "She flew into Corvo, Mrs. Bettencourt. It makes no sense that she'd take the ferry to leave."

Through narrowed eyes and a clenched jaw, she made her distaste clear. "It makes perfect sense. She is on a lineage search, as are many Americans who come to the Azores. Bettencourt is as common a name on these islands as Smith is in the United States. Perhaps she went sightseeing to the other island. There's absolutely no reason to accuse me of anything."

He notched a brow. "I didn't accuse you. I questioned your logic."

"Well, I don't like your tone." She finally glanced at Lizzie. "I'm sorry about your sister."

It sounded oddly like a condolence. Solange walked around Con, marching to the front porch without a glance back. As much as he wanted to grab her arm and demand entry, he knew he couldn't. He had no right or reason.

"Come on." He placed a hand on Lizzie's shoulder to guide her toward the bike, slowly. The front door closed with a deliberate slam.

"Jeez," she said.

"Give it a sec," he said, getting on the bike and waiting for her to settle in before he started it up and headed toward the road. At the last second, he turned toward the windmill.

"What are you doing?" Lizzie asked.

"I don't want to leave yet." He parked the bike behind the structure, where it couldn't be seen from the house, and climbed off. "We'll stay in here for a while and see what she does. If she leaves the property, we might walk through her house to see what gives."

"What are you looking for?" Lizzie asked.

"I don't know. She gave me a bad feeling."

"No kidding. Who let *her* out of the bitch factory?"

He smiled, pushing the door open with one hand, peeking in before entering. The grind of gears and wheels echoed over the stone.

"This is a different kind of windmill," he observed, peering up at the mechanism in the middle and then at the stone stairwell that lined the wall.

The door popped open with a crack and he whipped around, blocking Lizzie.

"Get the hell off my property." This time, the bitch was armed. She raised a revolver, cocked and ready, and pointed it at him, earning a gasp from Lizzie.

"We're just looking at the windmill," he said, holding up his hands, considering what it would take to get her gun.

"You are trespassing, and I will shoot you both if you don't leave this minute."

He couldn't take a risk with this madwoman. "All right."

Still protecting Lizzie with his whole body, he led them out, never taking his eyes off her or the gun, ready to dive in front of a bullet if he had to.

"Get in the front," he said softly, nudging Lizzie there when she gave him a questioning look. "If she shoots, it's going in my back."

She hesitated, then climbed on, and he got behind her, reaching forward to turn the ignition on.

Mrs. Bettencourt never lowered the gun.

Lizzie twisted the handle, her body bracing as though she expected the gun to go off any second, then she drove down the dirt path and onto the road to the village.

As soon as they were in the clear, she put a hand on his leg and squeezed. "Con, you're officially off my shit list."

"It's about time." But his mind was on that woman. She was scared of something, and it wasn't a couple looking for a missing tourist. So what was it?

He wasn't leaving this island until he found out.

* * *

She really, really wanted to hate him. It should be so easy.

Lizzie kneeled on the twin bed in the attic room on the third floor of Sousa's restaurant, her elbows propped on the windowsill with a direct view of the rooftops to the sunset over the Atlantic Ocean.

Sitting on the floor, Con was making another phone call. On the last one, to New York, he'd ordered background information on Solange Bettencourt. Now he was talking to the pilot of their plane.

She turned to look at him, elbows propped on bent knees, sitting against the wall, his eyes closed as he spoke softly. His whiskers had grown in enough to give his angular jaw a menacing shadow. Long, strong fingers held the phone, and she couldn't help studying those hands for a moment, remembering how he touched her, entered her, made her whole body—

"Do you want to, Lizzie?"

She pulled herself from sexual la-la land and blinked at him.

"Do you want to fly to Flores now? It's bigger than Corvo, so we could fan out and check the hotels and inns there. Or we could stay here to get some rest and see if she comes back on the morning ferry, or even fly over at daybreak." He closed the phone. "You look like you could use some rest."

"I'd really like to talk to Gabby, too. *Senhor* Sousa said she comes back every night, even if she's left for the day. She might know exactly where Bree is, saving us a ton of time and effort."

He gave a quick nod and spoke into the phone.

"We're going to stay put for now, Captain. I'll keep you posted." He ended the call, then stood to stretch, his gaze on her. "What's the matter?" he asked.

"Why?"

"You're looking at me funny."

"Am I? I was just trying to hate you."

He laughed softly, dropping down on the bed next to her. "Anything I can do to help that along, just let me know."

"That's just the problem," she said, scooting to lean against the headboard. "You do *everything* to help."

"I didn't come along to be a hindrance, Lizzie." He reached over, closed his hand around her ankle, pulling one bare foot and then the other to straighten her legs. "Although you probably hate me because the room only has one little bed."

He applied pressure with his thumbs on the balls of her feet, making her toes curl with the wonderfulness of the simple, strong massage.

"And a floor," she said.

"You'll do fine on the floor," he teased.

"Right. You'd never make me sleep on the floor while you're on the bed."

"Who said I'd be on the bed?" He grinned. "And I might make you sleep down there, but I'll give you the comforter."

"No, you wouldn't—and that's just the problem."

His fingers stilled as he frowned. "Not following, Lizzie. Why exactly is that a problem?"

She wiggled her toes and he got the message, rubbing again. "It's really hard to hate someone who is so . . ." Thoughtful. Competent. Protective. Gorgeous. Smart. The list was laughably long, so she went for the obvious. "Good."

He shook his head. "Just think about Judd and you'll hate me fast enough."

"I tried. Then you go and do something like sit on the back of the bike so you can take a bullet for me. How am I supposed to hate that guy?"

He chuckled. "I see your dilemma."

"Anyway, I thought the job for Paxton was done." Lord, was she that pathetically attracted to him that she could forgive him already? He worked his way up to her ankles, his fingers melting her feet with each touch. Yes—she was that pathetically attracted to him.

"The job on the ship is done," he said. "We're here and the job is to help you track down your sister, and get the information you need and want regarding your great-times-many-grandfather."

And she had to admit, he was going after that mission with determination and direction. She could never have done this alone. Not this quickly and efficiently.

"And deep down, to the bone, Paxton out of the picture . . . you really are one of the good guys."

Something darkened his eyes. Pain? Regret? Longing? "No, I'm really not, honey." But he looked like he wanted to be. "And let's be honest; Paxton could never be out of the picture."

"If he were . . ." When she let the words trail, he looked up from her feet to catch her gaze, his own suddenly smoky.

"If he were," he finished for her. "We'd share this bed."

Somehow, nothing could have been as flat-out sexy as that simple, straightforward statement.

The power of it shot right through her and rattled her nerves. She tried to swallow, but her mouth went dry, her heartbeat steadily increasing with each roll of his thumbs under her foot.

"But he *is* in the picture," he said roughly. "I won't lie to you about that again."

Taking a slow breath, she held his gaze. How could she say this and save her pride? *Could* she say this and save her pride? Did she even give a damn about her pride anymore?

"What if we . . ." The words lodged in her throat and his fingers moved slowly, intently, as though he could coax the words out of her. "What if *I* were willing to forget about him? To put the whole Paxton thing aside. Temporarily."

He released her feet and placed his hands flat on either side of her calves. Slowly, deliberately, he got onto all fours, then started moving forward, his eyes locked on hers like she was prey and he was a starving animal.

She couldn't move. Couldn't look away. His body was right above hers now, his face dark and set in an expression of control and intent. Breath caught in her chest, she lifted her head to hold his gaze, not certain what to expect, but knowing that whatever it was, she'd let him do it.

"Then . . ." He lowered his face, kiss close. "You . . ." One more inch, the heat rolling off him. "Would still be . . ." He put his mouth over hers. Not a kiss, just a whisper of a touch. "Very wrong . . . about what you think I am."

"I don't care." She let her lips move against his, putting the words right into his mouth. "Right now, this minute, I don't care, Con."

He completed the kiss, sucking in her admission and her tongue. Instantly, she wrapped her arms around his neck, trying to pull him down, wanting all of him on top of all of her.

He resisted, breaking the kiss. "You will care tomorrow, Lizzie. You will. And you have no idea how *not* good I am."

She searched his eyes, looking right into the depths of them. "I want to know."

"No, you don't."

"I want to know *you*." She put her hands on his face, the whiskers scratching her palms. "I want to climb right inside your head and figure you out."

"No, you don't."

"Would you ever let me? Would you ever let anyone?"

He opened his mouth, clearly ready to say no, but then he stopped.

She seized his hesitation. "Would you, Con? Because if the answer is yes, I want it to be me." Tears burned behind her lids. "I want to know who and what you are, and why you think it's so critical to hide it from me."

"Who I am?" Under her fingers, his jaw clenched. "I am Constantine Xenakis. What I am?" His eyes narrowed. "For the past six years I've been a professional thief."

Pain splashed in her chest, but she didn't move. She had to know this.

"And why it's critical to hide it from you? Because you deserve better."

He rolled off her and stood, leaving her cold and bereft and confused.

A professional thief. It fit perfectly. At least it fit with what he was able to do, but not with what he was doing right now.

And she *did* deserve better.

"Then what are the Bullet Catchers?" she asked.

He leaned against the wall and crossed his arms. "It's exactly what I told you—the best security and investigation firm in the business. I'm trying to join the company."

"And they hire former thieves?"

"They might. That's what I want."

"Why? To clean up your act?"

"So to speak."

A million questions formed and she went with the first one. "What did you steal?"

"Whatever people like Gerry Dix wanted. Art. Information. Jewels. Money." He lifted one eyebrow. "Treasures."

The word punched her chest. "Why? Just for money?"

"Because I could," he said gruffly. "Because I learned how as a kid, and after my brother Alix died, I left the SEALs, and the first thing I did got screwed up by somebody else. I got accused of stealing, because that's what I was, so that's what people thought I would always be."

"So you thought, what? Can't fight 'em, then be one?"

He shrugged, his defensive walls up so high Lizzie could practically see them. "More or less."

"I suspected something," she admitted. "Not that, exactly, but you know an awful lot about stealing stuff."

"I know everything about stealing stuff. I'm wanted in four states, and well connected to some of the people you hate most in the world—Judd Paxton and others like him, private collectors rich with money and greed." He gave her a sharp look. "You wanted to know, Lizzie. And now you do."

She certainly did. "Have you . . ." The words wouldn't come out. Did she want to know this?

"Have I what?" he prompted.

"Ever killed anyone?"

"No."

Relief rolled through her.

He smiled. "So maybe there's hope for me yet."

"I appreciate the honesty."

"And I appreciate the desire to . . . what was it? Get inside my head and figure me out." He lifted one shoulder. "Now that you have, no doubt you'd like to get right back out again."

Had she figured him out? She knew his past now, and it was ugly.

But the man in front of her was still made of something good. Wasn't he?

"I don't know," she said honestly. "I don't like what you've done, But I like the potential for what you could be."

He said nothing, but his face said it all. Gratitude. Surprise. Hope.

Outside the door, loud footsteps broke the moment, along with a hard rap on the door. "Miss Dare?"

"Gabby!" Lizzie rolled off the bed as Con let her in.

Gabby filled the little doorway, shouldering a large bag and greeting them with a concerned look. "I heard you didn't find your sister."

"Mrs. Bettencourt said she left on the ferry to Flores."

Gabby glanced at Con, then back to Lizzie, frowning. "That's not possible. I was on the ferry this afternoon and just came back. That ferry's small, maybe twenty people."

"She said she left this morning."

Gabby shook her head. "The morning ferry was canceled because of high chop in the seas, or I would have been on that one. She was not on the ferry."

"Could she have flown out?"

"No," Con said. "I already checked that. We got the names of every person who left via the Corvo airport today, remember?"

"There's no other way to leave the island, unless she had a private boat." Gabby frowned. "I don't like it."

"What do you mean?" Lizzie asked. "What don't you like?"

"That woman, Bettencourt, is certifiable. And I seem to be the only one who thinks Ana's trip off the top of the windmill was not the suicide everyone's claiming it was."

"Think we can get that scooter again?" Con asked.

Gabby nodded. "No problem."

"I'm going up to pay a visit to Mrs. Bettencourt." He reached under the bed and got his Glock. "This time I'll be the first to pull the gun out."

"I'm going with you," Lizzie announced. At his look, she held up her hand. "Don't even think about it. She's my sister, and I'm going."

CHAPTER
TWENTY-ONE

WHITE-HOT PAIN BURNED Brianna's shoulder, a vicious, blinding hole of hurt that seared through from front to back.

Which meant she was still alive.

Digging deep, she attempted to open her eyes, fighting the darkness of unconsciousness, desperate to awaken. She blinked, but that didn't clear her blurred vision. Shades of gray swam before her eyes, the smell of earth and sea and something metallic filling her nose.

Gunpowder.

The thought forced her head up, causing a suctioning sound as her face separated from a sticky, wet floor. Sticky with . . . blood. Her blood.

"Oh, God," she whimpered. She'd been shot by that lunatic.

Where did she go? Was she standing over her right now, aiming that gun at her head, ready to push Brianna into that grinder thing that belonged in a horror movie? Why didn't she say something?

Using every drop of strength she could muster, Brianna lifted her head higher, a wave of dizziness and nausea rolling over her as the sound of a gear a few feet away passed by then headed around the other side.

She managed to tilt her head back, her knees digging into the stone floor, one hand smashed against her wound. The bitch missed her heart, but left a hole in her shoulder. Was the bullet still in there?

She couldn't tell. And she couldn't see where that woman went. The door to the sweeps was closed, blocking out light. But she could see the ledge, only six inches away. And if she fell over it . . .

The nasty gear groaned as it rolled by again.

The teeth of the two gears meshed on each pass, crushing anything caught between them. *Not* the way she wanted to go.

Crazy Lady appeared to be gone. Brianna forced herself up on her knees, finally letting go of the wound, another whimper escaping her as she stared at the blood all over her hands.

But she was *alive*. And if she was alive, she could get the hell out of here before her killer returned. She didn't dare call for help. Solange might have left her thinking she was dead. She might just be planning to let her rot up here.

No one ever comes up here.

But what about Gabby? Maybe she'd come back. Had she sent the e-mail to Lizzie, telling her all was fine?

Lizzie. A whole different kind of pain gripped her. This would be Lizzie's worst nightmare: Brianna being impulsive and adventurous and getting herself killed.

Just like Dad.

No. She wasn't going to die like this! The thought was all she needed to ignore the pain and push herself higher, her knees sliding on blood.

The wheel moved by again, like a beast reminding her that he was right there to bite her. Carefully, she pushed herself up higher. The knife of pain cut through her shoulder again, making lights burst behind her eyes.

With a grunt, she slowly pushed up, her legs wobbling, her one sneaker slipping on the blood, the toe right at the edge of the ledge. She flailed, fighting for balance, the movement firing pain in her arm.

That sent her right back to her knees, cracking them on the stone.

"Son of a bitch!" she hissed, tears soaking her face.

She'd never make it to the damn door and down all those stairs. Despair clutched her, and she squeezed her eyes shut to push it away. She couldn't think *never*. She had to get out of this place.

Outside, the giant sweeps made a higher pitched whine that turned to a shriek when the wind gusted. Could she climb down the side of the windmill? The stones were irregular and jutted out here and there, and it wasn't that high. Not more than a three-story building.

She had no choice. That way, there was less chance of running into Solange and her gun.

Once more, she dipped into the last bits of her strength to force herself up. This time she made it, straightening her legs and finally getting control. It was just pain, she told herself. Just pain, not death. She could do this. She took one step, then another, reaching the door. She closed her fingers over the handle, turning it, bracing for the wind. A strong gust would send her right back into the gears.

She managed to open it, the wind whipping her hair and face, an eerie coldness shooting through the hole in her upper chest. She leaned out to look down, the angle too awkward to really see how steep a drop it was.

The other door flew open, creating an instant wind tunnel, pushing her like an invisible force straight back to the ledge. She tried to grab the doorjamb but just missed getting a grip, the wind ramming her backward, folding her almost in half. Two steps, three . . . her sneakers were at the edge.

She threw herself flat on the ground to keep from falling back into the gears, just as another deafening crack echoed. She looked to the entry door, but it had slammed shut before anyone had entered, leaving her completely alone again.

For a second the wind died down, and the door to the sweeps started to close without the force of the breeze. Then it squalled again, more forceful than before, slapping the door wide open and gusting over her like a freight train.

Her whole body slid over the edge. With nothing but the blood-slickened stone floor to grab, she went sliding into the pit of the gears, her foot jamming into a wooden wheel as it turned.

She opened her mouth to scream, bracing for the

pain, the sound of her bones breaking, the blackness of inevitable death.

But the groaning machine stuttered . . . then whined. She was lodged just enough to hold the gear back. But the beast was fighting her, and something told her that one killer gust of wind would finish her off.

"Help!" she screamed, her word drowned out by the cry of the machinery. "Someone help me, please!"

But no one could possibly hear her over the endless, deadly wind.

"That was a gunshot," Con said sharply.

Lizzie's heart clenched. Would that woman hurt Bree. *Why*? "I didn't hear anything."

"I did." Con squeezed even more speed out of the bike, powering up the turnoff to the Bettencourt farm. At the windmill, he vaulted off the scooter and instantly pulled her off. "You need cover. Inside, now."

"What?"

"I heard a gunshot. You'll be hidden and safe here, and I'll find out what I just heard."

As much as she wanted to believe he was wrong, she'd been with the man long enough to know not to question his hearing.

They darted over the gravel to the door, only to find it locked.

Con swore under his breath, reaching for his gun. He pushed her behind him with one hand and fired twice at the lock, the shot so loud she had to cover her ears. The door popped open and he pushed her in, then froze.

"What—"

"Shhh!" He held a hand up to her mouth to silence her, closing his eyes.

All Lizzie could hear was the infernal growl of the wheel, the moan that sounded like a woman—

Calling for help!

Con launched toward the stairway, disappearing into the darkness as he took the stone steps three at a time. Lizzie followed, the sound even clearer as she entered the echo chamber of the stairwell.

She rounded the curve, blinking in the dark, but seeing Con bent over a body.

"Bree!" She threw herself to the ground just as Con turned the woman over and two lifeless eyes stared up at them, blood oozing from a hole in Solange's chest.

"Help me!"

For a split second they stared at each other in shock, then simultaneously jumped up and ran up the last of the stairs.

"That's Brianna!" Lizzie cried, her foot slipping as she tried to take the stairs three at a time like he did.

Con beat her to the door, lifting a leg and slamming the wood with a solid kick. Lizzie practically pushed him out of her way, but he held her back. The area was nothing but an open pit, the stairs turning into a three-foot-wide ledge with no railing or inside wall.

"Bree!" She took a step toward the center, but Con yanked her back, diving to the edge himself.

Lizzie followed, falling to her knees, a scream welling up inside when she saw Bree four feet below, trapped between two massive cogs, her legs extended to hold back the turning wheels. Blood oozed from her shoulder.

"Oh my God!"

Con thrust her back. "Find the brake, Lizzie! There's a brake outside, under the sweeps! A lever, a rope, something turns this off. Find it while I go down there to get her." He flipped himself over the ledge so fast she barely saw him disappear, stunned as he dropped through the air and landed right on the cog of one of the wheels, his weight taking over the job of holding off the machine from squeezing Brianna any more.

"Find the brake!" he yelled.

She shot downstairs.

"Go below!" Con yelled after her. "You have to look below the sweeps!"

Leaping over Solange's dead body, she stumbled once on a loose step, bracing against the wall to save herself. Spinning around the wall as it ended, she tore outside.

Below the sweeps. *Below* them?

Flat against the stone building, she made her way around toward the front, the giant blade whooshing by her head at what seemed like fifty miles an hour, the wind pressing at her.

Peering up, she saw a rope, frayed and shortened with age, fifteen feet above her head.

The only way up there was to scale the stones. If she fell backward, she'd be sliced in half by one of the sweeps. She glanced down the cliff, which was equally dangerous.

There was no way Con could get her sister out of that machine if they didn't stop it.

She grabbed hold and started to climb the wall, every muscle quivering as she scaled one stone, then the next. Her fingers dug into the cold, hard wall, barely able to find a grip as the next blade whizzed by. She put one foot up, then the other. Using all her strength, she hoisted herself higher. The next possible step was hip high, requiring her to lift her knee up as far as possible, pull with both arms, and find her footing as the sweeps sailed by and the wind whipped off the ocean.

Forcing herself not to shake, she continued to climb, grunting with the effort, determined to make it.

The rope was within reach. One more step, one more pull, one more huge push . . . she finally got high enough and reached for the bottom of the rope, but she just couldn't . . . get . . . it.

A gust of wind fluttered the rope, catching the un-latched door above the windmill shaft and blowing it open, sending Con's voice out into the air.

"Hurry, Lizzie! Hurry!"

They were still alive! She stretched her arm farther than it seemed possible, closing her hand over the rope to pull.

It didn't budge.

Horror rocked her. Wasn't it the brake rope? Or was she just not strong enough? She needed all of her weight to pull on it, and if she grabbed it with both hands, she could swing right into a passing sweep.

She couldn't let them die.

Using every muscle in her body, she levered herself

against the wall, grasped the rope with the other hand, and hung from it.

It was coming down! It was *moving*! A grinding sound echoed as the sweeps slowed, and she looked up to see the lever attached to the rope moving down, down, down.

The sweeps grew slower. The groans lessened. The odds of Bree and Con living increased. Finally, when the brake lever was parallel to the ground and the rope had dropped so far that Lizzie was only two feet in the air, the sweeps stopped.

She did it. She *did* it!

"Can I let go?" she yelled up to Con. Her arms were burning, but if she let go and dropped to the ground, would the sweeps start back up again?

There was nothing but ominous quiet in response. Was she too late? Had one of them slipped and let the gears crunch them both while she was scaling the wall? She barely breathed, hanging on to the rope as if it was hope itself.

"You can let go," he finally called out. "I've got her. We're out."

She tumbled to the ground with a moan of relief, then ran into the building, seeing images of Bree, bloody and inches from death . . . and Con diving into the deadly machine to save a woman he'd never met.

He'd risked his life without a second's hesitation.

Who cared what mistakes he'd made in the past? He'd just erased them all.

CHAPTER
TWENTY-TWO

BY THE TIME the Azorean police officers left the scene, the sun was rising.

Lizzie had left with Brianna by way of the Azorean version of an ambulance, once they'd determined that the bullet had passed through her muscle tissue and the wound could be tended without airlifting her to another island. Con stayed with the police, participating in hours of frustrating communication in broken English and Portuguese, explaining that Solange was dead when they arrived.

That was, oddly enough, the easiest task of the night. The police believed her to be a recluse psycho who was rumored to have attempted suicide at least once in the past, and they were opening an investigation into the death of her nurse earlier in the week. Now they were gone.

He'd ride back to find Lizzie soon, but there was something he had to do first.

He had to call Lucy. He had to tell her he'd changed his mind.

Exhausted by the fight with the wheel to keep Brianna from being crushed, and the fight to communicate with the police, he dropped onto the stone step and reached for his phone, mentally preparing for one more battle.

His pocket empty, he tried the other one, glanced around, and realized his phone was gone.

A sign that he should skip the call?

Blowing out a breath, he stood to go back up to the top floor of the windmill where it had probably been lost in the battle to keep Brianna alive. That was probably the moment he'd made the decision, come to think of it. As he saved the life of one woman, and got blown away by the strength and determination and power of another.

He'd underestimated Lizzie Dare on every level. He'd truly thought he could use her, betray her, lie to her, take from her, and walk away—but all of that had changed tonight.

Especially after he'd thrown down the gauntlet of his inescapable past and she'd picked it up.

I don't like what you've done . . . but I like the potential for what you could be.

The words had annihilated him, and the moment she spoke them, he made a decision. He might walk away from this woman, but he wasn't going to screw her out of her scepter and diamond.

Looking down in case his phone was on the stairs, he noticed that one of the stones was knocked askew, leaving a gap beneath it. Great. His phone could be anywhere. He kicked the stone to put it back in place, but that just made it slide out farther. Kneeling down to do the job right, he discovered that the stone slid out of the opening as if it was designed to do that—and underneath it was a square concrete hole, the width of the stair and a few feet deep.

He looked up the rest of the curved steps. Were they all like this? He tried the next step, but it didn't move. He tried the rest on his way up, and found another one that opened, revealing . . .

A metal box.

Taking it out and laying it on top of the step above, he twisted the wire latch keeping it closed, then lifted the lid. Parchment papers with dark script handwriting lay inside. He took out the first one, but it was too dark inside to read. Taking the box down to the main floor, he read by the light of a window.

And felt his jaw drop.

The *El Falcone* manifest. Exactly the same as the copy the Bullet Catchers investigator had found in the Havana library, but this looked like the original.

The next paper was a detailed contract between Captain Aramis Dare and Carlos Bettencourt for payment in gold bullion for the delivery of two identical scepters topped with blue diamonds for presentation to the king and queen of Portugal upon their marriage.

After that, a letter written by Captain Dare demanding payment for the scepters, stating that he waited off the coast of Corvo Island.

Con read every word as the sun rose higher and the story became clearer. According to the paperwork, one of the scepters was delivered to Bettencourt, but Captain Dare was holding the second one until payment was received.

In addition to the letters, the documents included pictures of items. Some that he'd seen in Malcolm Dare's journal, some, like the Our Lady of Sorrows medallion, that he'd held in his own hands. And according to this, *El Falcone* took off in the middle of the night with only one scepter and diamond on board.

So was the other one . . . here?

Replacing the papers in the strongbox, he headed back to the stairs, checking every step on the way up. As he rounded the second level, he found another loose one. Pushing it to the side, he saw something white filling the hole. White velvet, he discovered. Closing his hands over the fabric, he felt something hard inside. Long and hard and familiar.

Lifting it gingerly, he laid the bundle on the stair, slowly unwrapped it and stared at the scepter that was indeed a perfect match for the one he'd already handled, topped by the very same breathtaking blue diamond.

Holy hell. It was right here under their feet all along.

He touched the gold, far brighter than the one that had spent its years underwater, and then the diamond. The value of just the diamonds was truly incalculable, he knew.

And he also knew what he had to do, to get everything he wanted.

He jogged up to the top, spied his phone, snagged it, and had Lucy on the line in a minute.

After relaying the entire story of Solange Bettencourt and making arrangements to get Brianna to a hospital in Lisbon as soon as they could, he added his final announcement. "I'll deliver the scepter and diamond to Paxton as soon as I get back."

"Are you certain you can get your hands on it?"

He touched the gold again, tracing the elaborate markings. "Without a doubt." He would hide this one from Lizzie and give it to Judd Paxton, satisfying Lucy's edict. And Lizzie could keep hers, and at least have half of what belonged in her family. He wouldn't have to betray her.

"That would be a real coup," Lucy said. "Exactly the kind of performance I want and expect from a Bullet Catcher."

Well . . . not *exactly*.

"How are you going to do it?"

"Just consider it done, Lucy."

For a moment, she said nothing. Then, "Fine. And talk to Avery as soon as she gets in this morning. She's unearthed quite a bit of information that you'll want, which might even help with the Azorean investigation. Mostly about Solange Bettencourt, but also Dylan Houser, who was connected with Malcolm Dare's death."

"Good. If you talk to her first, can you have her check something else? The police took Solange's cell phone, but before they did, I checked her call history. One number from the U.S. showed up quite a few times." He pulled out the paper and read it to her. "I want to leave here as soon as they'll let us, considering that we are witnesses in an open investigation."

"I have contacts in the Lisbon police department,"

Lucy said. "They are in charge of the Azorean police. I'll make sure you are all able to leave."

"Great. I'm going to check on Lizzie and her sister."

"Lizzie sounds like she's quite a fearless woman."

"Add it to a long list of attributes."

"And it sounds like you've grown fond of her."

Slightly. "Yep."

"So how is it going to be received when you take something she wants, and give it to a man she considers a mortal enemy?"

"I'll smooth things out with her," he said, rewrapping the velvet around the scepter. "I've figured out a way to keep her happy."

"Be careful about getting involved with a principal, Con. I don't like it."

"She's not a principal, Lucy. She's a target. And if I don't get involved with her, how else can I smooth things over?"

"She's going to hand over those scepters just for the joy of sleeping with you?" She laughed softly. "You *do* belong in this organization."

He smiled. "I knew you'd figure that out sooner or later."

Signing off, his smile was still in place. If everything worked according to plan, he'd get what he wanted, Lizzie would get what she wanted, and even Judd Paxton would be happy.

The truth would come out eventually, but by then he'd have given Lizzie all this paperwork, and she'd have what she needed to make a compelling argument that the other scepter belonged to her. She could take it public; the media would eat that up. She'd win by virtue of her name and her nature, and Paxton would be shamed into giving the other scepter to the museums where she wanted to exhibit them. Aramis Dare's name would be cleared, and Con would be a full-fledged Bullet Catcher.

And if she could see his potential now . . . she could actually *love* him then.

He hid the scepter in the step again, making sure the stone was secure. The papers in the metal box were coming with him.

Lizzie would go absolutely crazy with happiness. But first, he was going to make her absolutely crazy in a totally different way.

Lizzie curled up under the cloud of duvet, her hair wet from a shower, her body screaming for rest. She'd wanted to stay at the clinic longer, but there wasn't anything she could do for Brianna except let her sleep, and the two nurses were quite capable of watching over her.

Remarkably, Bree was in stable condition, drifting in and out of sleep, but not in any danger. The doctor in Corvo had been competent and spoke English, but Con promised to get her to a specialist in Lisbon as soon as possible and then back to the States. She'd have a scar just in front of her armpit, but with plastic surgery and physical therapy, she'd be fine.

An inch or two lower . . . or a few minutes longer in that mechanism . . . and Bree would have been dead. Lizzie shivered and tucked deeper into the mountain of down, just as the door opened.

She peeked out from the comforter to see Con filling up the doorway, a dark expression on his face, dried blood over his eyebrow from a cut he'd sustained in the windmill.

"Con." She barely breathed the word.

He just looked at her, his eyes narrowed, his chest rising and falling. No smile. No greeting. Nothing but waves of intensity rolling off him and threatening to flatten her.

He kicked the door closed behind him and dropped a box of some sort on the floor with a clunk. All she could do was stare at him, gripping the duvet in her fists as her heart rate climbed with each second.

He ripped off his T-shirt and threw it on the floor.

Her stomach took a roller-coaster dip.

He unsnapped his pants, kicked off his shoes, and pushed his jeans down, naked and fully erect underneath.

She opened her mouth to say something but nothing came out.

He stepped out of the pants and closed the space between them, the only change in his expression a tightening of his jaw, dark with whiskers and smudged from the battle with the windmill.

"Whatever you have on under there," he said gruffly, "it's coming off."

She dropped the duvet cover, letting it fall to her waist.

His gaze burned her bare breasts and he took a slow, deep breath. "That's a good start."

She removed the cover deliberately, exposing more and more of her bare skin.

A whisper of a smile curved his lips. "That's even better."

"Con . . . what . . . why. . . ."

"Lizzie, *what* is obvious, *why* should be obvious, and anything else, you can ask later." He set something on the nightstand that she hadn't even realized he held. A condom.

He put a knee on the bed and then straddled her, his hard-on pulsing over her stomach, his chest looming like a rock wall. He cupped her cheeks as he lowered his whole body onto hers, holding her gaze.

"This," he said as he closed in for a kiss, "is the last gentle thing I'm going to do until after you scream."

He kissed her mouth with . . . love. That was the only way she could describe the tenderness, the sweetness of the kiss. His eyes stayed open, locked onto hers, both of them lost and completely connected.

Her heart hammered, and so did his. Their tongues touched in a caress, a delicious silent overture that made her body warm and achy. She closed her arms around his shoulders, pulling him against her, opening her legs to get every inch of him against every inch of her.

He finally lifted his head, lasering her with his intention as he took her arms from around him and pinned them with one hand over her head.

His smile was dangerous as he licked his lips, tasting her kiss, then coming down for another—much hotter, much more demanding. If the first one was love, then this kiss was pure sex, burning, wet, slanted, deep, mouth-to-mouth fever.

And he didn't stop there. Still holding her wrists in his hands, he trailed fiery kisses down to her chest, making her gasp and moan as he licked one nipple to a peak, then the other. She pushed against his hand, dying to have hers free so she could guide his head, dig her fingers into his hair, somehow have some control, but it was impossible.

He suckled and kissed her breasts and flesh, his left hand sliding down her waist and over her hip.

He cupped her buttocks and moaned as he kneaded the flesh, and she bowed her back in helpless response, his hot hands making her rock with need for more. He finally slid his fingers between her legs, letting out another groan of pleasure when he touched her wet, swollen center.

He murmured her name, circling his finger over her clitoris, then rolling it gently, kissing her just to make her completely insane. He slid his tongue between her lips the very second he slipped his finger into her, in and out in precisely the same rhythm but in opposite strokes. Tongue in, finger out. Tongue in . . .

And she couldn't touch him. He still hadn't released her wrists, heightening the sensation of being taken by him, maddening her, torturing her, blissing out every pleasure center in her body.

"Con, let me touch you," she urged when he returned his mouth to her budded nipple.

He just looked up, a smile threatening as he shook his head. Moving to the other side, his fingers curled inside her and twisted more pleasure out of her.

"This is me . . ." He stroked her flesh. "Doing you." He nibbled her nipple. "And you . . ." He thumbed her clitoris. "Coming apart."

"I am," she admitted.

"Not yet, you're not." He flattened his tongue over her breast, then sucked again, shooting sparks behind her eyes, in her belly, between her legs. His thumb twirled over her, his fingers flicked and fluttered, over and over until the need to free her hands was long forgotten, her brain only able to focus on bits and pieces.

The smell of salt on his skin. The achy thrum in her core. The zing of her nerve endings, the tickle of his leg hair, the wetness of his kisses, the moans from his chest, the feel of flesh against flesh, mouth against mouth, man against woman. His erection pressed against her thigh, burning and branding and making her beg to touch him—but he didn't relent.

"Now you come apart." One more shocking kiss. *"Now."*

The demand was incendiary, intoxicating, impossible to ignore as he stroked her inside, licked her outside, fired her everywhere.

She panted breathlessly as the shudder started low inside her and built, the orgasm almost within reach.

Her eyes closed, she couldn't think, couldn't let go of the sensation about to overtake her.

She felt his fingers withdraw, heard a condom packet rip, and opened her eyes to see him position his hard-on between her legs. He thrust into her, all the way, shocking her, taking her, owning her.

He plunged in again, holding perfectly still, suspending them both, then pumped fast and furious until her orgasm exploded deep and intense and long, making her cry out.

Then he finally let go, releasing himself into her with crushing, insistent strokes and a sweet, sweet moan of satisfaction.

Lax and spent, he laid on her, their breathing labored and ragged, their skin heated from the rush.

After they finally quieted, he said, "Now you can ask questions."

She smiled. "You answered them all."

Con shifted to his side. "But I need to tell you something, Lizzie. I shouldn't have waited, but I couldn't help it."

She put her hand on his lips. "Don't."

"You don't know what I'm going to say."

"It doesn't matter what you're going to say. I want to say something first, without you making any speeches or statements or confessions or announcements."

He fought a smile. "You'd like the one I'm about to make, trust me."

"You'll like the one *I'm* about to make," she countered, sliding over him to pull his whole body into hers. "It doesn't matter."

He waited for her to continue. "That's it?"

"What else is there? The past is past? You're clearly doing everything to change your life?" She stroked his cheek gently. "Your colors are true, Con. You risked your life to save my sister. You couldn't have shown me what you're made of better than that."

"Funny thing. I was thinking the same thing about you."

She smiled. "We're a good pair."

"We are."

"And you . . ." She just had to know this. "You aren't planning to take my scepter and diamond and give it to Paxton."

"No."

There was just enough hesitation to give her a squeeze of doubt. "Con? Are you lying?"

"No, I'm not. That *was* my plan, but not now—I swear it. The truth will come out. I promise."

She saw nothing but honesty in his eyes. "Then you're going to prove it."

"How?"

"I'll tell you who has it. I'm going to trust you with that information, and you're not going to do anything with it."

"All right."

"I gave it to Sam Gorman."

"And he'll keep it safe?"

"Of course. He certainly won't give it to Paxton. He's on my—our side."

"I give you my word I won't touch it." He kissed her softly.

She smiled. "We *are* a good pair. Now, what were you going to tell me?"

"You know that box I brought in?"

She rose up a little to see it on the floor. "Yeah. What is it?"

"The original manifest of *El Falcone*. Letters between

Bettencourt and Captain Dare. Proof that your great-times-many-grandfather was legit. Everything you need to clear his name when you take your scepter and diamond on its exhibit tour."

For a few seconds, she couldn't even process what he was saying. "Letters? Proof?"

"And if the other one is ever found, then you have a claim to it, wherever it is."

She pushed herself up, the words still barely sinking in. "You have proof and you didn't tell me when you walked in?"

He smiled. "I knew that once you opened that box, you'd forget all about me."

She nearly shoved him off her, rolling out of the little bed and landing on her feet, pouncing on the box. She kneeled in front of it, staring, then turned to Con.

He sat on the bed, as naked as she, grinning. "Go ahead. Open it."

She did, almost afraid to touch the parchment papers inside. She lifted the first one, the words swimming as if they were underwater, the Spanish slowly making sense.

El completos manfiestan El Falcone, Aramis Dare, el capitán. Sin registrada.

She blinked, sending a tear down her cheek, and she automatically moved the paper so it wouldn't get wet.

"I told you you'd forget about me when you saw it."

She looked up at him, another tear escaping. "No, Con. Nothing in the world could *ever* make me forget about you. I believe in you. And I know you'd never do anything to break that trust."

"No." Con's smiled wavered, then disappeared. "I wouldn't."

"I have to tell Bree. I have to show this to her."

"Go ahead," he said. "Take it. I need to hit the shower anyway."

As she stood, her gaze fell on the open bag near the foot of the bed, her *Gold Digger* baseball cap tucked into the side pocket. Scooping it up, she bounded over to the bed.

"Here you go, sweetheart." She placed it on his head, tugging on the bill. "For 'first hands' on the best recovery of the trip so far."

He just smiled. "Thanks."

CHAPTER
TWENTY-THREE

FOR A LONG time after Lizzie left, Con sat on the bed folding the cap in his hands.

How did this get so freaking complicated?

Was it when he agreed to accept Lucy's challenge and get that scepter from Lizzie and give it to Judd Paxton? Or just a few hours ago, when he found the second one, and cooked up a scheme that suited his needs but no one else's?

Life was easier before he grew a conscience. Life was easier before Lizzie.

Empty, quiet, lonely, boring, and bland—but easier.

The bottom line was that as long as he gave either scepter to Judd Paxton, he was lying to her. And he cared too much for her to do that anymore.

Lucy wasn't going to like it, but—

The phone vibrated in his hand, and he swore when he read the ID. He wanted to call her first, damn it.

"Hey, Luce. I was just about to call you."

"It's getting late and Avery has compiled a lot of

information for you. I spoke with my contact at the Azorean police, and you'll be cleared to leave there this afternoon."

"Fine, we can do that, but I have to tell you something. There's been a change—"

"Yes, there has, because I'm not finished."

Damn, the woman liked control.

"Solange Bettencourt's husband, Jaeger, is the man Judd Paxton has lined up to buy the scepters and diamonds should they be recovered from *El Falcone*."

"Really."

"In fact, he financed this dive, because he is the person who first found the map that pinpointed the location. Clearly there is a connection between his wife's awareness of the recovery effort and her death."

"There's a connection, all right. She had the other scepter."

"Excuse me?"

"I found it, hidden in her windmill." It wasn't how he'd wanted to tell Lucy, but all his plans seemed to implode the minute Lizzie forgave him his past.

"You're serious?" Lucy said when he didn't offer any more details. "You found it there?"

"Along with original documentation that supports Lizzie's theory that Bettencourt tried to rob Aramis Dare, and in the process the scepters got separated."

"Are you sure it's authentic?"

"We can have it checked, but it looks real. And it explains a lot."

"Like what?" Lucy asked.

"My guess is Jaeger Bettencourt didn't know that one

of his treasures had never made it to that ship, and that his ancestor had hidden it. Then, his estranged wife found it. And I don't think she killed herself. Unless the police are complete morons, they are going to figure that out when they examine the body. I don't know how long she was dead when we found her, but there was no one around, and no one passed us on the road down. I don't know who could have been up there—"

"I do. The phone calls she made to the U.S. were to someone on *El Falcone*."

"Who?"

"Sam Gorman."

Sam . . . *who had the other scepter.* "How does he know Solange?"

"It's not clear he did. But Charlotte Gorman did some conservator work for the Bettencourts' art collection, and they may have stayed in touch. But there's another connection that troubles me even more."

"What's that?"

"Recently, the Gormans donated a considerable amount of money to sponsor a diving expedition off the coast of Mexico."

"Is that unusual?" Con asked.

"The expedition was run by Dylan Houser, the man who was with Malcolm Dare on his last fatal dive. So, what's unusual is that the Gormans and Houser have at least a monetary connection. And the Bullet Catcher research database showed at least one other identity for Houser: a Douglas Haberstroh, who checks out as a free-lance diver, mostly out of the country, where he allegedly is now. None of this proves anything, of course, but it all makes me uncomfortable—especially since Sam and Charlotte Gorman are on Corvo Island right now."

"*What?*"

"They flew in directly and went through customs early today."

"Then they couldn't have killed Solange." But the fact that they were there made him want to race to be sure Lizzie was safe.

"They still need to be brought in for questioning. I want you to find them and get them to the authorities, and arrange for them to be transported back to the States."

"Will do."

"And congratulations on getting both scepters," Lucy added. "Judd will be thrilled. Great work."

He was already checking his weapon and pulling a shirt over his head with one hand. "I'm not giving them to Judd Paxton, Lucy," he said simply. "They belong to Lizzie Dare. The docs I found prove that. She's keeping them." End of discussion.

"The documentation has to be verified as authentic," she said coolly. "And one was located during a dive sponsored and managed by Paxton Treasures." She waited a beat. "Have you changed your mind about working for me?"

"I have had a change of heart, period. I'd very much like to work for you, but my position on this isn't going to change."

"That's very noble, Con, but in this company, I call the shots. If you can't work within those parameters, then you can't work for me."

"Fine." The Bullet Catchers weren't the only game in the world. Just the best.

He heard Lucy's soft sigh of disappointment. "You told me you could do this. And I believed you wanted to dig deep and find the good man that lived inside a thief's body."

He laughed softly. "I did, Lucy. Only you weren't the right woman to help me with that." He hung up, and set off to finish the job—his way.

"You're awake!" Lizzie peeked into the only patient room in the back of Corvo's tiny clinic. "How do you feel?"

Her sister turned slowly, obviously still in pain. "Like I was shot at and blown into a gristmill."

"Well, you were, sweetie." Lizzie sighed with relief and love. Leaving the door open in case she needed a nurse, she approached the hospital bed, taking in Bree's pale skin and heavily bandaged arm.

Bandaged and hurting, but alive. Once again, she closed her eyes and thanked Con.

"What's that?" Bree asked, her gaze on the box.

Lizzie grinned and lifted it. "A little something to improve your mood."

"Painkillers? Massive amounts. Street grade. Throw in a martini, and I'll be happy."

Lizzie laughed. "Okay, I'll ask the nurse for meds."

"Don't worry, she just left to get them. What is it?"

"You will not believe what Con found."

Even in her weakened condition, she managed a raised eyebrow. "Where did you find Con? *That's* the question."

"I told you, on the *Gold Digger*. And he's not just another diver, Bree."

"No shit. He's a really hot diver."

"He's a consultant for a security company. Like a high-end bodyguard and protection specialist."

"Are you sleeping with him?"

She grinned enough to answer the question.

"So you got to go on the dive, find the most amazing treasure, *and* do some Greek god while I sifted through Daddy's paperwork? *That* was fair."

"Your sifting days are over. This is the *real* treasure."

Bree tried to sit up and cringed in pain. "What is it?"

"Proof that everything Dad believed about Aramis Dare and *El Falcone* was absolutely true."

She got up then, eyes widening, broken ribs forgotten. "What? How did you get it?"

"Con found it after he finished his interviews with the police."

"Oh my God. Show it to me."

"No, show it to *us*."

Lizzie whipped around, shocked by the familiar voice as the door opened the rest of the way. "Sam! What are you doing here?"

Sam's blue eyes twinkled as he stepped in, followed by a smiling but tearful Charlotte, who reached for Brianna. "Look at you! It's even worse than they said."

Lizzie stood, still trying to accept that they were there. "How did you ever find us?"

Sam nudged his wife. "Thank Miss Relentless here."

Charlotte gave a gentle pat to Brianna, looking up at Lizzie. "Sam told me everything, and I was worried about you. After what happened to Alita and the whole dive going south, I just had a bad feeling. When he told me that you were planning to come here to fetch your sister, I just thought . . ." She angled her head, her eyes sympathetic. "You two have no parents. This is what your parents would do."

Brianna gave her a strange look. "Did you even know my dad?"

"Not long enough," she replied, ignoring the rude tone in Brianna's voice.

Lizzie noticed it, though, and chalked it up to pain. And the fact that Charlotte and Sam hadn't been married that long and Brianna might not have been on any of the dives they were on with Dad.

"You didn't answer your door the next day, and this one had me on a flight in hours," Sam said. He moved closer to the bed, glancing at the unopened strongbox. "You look pretty beat up, young lady. They told us you had an accident in a windmill."

"Who told you?" Lizzie asked, still trying to figure out how they got there, and in so little time. It seemed impossible that they could have waited for her to leave.

"The men in customs," Sam said. "As soon as we mentioned we were looking for two American women, they knew you'd been brought to this clinic."

"It's a very small island," Charlotte said, sitting on the bed and stroking Brianna's leg. "Everybody knows everybody's business."

"So what *is* that?" Sam pointed to the box.

"Treasure," Lizzie said.

Sam's eyes lit up as they always did at the mention

of the word. "I like the sound of that. What kind of treasure?"

Lizzie hesitated. But after handing over the scepter to Sam, it seemed a little crazy not to tell him everything. She flipped the latch and slowly opened the box. "Everything we need to vindicate Aramis Dare is right here. All we need now is the other scepter and diamond, and all of Dad's dreams will come true."

CHAPTER
TWENTY-FOUR

CON JOGGED TO the Posto de Saude do Corvo, barely acknowledging the young woman at the front desk as he threw Brianna's name at her and headed toward the back.

There was one patient room with the door closed, a nurse at a small station nearby. She stood as he approached, but he just headed in, expecting to see Lizzie.

The room was dark and Brianna was asleep. He glanced around, but there was no sign of Lizzie or the box of documents she'd taken.

"Brianna?" he whispered, stepping toward the bed.

"*Ela está dormindo,*" the nurse insisted, coming up behind him. "Asleep."

"I need to wake her." He touched her hand and gave it a little shake. "Please, Brianna. I need to know where Lizzie is."

"*Senhor!*"

He ignored the nurse and leaned closer. "Bree, wake

up. Lizzie's not safe. Neither of you are. Please tell me where she is."

Her lids fluttered and she let out a soft moan. "Lizzie . . ."

"Where is she?"

Her eyes slowly opened, dilated and unfocused, then closed again.

"Is sedative of pain," the nurse said, her hand on his arm. "No wake."

"The other woman? Sister?" He searched for the word. "*Irmã*. Sister—she left?"

"*Irmã!*" She brightened, nodding. "*Sim! Irmã.*"

"Her sister, yes. Did she leave? Go?" He made his fingers walk off, then tapped his wrist. "When?"

She shrugged and shook her head, responding in Portuguese, enough to communicate that she had no idea when Lizzie left.

"Alone?" he pressed. "Others? A man and woman? *Homem* and . . ." He couldn't think of the word for woman.

She nodded again, getting it anyway.

She held up two fingers. "*Homem e mulher.*"

Man and woman. A fist slammed his chest. *She was with them.*

There was only one place they could have gone. He thanked her and looked at Brianna. She wasn't safe here. He pulled out his satellite phone and called the pilot waiting at the airport, instructing him to come guard Brianna until he returned. Then he waited until the pilot arrived, an eternity that was probably less than fifteen minutes.

Outside, he scanned the streets. A cab was unheard

of, and unacceptably slow. There was no time to get the scooter, and even if he did, it wasn't fast enough, either. He needed—

A Ducati.

The speedy little sports bike was parked directly across the street, the key in the ignition. Of course. There was no crime in Corvo.

Well, there was some now.

He looked left and right again, the only people in sight an older woman walking toward the church with a white-haired priest.

He jogged across the street, threw a leg over the seat, and closed his fingers around the keys. The engine turned over with the distinctly mellow growl of an Italian bike and Con took off, knowing exactly where he had to go.

As he passed the priest, he silently asked the old man to pray he wasn't too late.

"He's a thief, Lizzie, and the sooner you realize that, the better off you are." Charlotte looked up from Solange's open desk drawer, where she'd been rummaging since they'd arrived at the farmhouse, her normally calm demeanor agitated as she searched for something she claimed could really "help them understand the documentation" that Con had unearthed.

But every time Lizzie or Sam tried to press her on exactly what it was, her answers were vague and she changed the subject to harp on Con.

The facts she'd somehow managed to get on Lizzie's lover were irrefutable. Any claims that he was not a former thief would sound as hollow to them as they did in Lizzie's head.

Especially once she'd convinced them to stop by Sousa's to tell Con where they were going, and he was gone. No note, no explanation. Just gone.

Where would he go without stopping by the clinic to tell her? It was possible she'd missed him between the restaurant and the clinic; there were plenty of winding back alleys throughout the town. Still, worry and uncertainty pushed at her heart. And the accusations didn't help.

Charlotte slammed a drawer shut and stood, shaking her head. "Let me check the bedroom."

Lizzie dropped onto a window seat that looked out over the property, stretching all the way to the windmill and the sea beyond. At a distance of what was probably the length of two football fields, the windmill looked small and sweetly picturesque. But it wasn't so small when she was scaling the side to get to the brake. And it sure as hell wasn't sweet when those gears nearly crushed her sister.

And Con had risked his life to save Brianna. He'd been a thief at one time, but he was a hero to her. She blew out a breath.

"If it's any consolation, Lizzie Lou, I like him." Sam had come up from behind, placing a gentle hand on her shoulder. "I know Charlotte has all these connections in the world of art and collectors, so this dirt on Xenakis undoubtedly has some merit, but I've seen the way he looks at you, honey. A man who feels that protective about a woman can't be all bad."

She smiled wanly up at him. "If he's so protective, why did he disappear?"

"He couldn't have gone far on this island. Give him time."

She nodded, looking out again. "This is when I miss my dad the most, you know. He was a great judge of character."

"I don't know about that." Sam chuckled. "He liked me."

"He did like you, a lot." *Never liked your new wife, though.* But there was no reason to hurt Sam.

"That thief's probably already been here." Charlotte's voice floated in from the bedroom down the hall.

"What is she looking for?" Lizzie whispered to Sam.

He lifted a shoulder. "She says she'll know it when she sees it. You know how she is with treasure and art. Has a nose for it."

"Did you tell her about the scepter?" she asked softly.

His expression grew pained. "Actually, no. I should have, but . . ."

"You were smart not to," Lizzie assured him. "For her own protection."

"Yeah." He didn't sound so convincing, but before she could pursue it, Charlotte made a disdainful *tsk* from the bedroom.

"He was probably here cleaning this place out while we were in the hospital with your poor sister," she said loudly.

"My sister whose life he saved," Lizzie said under her breath.

Sam put a hand on her arm. "If you like this man,

or even if you love him, go with your gut, honey. Be honest with him. Give him a chance to explain who he is and why."

"I did."

"And did you like what he had to say?"

"Most of it."

"Well, there you . . ." Sam's voice faded as his attention shifted outside.

A figure moved in the far distance of the road. Lizzie sat up taller, squinting to see more clearly. She was able to make out the shape of a man in dark clothing with dark hair or a hat, dropping a motorbike to the ground and then bending over, running as though he were trying to maintain cover, as he headed toward the gravel drive that led to the property.

Was that Con? It was too far to make out any detail, but it sure looked like he wore a dark baseball cap—exactly like the one she'd playfully put on his head when she left to see her sister.

But why was he trying to hide?

"That your boyfriend?" Sam asked.

"I don't know." She narrowed her eyes, trying to focus on the way he moved, the shape of his body. "From this far away, I think so."

Relief rolled over her. He'd come to find her.

"What's he doing?" Sam asked.

"I wish I knew."

He reached the gravelly perimeter surrounding the windmill, and hesitated. Was he looking up here? She couldn't tell. If he was looking for signs of life, he wouldn't see it, as Charlotte had insisted on parking their borrowed four-wheel drive in the back. Con had no way of knowing she was there.

She started to reach for the window, to open it and call to him, but something in the way he moved—or didn't—stopped her. Then he disappeared into the windmill.

"Maybe he thinks I'm in there."

"I'm going up to check the attic," Charlotte called as she passed, pausing at the doorway. "You ought to listen to me, Lizzie. The man is a known thief, and nothing is ever going to change that. Be glad you found out before he could rob you blind and break your heart. Can you imagine how badly he'd like to get his hands on those scepters and diamonds? It's no wonder he glommed onto you—"

"Char," Sam said softly. "Stop."

She just headed down the hall, her footsteps heavy on the wooden stairs at the end.

"I trust Con," Lizzie said emphatically, as though saying it out loud made it even truer.

Then he stepped out of the windmill, a swath of something white in his arms. Lizzie stared, leaning as close to the glass as she could to make out the man and what he carried. As he turned, a gust of wind fluttered the fabric, and the sunlight glinted a flash of golden light, a prism of blue. Brilliant, even from this far away.

"Oh my God," she said.

"Well, look at that." Sam's voice was stunned, and sad. "Oh, honey, maybe Charlotte was right about him."

"No." She refused to believe that.

Come to the house now, Con. She willed him to run

toward the farmhouse, looking for her. Or pull out his satellite phone and announce what he'd found.

But he didn't. He turned toward the road—away.

Her heart thudded in her stomach as realization hit.

"He knew it was in there," she whispered to herself. "He knew all along." While they made love. When he showed her the documents. When he playfully kissed her good-bye and . . . never said a word. For a second, she could barely breathe.

He had *used* her. He'd used the documents as a decoy, then sent her to see her sister and . . .

Partially covered by the thick lilac bushes, he slowed his step, pulling something—a phone, she realized—out of his pocket. Who was he calling? Lucy? Paxton? Another buyer?

"I can't believe this." The words were strangled in her throat.

"You have to find out the truth," Sam said.

She turned to him. "I'm looking at the truth."

"The truth is not always what it seems to be," he said, his blue eyes fierce on her. He stood and pulled out a set of keys. "I'll stay here with Charlotte. Can you drive that Portuguese Jeep? The Gurgel?"

She nodded.

"Go." He put the keys in her hand. "Go find out what he's doing and why. I just don't believe that man would hurt you. I saw good in him."

"Oh, Sam." She blinked back tears she hated, and put her arms around the other man. "So did I."

"Go." He gave her a little nudge, and tilted his head toward the hall. "Before she gets back and changes your mind. I'll tell her you . . ." He stared beyond her again. "He's headed north. What the hell's up there but rocks and cliffs?"

She shook her head, trying to remember the map she'd studied on the plane. "Nothing but hiking trails and farmland," she said. "And a mile-wide volcanic crater at the tip of the island. There's only that one road, as far as I know."

"Then go catch up with him, Lizzie. Find out what the man's made of. Your dad would want you to."

Would he? Or would he tell her to run as fast as possible in the opposite direction?

"And maybe get that scepter and diamond back," Sam added with a wink. "You know what they say, Lizzie Lou?"

"The blondes find the gold." They said it at the same time and she gave him another squeeze, jumping off the window seat. "See ya, Uncle Sam."

She hadn't used the name in many years, but he'd earned it.

Lizzie trotted quietly down the steps, out the back door, and leaped into the topless Gurgel.

This was definitely the right thing to do, she told herself as she turned the key. Regardless of what he was doing, who he was double-crossing, or why, he would never hurt her physically. Emotionally? Yeah, he could do some damage—some major damage—to her heart.

So what's the worst that could happen? She could hear his voice posing the question as she drove to the front.

Well, she could find out that he was a lying thief, or still on Paxton's payroll.

"That wouldn't be the worst thing," she said into the wind, her heart rising with the speedometer. "Better to know now than later, when I'm in love with the rat bastard."

Mud sloshed under the wheels as she powered down the drive and reached the road. Why would he go north and not toward the town where he thought she was?

The man is a known thief and nothing is ever going to change that.

She hesitated at the intersection, thinking she heard another engine around the curve in the opposite direction. After a second, when nothing came around the corner, she hit the gas to head up the hill, silencing Charlotte's voice in her head.

Yanking the wheel to the right, she slammed her foot on the pedal, shooting up the winding asphalt, the emerald foliage and lavender-blue flowers blurring as she focused on the road. She twisted around one corner, then another, still not seeing him. At a straightaway, she squinted into the wind, seeing a spot on the road maybe a mile away. Was that him?

He turned the next corner and she powered on, her hair blown straight back as the wind smacked over the windshield and pounded her. All that was left was the narrow, steep road up to the perimeter of the volcanic crater, the asphalt cracked and pitted up here.

Where in God's name was he going with that scepter?

With each quarter mile, new emotions took hold, numbing the pain in her chest. Fury. Resentment. Disgust.

She'd been duped.

So what? She wasn't the first woman in history to fall for a con man, and she wouldn't be the last. But she wanted that goddamn scepter, and when she got it, she was gonna smack him with it. Just so he knew exactly how she felt.

She spotted him ahead.

The road disintegrated at the top of the mountain into gravel and rocks, and she stopped the Gurgel, knowing she couldn't make it as far as he had on the motorbike.

She jumped out and started hiking, watching him in the distance as he climbed, still holding the white-covered scepter, over the last crest of the cratertop.

Why the hell hadn't he heard her? He had the ears of Superman. Was he that focused on his job? Or was she still too far away?

He disappeared over the edge.

Panting, sweating, burning inside and out, she finally reached the top of the crater, a hump of dirt about five feet wide. On one side was a steep, fifty-foot drop straight down to the ocean, on the other, a sloping grassy bowl leading down to a group of lakes at the bottom of the crater.

Lizzie pulled herself over the top, staying low to surprise him, trying to be quiet.

He was about twenty feet away, crouched over a large black bag. He'd left that there? When? How long had he planned this treachery?

Angled away from her, his face blocked by the low bill of her *Gold Digger* cap, he opened the white fabric to reveal the scepter. A soft laugh of victory escaped from his lips, the sound bruising her heart.

How could she have misjudged him so completely?

He stood and she did the same, ready for the confrontation. She opened her mouth to call his name just as he whipped off the cap . . . and shook out long surfer-blond hair.

"Dave?" The word was barely a croak. *Divemaster Dave?*

Instantly he swooped to the ground, picking up the scepter in one hand, a gun in the other.

Her jaw dropped, disbelief rolling over her.

She took a step backward, chills running down her back. "What are you doing?" she asked.

"*We're* hiding some treasure in the crater lake caves." He pointed the scepter toward the calm blue waters of the lakes. "But you're going to have to stay down there with it, Lizzie. For a long, long time."

"What? Why are you . . . I just don't get it, Dave."

"Not Dave," he said, climbing the slope to close the space between them. "Most people in the diving world call me Dylan. Your dad did."

CHAPTER
TWENTY-FIVE

THE INSTANT HE turned into the Bettencourt farm drive, Con saw the muddy tire tracks. A four-wheel drive.

Someone had recently left the farmhouse, headed away from town.

He motored past the windmill, not caring about the scepter he'd left behind. That didn't matter now.

Nothing mattered but Lizzie, and getting Charlotte and Sam Gorman in for questioning.

He parked the bike close to the house and had his weapon out by the time he reached the front porch. The door popped open before he knocked.

"Where is she?" Sam asked, scowling. Then his gaze dropped over Con's shirt. "Why'd you change?"

Con just looked beyond him into the dim front room. "Where's Lizzie?"

Sam blinked, his jaw slack. "I thought she . . ." He paled, stepping back to let Con in.

"What do you want?" Charlotte Gorman strode into the room, her hands locked behind her back.

Con wasn't taking any chances. He greeted her by raising his gun and aiming it. "I want Lizzie. And I want you two to take a ride with me. The Azorean police have a few questions for you."

"Get out of here, you thief," Charlotte snapped at him. Her fearless tone confirmed what he suspected: she had a gun of her own behind her back.

Sam held up a hand to her. "Char, I'm not ready to hang this man, despite the fact that he has a weapon pointed at us. Where did you go, Con?"

Con didn't know what he was talking about, so he looked from one to the other, measuring the dynamics, getting the impression these two were not in sync.

"We saw you," Sam said. "In the windmill. Lizzie and I were watching from the window."

Charlotte sucked in a breath so softly, anyone else would have missed it. But Con heard.

"It wasn't me. But *you* know who it was, don't you, Charlotte?"

"I most certainly do not."

He closed his finger over the trigger and pointed it to her face. "Tell me where Lizzie is right now."

"She doesn't know," Sam said, patting his hands in the air to silently beg for the gun to be lowered. "She went after . . ." He just shook his head. "She went after *you*."

Whoever she went after, it wasn't him. "When?" he demanded.

"A few minutes ago."

"Why didn't you tell me that?" Charlotte demanded. "How could you let her leave?" She threw a look at

Con. "I mean, it could be dangerous running after a man who's got . . . a . . ." Her voice trailed off. "A reason he could be dangerous."

Sam turned to her, his expression changing. "You know, Char, don't you?"

"Know what?"

"You know what he—what *someone*—took from the windmill." Sam glowered at his wife. "That's what you've been looking for, isn't it? That's why you insisted on coming here."

Con didn't have to ask any more questions; there could only be one thing someone would take from the windmill.

"Sam, you're wrong," Charlotte insisted. "I told you that I go way back with Solange—"

"Shut up," Con said, taking a step forward, the gun on her, his eyes on the other man. "Where did she go?"

"I really don't know," he said softly, shooting a vile look at Charlotte. "I don't know anything or anyone, anymore. Even my wife. Especially my wife."

"Not my problem," Con said. "But you two are. I need to take you in for questioning."

"All right," Charlotte said. "We've done nothing—"

"No." Sam cut her off and pointed at Con. "You need to find Lizzie. And you need to find her now. She's in danger."

The rightness of that punched him. But if he left these two, they might get away. They might get picked up in town, but he couldn't be sure. His assignment from Lucy was to bring them in.

But Lizzie . . .

He notched his head at Charlotte. "Put your weapon down."

"What?"

"Put your damn weapon down—fast!"

She brought both hands around to reveal a pistol. Con was about to pocket it when Sam reached out, his blue eyes burning at the woman he'd married.

"Give it to me," he said. "I'll keep her here until you get back."

Con almost laughed. "Right."

"I'm serious," Sam said, his expression underscoring that. "I've known this woman for two years, but frankly, I don't know her at all. And what I do know, I'm not sure I like."

"Sorry, not putting you in charge of security anyway." Con was already considering all his options. He could tie them up, lock them here until the police came. But that would take time, and Lizzie might not have time. He had seconds to make a decision.

"For the love of God, Charlotte, help the man." Sam's insistence surprised Con, both with its vehemence and its ring of desperation. "Who did Lizzie just follow? Where did he go?"

"I don't know," she said, her mouth pulling down. "I really don't. I mean . . . I think I know, but I have no idea where he's gone."

"Who?" Sam and Con demanded at the same time.

"A liar. A double-crossing thief."

Con wanted to throttle her, but forced himself to keep his voice calm. "Where did this double-crossing thief go?"

"I honestly don't know. He must have known where

the scepter is, and is hiding it." Her voice was heavy with defeat.

"I think he went north," Sam said, still holding his hand out to Con. "Please, Lizzie loves you. And I love her as a daughter. Please trust me to keep Charlotte here while you go get her. Go *now*. Every minute counts."

He handed Sam the gun. "Screw with me, and you'll regret it."

"You can trust me."

He had to.

Running from the house, he jumped on the bike to follow the tire tracks. When they dried up, he continued north on the only road on the island, imagining all the things that could happen to a woman who thought she was following a man to trap him in the act of breaking her heart.

Hopefully, Lizzie was mad enough at him to hurt the guy before he hurt her.

Because if he lost her . . .

He revved the Ducati over eighty and careened down the center of the road; every second counted if he was going to have the chance to tell her what he hoped she already knew.

The crack of a gunshot echoed over the rolling hills, the sound ripping through his heart. *Lizzie!*

Lizzie jumped a foot when Dave fired the gun at the ground near her feet, sending a small explosion of dirt and moss into the air.

"Thought I saw a snake," he said with a snide smile.

"You're scared of them, are you? You're lucky I didn't put two in that room."

She narrowed her eyes at him, backing up, aware that what was behind her was every bit as dangerous as what was in front of her. "The only snake on this island is you."

"And Charlotte." He pulled a dive mask from the bag, the gun still aimed in her direction. "She's snakier than anyone I've ever met."

"Charlotte?" Disappointment and shock weighed her down. "And *Sam*?" So much for her dad's great character judgment.

"Nah—Sam's not the mercenary his wife is," Dave said, stepping closer. "He's pretty clueless. You don't get one of these, Lizzie." He hooked a dive mask around his wrist, a movement she'd seen him do a hundred times aboard the *Gold Digger*. "But you can carry the tank. One tank—for me. Get down here."

She didn't move, still in shock. Dave had monitored the dive schedules and had access to the air compressor; he could remove an air intake valve and kill a diver.

All that time, all those inside diving jokes, all those days and nights and cakes and first hands celebrations . . . all that time, the divemaster had been her father's killer.

"Were you with him when he died?"

"It wasn't nice, Lizzie. I liked him."

She choked. "Well, I *loved* him, you son of a bitch."

"Hey, I was just following my benefactor's orders. But now that I've gotten rid of her, and you, I'll hide this." He took four more steps. "Now *move* it. I need you to carry the tank."

Dave Hawn. Dylan Houser. "How many identities do you have?"

"A few. Depends on the job, the treasure, the dive. Real name's Doug Haberstroh. That's what I'll use when I have both scepters."

"Are you kidding me?" She was horrified. "You killed a man for what? Fame? The recovered treasure? What?"

His expression changed. "Shut up, Lizzie. Talk time's over. Let's dive."

She shook her head again, backing up, sneaking a peek to see her options. Slim to none.

All she could do was take off to either side, get back down to the road she'd driven up on, and buy time. And dodge bullets.

"Don't even think about it," he said sternly.

There had to be another way. Another approach. Something he'd believe, something he'd fall for. A way to get him closer, away from the water, and . . . over that edge. She didn't dare look behind her to the cliffs.

But how?

Her gaze shifted to the scepter. She wet her lips, lifted a brow. "Can I touch it?"

"Very funny." Still, he glanced at the scepter for a second. "But I understand the appeal. It is amazing."

"Just . . ." She reached out her hand. "Once. I've never seen anything like it."

He was a ruthless killer but he was also a treasure hunter, and he understood the appeal of gold and gems. He raised the golden rod, the diamond capturing the pale blue of the cloudless sky.

"And worth gazillions." He looked at the diamond, grinning. "Can you imagine two of them?" He stepped closer and held it up, taunting her as he had with many treasures that other divers brought out of the sea. "Two of them will set me up for life."

But . . . Sam had the other one. "How do you plan to get two?"

"I'll be the divemaster when Paxton officially salvages *El Falcone* next season, and I'll get my hands on scepter number two then. Charlotte and I have it figured out."

So he *didn't* know she'd recovered the other one. Sam hadn't told Charlotte. Sam *wasn't* in on this. She sent up a silent thanks, because being betrayed by Sam would just be too much.

And Sam knew where she'd gone. Would he tell Charlotte? Oh, God, would he tell Con? She clung to the hope, but it could be hours before Con found her. She could be buried in a cave under water by then.

"Come on, Dave. Let me see it," she begged.

He tipped it back. "Come and get it, Lizzie."

She took a half step closer, not wanting to get too far from the cliff, her only weapon of defense at the moment. "How did you know the scepter was on Corvo?"

"I hooked up with that whackjob Solange ages ago in New York, and she put me in touch with Charlotte, who's so determined to get these things, she married Sam for the access. It's a small diving and treasure world, Lizzie, as you know." He indicated the lakes at the bottom of the crater. "You'll be missed, like your dad is."

White-hot anger spiked through her and she lunged for the scepter, yanking it from his left hand. He waved the gun, not able to hold onto the scepter and get his finger on the trigger, just enough of a hesitation that she grabbed the scepter with both hands, wrenching it from him. She instantly rammed it onto the gun, knocking it five feet away.

"Bitch!" He leaped toward her and she dove to the side, then whipped the scepter at his back with all her strength, knocking him forward to the very edge of the cliff.

His hand clamped on her shoulder and he pulled her with him, but she instinctively collapsed her knees, taking away his support so that he fell and slid over the edge. As he did, he managed to snag the hem of her jeans, yanking her toward him.

She kicked wildly, her shoe in his face, trying to lose him and push him over the edge, but he held tight, swearing and clawing his way back up and pulling her down at the same time.

She kicked again, then pounded the scepter on his fingers, cracking his bones and drawing a loud shriek of pain. Fury, hate, and the need to make him pay for her father's death exploded in her as she slammed at his hands over and over again, until he lost his grip on her. On the last whack, he managed to grab the scepter, using it to pull her down with him.

She cried out as she slid, grabbing the first jutting rock to hold her. He still held the bottom of the scepter, her hands clamped over the end with the diamond. She shook it hard, trying to make him let go, her other hand clinging to the rock that stuck out from the cliff.

He had nothing to hold on to but the smooth scepter.

One more violent shake, and suddenly all the weight was gone. She looked down to see his horrified face as he fell straight down onto the rocks far below, the ocean instantly closing over him.

She opened her mouth and screamed with every bit of power she had.

The waves crashed below her, and the endless, relentless wind of the Azores blew. She had rapidly draining strength left in one hand, and a priceless treasure in the other. Which hand would let go first?

Con shut off the Ducati's engine when he saw the Gurgel, determined to use his most powerful tool: his ears.

He heard waves against rocks. A horse neighing in the distance. The burp of a frog, the squawk of an exotic bird.

And a low, desperate plea for help.

Throwing the bike down, he ran up the path toward the top of the crater. Where was she? "Lizzie!"

A soft whimper was the only response, coming from . . . below? He dove toward the edge of the cliff, looking down a menacing drop. She clung to a jutting stone with one hand, six or seven feet below him, her body pressed against the almost vertical cliffside.

"I'm coming," he said, already rolling into position to climb down.

"Con." She could barely speak, tilting her head up to him, her face filthy with sweat and blood. "Dave killed my dad. And I killed him."

"Don't let go, Lizzie. Hold on." He couldn't find a foothold, and slid the toe of one shoe into a crack. There was no way to get closer than two feet, maybe eighteen inches, and still hold on to the rocks that formed the edge of the cliff. "Can you reach me with your other hand without falling?"

"I don't . . . know . . ." She twisted a little, and then he saw the scepter. He could reach that!

"Hold that up, Lizzie. Can you hang on to it and let me pull you up?"

She answered with a fraction of a nod and lifted her hand toward him, her grip tenuous around the diamond as she pointed the other end at him.

He closed his fist around it. "Hang on, honey. I hope to hell that diamond holds."

He used all his strength to haul up the scepter, his wet palms slipping against the hot gold. She rose a little, dangling for a second before her feet and legs hit the cliffside.

"Try again," she said. This time, she used the strength in her left hand to help, and he almost had her.

"Can you just get high enough to put a foot on that rock where your hand is?" he asked.

She nodded again, her face contorted as she worked with him, trying to get higher while he gave the scepter one more powerful pull. His hand slid and he squeezed, every muscle in his body taut with the effort.

"Your foot," he urged her. "Get it up there."

"I'm . . . trying . . ."

"You've got to let go of the rock, Lizzie," he said, seeing that she didn't want to trust the diamond. "You need to hold this thing with both hands to be able to get your foot up."

She looked up at him, tears and sweat streaming down her face. "I'm scared."

"I know, Lizzie. But try. It's our only shot."

She closed her eyes and let go of the rock, reaching up to the scepter and hanging on, giving him her entire body weight, her whole life depending on that diamond staying in the prongs.

He heaved her up and she barely got a toehold on the rock. Her body lurched a little, pulling at the scepter, and she threw her weight toward the cliff for balance.

Suddenly, her eyes widened in shock as the diamond popped off into her hands. "Con!"

He swooped down to seize her hands, grabbing her. Her fingers flew open to take his, the diamond sailing right out into the air, falling and bouncing against the lava rock all the way down to the sea.

With Lizzie in one hand and the scepter in the other, gritting his teeth, he wrenched her up to his level, then pushed them both up the last two feet.

She fell face-first to the ground, fighting for air, spent, bleeding, and filthy. With his last ounce of strength, he thudded the scepter onto the dirt between their faces.

"All that," she said, struggling for a breath as she closed her hand over it, "and it's not a matched set anymore."

He covered her fingers with his. "No. But we are."

CHAPTER
TWENTY-SIX

"NICE OFFICE." LIZZIE'S eyes widened as Con rounded the drive to a massive three-story Tudor mansion high above the Hudson River Valley. "You'd be a fool not to take this job."

"We'll see." He reached over and took her hand. "I have some very tough contract stipulations."

He parked in the circular drive by the fountain, noting the limo at the other side. Maybe he shouldn't let her be surprised by this.

She didn't seem to notice the car, since it fit right in the surroundings anyway, but leaned forward to drink in the rustic beauty of Lucy Sharpe's home and the Bullet Catchers' headquarters. He used the excuse to draw her closer, kissing her hair, then tilting her face up to get to her mouth.

"What was that for?" she asked.

"I need a reason?"

"No, but that kiss had a purpose."

"Every kiss has a purpose. To show you how I feel about you."

She smiled. "I know how you feel about me."

Then maybe she wouldn't want to kill him when she walked in. But if he had told her, she would have refused to come. And having her here was critical to their success.

As they reached the front, the door opened, held by Avery Cole, a young woman with wide-set brown eyes and sleek dark hair, her dimpled smile warm.

"Hello, Con," she said, inviting them in with a glance toward Lizzie. "I don't think Lucy mentioned that anyone else was coming to the meeting today."

"This is Lizzie Dare, Avery," Con said. "I thought she should be here."

After they greeted each other, Avery warned Con, "Lucy's not big on surprises."

"I've heard."

"I'll let them know you're here." She disappeared up a wide set of mahogany stairs, leaving them in an over-size entryway alone.

He should tell her now, but that would still give her time to bolt.

Taking her hand, he pulled her closer. "We're a team, Lizzie," he said in her ear. "Don't forget that."

She looked up at him, confusion darkening her eyes. "I still don't know why you want me here to negotiate your contract."

"That part of the meeting is later. *This* part is why I want you here."

She frowned. "What part?"

Avery appeared at the top of the stairs. "They're in the war room, Con. Come on up."

Still holding Lizzie's hand, they walked up the oriental carpet that hushed the sound of footsteps. To the right, Lucy's library door was open, but the large antique writing table she used for a desk was empty. He led Lizzie to the conference and meeting room next door to that. When they reached the arched opening, she froze.

"Elizabeth Dare, what a wonderful surprise!" Judd Paxton's voice boomed his greeting as he crossed the room, hands outstretched, gray eyes twinkling. "I'm so delighted you are going to join us."

She turned slowly, her eyes narrowing at Con.

"Trust me, sweetheart," he whispered.

She had no choice but to return Paxton's handshake.

Con introduced her to Lucy, who seemed unfazed by the unexpected addition, but she'd make her feelings known later.

On one side of the room, a world map monitor marked the whereabouts of every Bullet Catcher. The rest of the screens that took up most of the walls were dark, a sign that, for one brief day, anyway, there were no major crises underway for the company or its clients.

Just the one brewing in the war room itself.

Avery returned, carrying a large container that she set on the table, opening it to reveal the scepters resting on black satin, the single blue diamond nestled between them.

Lizzie folded her hands and stared across the table at Con.

"Let's start out this meeting with a tribute to a very great and astute man," Judd said, settling in next to Lizzie, either oblivious or unconcerned with the palpable waves of discord from her. "A man I always admired for his dedication to the archaeological aspects of treasure hunting."

She dropped her eyes to the treasure on the table, working for control.

"That man," he continued, "had a saying I always liked. *Posterity, not prosperity.*"

Judd held out his two hands in a generous gesture of benevolence, as though he were blessing the scepters. "In honor of Malcolm Dare, I propose to have these donated to the country of Portugal." He beamed with the announcement. "Lucy, I would like someone from your company supervise the safe delivery of these to the proper officials and ensure that a Bullet Catcher team is part of the exhibit security when they are displayed to the public."

Lizzie shifted in her seat.

Con knew what she was thinking: without the matching Bombay Blue diamonds, the scepters weren't the world-altering treasure they once were.

"We can certainly handle that, Judd," Lucy said. "And what about the dives you're planning next season?"

"I don't think I'll need that level of on-board security again," he replied, his attention on Con. "But I owe you a debt of gratitude, young man, for identifying the real problem on my dive."

"And Lizzie," Con added.

"Of course, Lizzie."

"It was a team effort," Lizzie said. "Without Sam being willing to hold a gun to his wife's head, and then turn over evidence that will convict her, God only knows how Charlotte would have wormed her way out of this. Since the FBI investigators were able to trace Alita's death to Dare Hawn, we finally have some closure on my father's death."

"I agree," Judd said. "And as far as my stepson, I know he has personal problems, but his mother and I have decided to give him another chance, with additional responsibilities in the company."

Not as the manager of the *El Falcone* dive, Con thought. But there'd be a more effective way to drop his bomb, so he said nothing.

"Everyone deserves a second chance, Judd," Lucy said pointedly. "I think that's very wise of you."

"I'm sure I'll have a lot more business for the Bullet Catchers, however," Judd assured her. "And I'll add you to my list of preferred specialists, Con. Assuming you are signing on permanently with the operation."

Lucy smiled. "We're working out the details in our next meeting."

Con leaned forward. "No."

"Excuse me?" For once, Lucy was fazed. A little.

"I'm saying 'no' to giving these to Portugal," Con said.

"Con." Lucy put a calming hand on his arm. "We understand your position that they belong to Ms. Dare's family, but the fact is that the scepter that is intact was recovered on a salvage dive sponsored by

Paxton Treasures. And, Lizzie,"—she turned to address the other woman—"you really have no claim to it without a long and arduous legal battle. The other scepter is not that valuable without the matching diamond. This is the best solution, giving you exactly what you want: the treasure in a public museum and not in the hands of a private owner."

"Not enough," Con said quietly.

"Con, we don't negotiate with our clients."

"I'm not part of this company yet, Lucy, so this man is not my client." He turned to Judd. "And, frankly, this isn't a negotiation. And this isn't just about the scepters; it's about the entire *El Falcone* salvage effort."

Lizzie sat up straighter, a soft intake of breath.

"Every single item recovered is going to be donated for exhibit and display in a museum." Con crossed his arms and leaned forward, meeting her gaze. "And Elizabeth Dare is going to oversee the dive, the recovery, the conservation and cleaning, the processing, and ultimately will control the setup of the public exhibit. Paxton Treasures will finance the entire project."

The first hint of a smile teased Lizzie's lips.

Judd's jaw dropped open. "I'm afraid that would cost me millions and make me far less. I didn't get where I am in this world by doing business that way."

"No, you didn't," Lizzie said quietly. "You got there by muscling others out of your way, by forcing your agenda on the salvage and recovery industry, and by making your name synonymous with treasure hunting."

Mouth turned down in mock self-deprecation, Judd

shrugged. "I didn't do all of those things on my own, my dear."

"Of course not. You've had help from people like my father. From hundreds of divers and treasure hunters along the way, and quite a few wealthy people who bought what your teams brought up from the bottom of the ocean."

Paxton backed up. "Look, if this is going to turn into some kind of name-calling argument, I'm out of here. As Lucy said, there can be a legal battle. And you will lose."

"*El Falcone* is the biggest recovery effort in a decade or more," Con replied, ignoring the threat. "This is your chance to do the right thing, for *posterity*, not *prosperity*."

"Why would I do that?"

Con opened the file he had in front of him and slid a piece of paper across the table.

"This is a list of people I know personally. Some I've worked for; some I've worked . . ." He glanced at Lucy with a half smile. "Against. You'll notice they are some of the wealthiest art collectors in the world, as well as quite a few individuals who deal in the gray and black market of treasure hunting."

Judd read the list, his fists clenching tighter with every name. "What's the meaning of this?"

"Those people have personally guaranteed me that they will not purchase a single item of treasure salvaged from *El Falcone*. They are also spreading the word among other acquaintances to do the same."

The friendly gray eyes weren't so warm now. "That's . . . preposterous."

"As you know, the world of collecting treasure is a small one," Con continued. "This recovery effort is going to receive massive media attention and generate enormous goodwill as a worldwide traveling exhibition. The benefits to Paxton Treasures are intangible but tremendous. And, of course, there's the small problem of finding buyers . . ."

Judd read the page again, and while he did, Lucy's expression remained impassive. She wasn't happy, but she wasn't arguing, either. Big point for the boss.

"You're right," Judd finally said. "It's a PR move that will give Paxton a wholly different kind of payback." He turned to Lizzie and held out his hand. "Congratulations, young lady, you've got the job."

"Thank you." She shook his hand.

"I think we've wrapped this up for now, Lucy," Judd said, standing to shake her hand and Con's. "Why don't you walk out with me, Lizzie, so we can iron out some of the details."

"I'd love to." She gave Con a warm smile, her golden brown eyes dancing. "Excuse me for a few minutes."

When they left, Con turned to Lucy, bracing himself for the dressing-down.

"You love her," she said quietly.

He smiled. "I do."

"Enough to fight this battle, to risk infuriating me, and to threaten a client."

He shrugged. "Having me work for you won't always be easy, Lucy."

"I don't need easy," she said. "I need smart. And

that was *very* smart." She pushed away from the table. "Come into my office. I have the contract drawn up."

He followed her through a side door into her library, crossing to the antique chair in front of her desk.

After Lucy sat behind her writing table, she smoothed her loose-fitting jacket. "As you know, I'm expecting a baby, and I've decided to make some changes in the organization."

"Really? I didn't imagine having a baby would change anything for you, Lucy."

"It won't change me, and it won't change this company. I'm just going to structure things slightly differently and give up some measure of control." She held up her thumb and index finger a fraction apart. "Some *small* measure."

"What do you have in mind?"

"I'm dividing the company into specific departments, with capable individuals at the helm of each. All department heads will report to Dan Gallagher." She flashed a smile. "I believe you mentioned wanting his job."

"Gallagher's a good guy." Fair and smart.

"He'll report to me, as will a few others," she continued. "One of the new departments will specialize in preventing and investigating art crimes—something we've done on an ad hoc basis, but I'd like to formalize it."

"I know a little about art crimes."

"And every player in the world of collecting, as you just proved. I'd like you to head the Bullet Catchers Art Crimes division, Con. I think you'd be masterful both in the field and as a manager."

"*Head* it?" he asked, surprised.

"You'll report directly to Dan. Then you two can start arm wrestling for his job anytime you like."

"Thank you, Lucy. I'm in."

"Great. And I have your first assignment, which happens to be in the Azores."

"You're kidding, right?"

"Perfectly serious. I just got a call from my friend on the Lisbon police force, who knew I'd be interested in this one. It seems someone on Corvo found something of great worth and is trying to sell it." She handed him a file. "You might want to retrieve that—it should be a huge boon to the *El Falcone* exhibit. I didn't mention this to Judd because it seemed . . . premature."

He took the file, fighting a grin. "You're a good woman, Lucy."

"And you, I've discovered, are a good man."

He just laughed softly.

EPILOGUE
One Year Later

"Lights out, Lizzie?"

From the back of the cavernous hotel ballroom of the Fontainebleau Miami Beach, Con stood at the wall, his voice as anxious as the hand on the light switch.

"Not yet," she said, crossing the room, eyeing each display, making sure the treasures were laid out just the way she wanted them to be. "This is the calm before the storm, and I want to enjoy it."

"This is the last night we're going to be together for a week and a half," he said pointedly. "And I want to enjoy it."

She laughed lightly. "I do, too. But I'm not quite ready to give up this moment. It's been a long year getting here."

He flipped a switch, leaving only a few halogen spotlights on the most important pieces of the exhibit.

Tomorrow, when the television crews and journalists from around the world arrive for the launch of *El Falcone: The Life and Times of Captain Aramis Dare,* these will be the lights that come on first, with music and narration and all the drama befitting the most important salvage effort in the history of Paxton Treasures.

"I have to say," she mused, looking at the gold chains that winked under one light, "Old Judd kept his half of the bargain, giving generously to the exhibit."

"He's smart enough to know he's swimming in good press," Con said, walking slowly toward her in the middle of the room. "And you've done the same, sweetheart. You've given him quite a year."

"It was quite a dive," she agreed. "With Sam as my divemaster, Brianna as my lead diver, and all of my father's closest friends and colleagues on board, I can honestly say it was the best dive of my life." She reached for his hand. "The best *year* of my life."

"I personally liked the weekends when you let visitors on board." He threaded her fingers into his, pulling her knuckles to his mouth for a kiss. "And after this exhibit opening, we'll have a year where we never have to leave each other."

"Yep. There's another amazing year ahead." He'd arranged to travel with her as the security expert on the exhibit. And when they'd gone to New York to celebrate the birth of Lucy and Jack's baby girl, Dan Gallagher, the new Director of Global Operations, had suggested that Lizzie consider consulting for the Bullet Catchers as an underwater treasure expert.

She hadn't taken the offer yet, but a future with Con seemed possible and real, and so very right.

"You know, a year ago, this was a pipe dream—a reason for Brianna and me to keep my father's memory alive." She swept a hand toward the massive oil painting that Lucy had commissioned for the exhibit as the Bullet Catchers' donation. "Every time I look at that, I smile, because we did this for him."

Once they had all the documentation and most of the treasure recovered, they were able to fill in the historical blanks. Aramis Dare had been cheated and run down by the real thief, Carlos Bettencourt, and killed when his enemy sank *El Falcone* with cannon shot.

The painting recreated the battle at sea, with both captains at the helms of their ships. The image of Aramis was devilishly handsome, a perfect portrait of Malcolm Dare.

Lizzie and Brianna had cried when it was unveiled.

"*You* did this for him," Con corrected. "I'm not taking any credit, except to be smart enough to follow you into the lab and risk a nitric acid bath to see you naked."

She slid her arm around his waist and dropped her head to his powerful shoulder, the one she'd gotten so used to sleeping on, and leaning on. "I'm sorry I almost blinded you. You know it was an accident, and that I love you."

"I love you, too." He kissed the top of her head tenderly. "Though I bet you'd love me more if I hadn't lost the other Bombay Blue."

She *couldn't* love him more. "You saved my life, Con."

He held her gaze. "Then we're even, honey." He put his lips over hers and whispered into her mouth, " 'Cause you saved mine."

Her heart swelled with the familiar sensation of wholeness she had with him, and the growing belief that they could stay together forever and the whole world would just keep getting better.

Then she pulled him to the centerpiece of the exhibit where the scepters were propped up next to each other, the lone blue diamond on a sea of black velvet between them. "I'm used to the asymmetry now, and I like the presentation the curator came up with. It's still a remarkable recovery, and that beauty"—she nodded toward the diamond—"is getting a lot of press coverage all by itself."

The halogen light above the display had been placed to highlight the facets in the jewel, reflecting a million blue prisms that would always remind Lizzie of the color of Con's eyes.

"It would look better if there were two," he maintained. "They should be together for eternity—not separated by an ocean."

She smiled at him, getting his double entendre, warmed by the romantic notion. "I admit, it *would* be nice to see them together. We never did, you know. We've seen them both separately, but never together."

"Until now."

He reached into the pocket of his sports coat, then held out a large, misshapen diamond, part of one side chopped away.

"It's not perfect," he said, moving it closer to her. "But then, one of any set is sometimes flawed."

She blinked at it, afraid to believe what was right in front of her. "Is it . . . is it . . . the other Bombay Blue?"

"It is."

"I know you had some leads through some Corvo

locals, but I thought they all came up empty. I gave up hope."

"Big mistake, with me."

She laughed softly, reality settling on her. "I guess so." She finally touched the stone, warm from his body and hand, and definitely smaller than it had been. "Broken in the fall?" she asked.

"Blue diamonds are slightly softer, and lava rock is unforgiving." He showed her the jagged edge where a piece had chipped off, ruining the perfect sphere. "We only lost a carat or two." He opened the display case and slid it into the four prongs on one of the scepters. "It washed up on shore like this, and a local fisherman found it."

"How long have you had it?" she asked as he picked up the other diamond and worked it into its place.

"Long enough to make sure Paxton didn't change his mind." He smiled. "A year."

"A *year*? Did you really have to keep it a secret that long?"

"I had to do something else first," he said, closing the case and stepping back to admire his work. "And I had to be sure you'd understand . . . and agree."

"To what?"

He turned to her, this time reaching into his other pocket. "Since it was already chipped, I thought we might get something good out of a flawed stone. So I borrowed a little bit of that one . . . to make this one."

"Ohhh." The sound was no more than a sigh, one that couldn't begin to let out her happiness at the sight of a classic black ring box.

Opening it, he revealed a blue diamond solitaire ring. "I'm flawed, Lizzie, just like that diamond." His voice cracked just enough to break her heart. "But you took a piece of me, and made me exactly what I'm supposed to be. So that's what I did with that chipped diamond. I hope you don't mind."

She looked up at him, not even fighting her tears. "I don't mind, and you're *not* flawed. You're perfect, Con. And so is this ring."

"I'm not even close to perfect. But life could be, if you'll say yes."

"Yes, yes, *yes!*" She laughed as he slid the ring onto her shaking finger. "And yes again."

He drew her fingers to his mouth and kissed the ring, then pulled her into him, but she saw the glistening in his eyes before he buried his face in her hair. "You're the steal of a lifetime, Lizzie," he said, his voice husky with emotion.

She put her head on his shoulder and sighed. "And you are the greatest treasure I've ever found."

Experience the
excitement
of bestselling romances
from Pocket Books!

Eileen Carr
HOLD BACK THE DARK
When a clinical psychologist and a detective
investigate an unspeakable crime, they learn that
every passion has its dark side.....

Laura Griffin
WHISPER OF WARNING
Blamed for a murder she witnessed, Courtney
chooses to trust the sexy detective pursuing her.
Will he help prove her innocence...or
lead a killer to her door?

Susan Mallery
Sunset Bay

What if you got another chance at the life that got
away? Amid the turmoil of broken dreams lies the
promise of a future Megan never expected....

Available wherever books are sold or at
www.simonandschuster.com

20471